THE
NIGHT
BEFORE
CHRISTMAS

BOOKS BY MARIA FRANKLAND

MARIA FRANKLAND

THE NIGHT BEFORE CHRISTMAS

bookouture

Published by Bookouture in 2024

An imprint of Storyfire Ltd.
Carmelite House
50 Victoria Embankment
London EC4Y 0DZ

www.bookouture.com

Storyfire Ltd's authorised representative in the EEA is Hachette Ireland
8 Castlecourt Centre
Castleknock Road
Castleknock
Dublin 15 D15 YF6A
Ireland

ISBN: 978-1-80722-016-7
eBook ISBN: 978-1-83525-967-2

For Michael and fifty-two more Christmases together!

PROLOGUE

Fear catches in my throat. There's no pain, just blood. More blood than I've ever seen in my life.

Instinctively, I reach for my arm with my other hand. But within a split second, it's flooding in between my fingers.

The expressions of those gathered around me tell me all I need to know. It's nasty – seriously nasty.

'Help me.' The words somehow form themselves as I stagger back against the counter, looking for something, *anything*, to press against the flow of the blood.

They continue to stare, still as rocks, doing nothing, their eyes full of horror. How could one simple action, from the pierce of a blade, produce so much blood?

They'll know that there's nothing any of them can do to help me. An artery has probably been sliced.

There's nothing I can do to help myself either.

Other than to allow myself to slide to the floor and hope that death comes easily.

And without the pain that life has been bringing me.

NATALIE

ONE

'I'll never forget the first time I came here.' I'm trying to break the silence that's hung between me and Dominic for the last ten minutes, but he doesn't seem to be registering that I've just spoken to him. 'Earth calling Dominic.' I reach over the gear-stick and squeeze his leg.

'Huh?'

'You're miles away today. What's up?'

'Oh, I'm just having to focus harder in this.' He waves towards the snow, then grits his teeth as the anti-lock on the brakes kicks in. 'Sorry – what were you saying?'

'Just that, you know, it couldn't be more different than when you *first* brought me here – and I'm not just talking about the weather.'

He doesn't reply again. However, I'll cut him some slack – it makes sense that he's more focused on getting us safely to his parents' front door instead of wrapping us around a tree and I probably shouldn't be trying to distract him.

Eighteen months have passed since my first visit here, and as we head down this sweeping, tree-lined driveway that leads to the home of Dominic's parents, anxiety has replaced my initial excitement and anticipation. I didn't know what I was walking into then, but I definitely have more of an idea this time. Still, I've been promising myself that I'm going to make the absolute best of our visit and, if nothing else, at least Dominic and I can enjoy some proper time together where work doesn't get in the way.

Everything at The Elms was plump and green and lush for that first visit. The expectation of summer danced on the breeze as we arrived in Dominic's convertible with the sun on our faces. In meeting him, my life had already changed beyond recognition. I just needed the approval of his parents to offer the icing on the cake.

I was a mass of nerves and must have changed my outfit ten times – I was so keen to make a positive impression. I was hoping beyond hope that they'd be able to take me at face value instead of forming their judgements based on what they'd already heard about me. However, I never stood a chance.

'I hope your parents are going to be OK with me. Surely, because it's Christmas, they'll—'

'Just hang on for a couple of minutes, Nat? I'm really struggling to see my way through this. Sorry, love.'

I peer beyond the rapid windscreen wipers as they fruitlessly attempt to clear the ever-expanding snowflakes. They're falling so thick and fast, they're making me feel dizzy, so goodness knows the effect they'll be having on Dominic as he navigates the twists and turns that are taking us ever closer to the front door. As we get nearer and nearer, my chest is tightening with anxiety and I'm finding it increasingly difficult to regulate my breathing.

'Bloody hell,' he exclaims. 'As fast as it's settling, it's freezing. I can't imagine we'll be leaving here in a hurry.'

I don't reply to this. What could I even say? It's clear from his tone that the drive has stressed him out, but I've been getting the impression that something else seems to be bothering him as well, especially over the last couple of days. Hopefully, he'll be a bit happier after a shower and a beer and will talk to me about whatever it is.

As we approach the final turn, fairy lights twinkle between the snowflakes. I want to tell Dominic how I've never seen anything prettier against the darkening sky, but I'd better keep quiet so he can concentrate. There can be no doubt how magical and welcoming my in-laws have made their home look for Christmas. Or, as I should say, how magical their staff have made it look. I must make sure I comment on it when they open the door to us.

'So – it's our very first married Christmas Eve,' I say as Dominic brings the car to a halt. I'm trying to keep a note of excitement in my voice; after all, he'll be looking forward to seeing his parents even if I'm apprehensive. I only wish we were spending it on our own – just the two of us. Maybe when we have children, things will be different and we won't be expected to uproot them.

'It sure is,' he replies, staring at the exterior of The Elms, the house he grew up in. It looks so inviting from the outside that if I wasn't aware of the lukewarm welcome that will probably be waiting at the other side of the door, I'd be yearning to get in there.

Lamplight beams from every window and I can imagine the fires which will be lit beyond them and the smell of Christmas that will emit as soon as we get inside.

With our bags and carefully chosen gifts slung over our shoulders, we clamber the steps to the front door. I linger slightly behind, in the hope that Dominic will turn and offer me his hand. It works – it always does. No matter how stressed or distracted he often is, he is always a gentleman. 'Come on.' He tugs me up the last couple of steps. 'Let's get inside where it's warm.' He reaches for the bell.

Several moments pass.

'Where are they?' He turns to me, looking puzzled. 'I sure as hell don't fancy driving home again, I don't think we'd even make it.'

Perhaps they won't answer and we can just leave, no matter how long it might take and spend a lovely Christmas in our own home. However, I can't imagine in a million years that Dominic would get back in the car again and I certainly wouldn't be able to drive in this snow.

'I'll try again, shall I?' He presses the bell twice this time.

We continue to wait, both staring expectantly at the door.

'They know we're due to arrive,' I say. 'Surely they'll be listening out for us, especially in this weather?'

'I'll try around the back.' He lets go of my hand.

Just as Dominic's on the verge of skidding off the bottom step, the grand oak door in front of us is pulled open with a creak and with the sound, my heart drops.

TWO

'You could do with some WD40 on that,' Dominic laughs. I laugh too. Let's start as we mean to go on. Friendly and cheerful.

'You've done well to get here, son.'

I smile at Roger, my father-in-law, while telling myself I'm imagining the edge of disappointment his words seem to carry, as though he was expecting someone else.

He steps back to allow us to pass. I stamp my feet on the doormat, then squint in the sudden bright light as he points from Dominic's trainers to my snow-tipped boots.

'You'd better take those off.' His voice echoes around the hallway. 'You know how finicky your mother is.'

'It's just as well I've brought my slippers then.' I laugh hollowly, even though my comment isn't remotely funny. I feel about as welcome as a dose of the flu so far, and we've only just arrived. I find myself asking for the hundredth time how on earth I allowed myself to be talked into this.

'I can't believe how fast it's coming down out there,' Dominic says as we stack our footwear in the cupboard.

Passing my rucksack to Dominic, I reach my arms out to my

father-in-law. 'It's good to see you, Roger.' I'll try to hug him whether he likes it or not. Perhaps he'll be easier to defrost than Ann-Marie. 'Thanks for inviting us to spend Christmas with you.'

'Yes, erm, well...' He's as stiff as a board as I hug him, but I'm already used to that. Even on our wedding day, and after a few drinks, he still couldn't let himself go. I don't even recall him congratulating us – it was as though he couldn't bring himself to. I don't know whether it's just me he keeps at arm's length or whether he has trouble relaxing around other people as well. I must pick my sister-in-law's brains about it when she gets here. Her car wasn't outside, so she's probably battling her way here as well. Sophie's usually happy to answer my questions.

'We've been really looking forward to coming,' I add, my voice as bright as the fairy lights we've just driven by. If I say this often enough, perhaps I'll even convince myself.

When I was moaning to my brother about the situation a couple of days ago, his advice was to continue just being myself and eventually, he reckons, I'll thaw them out. His exact words were, *how could anyone not warm to you, Nat.* But ever since I got off the phone with him, I've felt guilty for complaining to him. After all, where I'm spending Christmas couldn't be more polar opposite to where he's spending it.

'It's good to have you here.' Roger steps back from me, leaving me to wish that his demeanour towards me matched his words. 'Let's just hope your sister can make it.' He looks over my shoulder at Dominic.

'Have you heard from her?'

Roger opens his mouth to speak, but then closes it again as the grandfather clock behind him begins to strike four. It gives me a moment to breathe in the aroma of whatever's cooking in the kitchen, causing my stomach to rumble.

My in-laws might not be over the moon to have me here, but

at least they have a team who know how to make everything warm and Christmassy. Their staff will have cooked up a storm, which I really am looking forward to. There'll be so many things I'll be able to compliment my in-laws about over the next couple of days that all will be fine by the time we go back home. In my most anxious moments, I've been telling myself that the next couple of days of family togetherness might provide the ties that will start to bind us. However, with the weather the way it is, I'm concerned we might end up staying for more than a couple of days.

'You made it then?' Ann-Marie steps from a door at the end of the hallway and strides towards us. Well, she strides towards *Dominic* and they briefly hug one another. 'It's a good job you set off early.' She gestures to the hallway window at the swirling snowflakes before moving her attention to me. 'Natalie.' She smiles a tight-lipped greeting before offering her arms for me to lean into. Even when Ann-Marie smiles, she appears to be scowling. It's probably something to do with the close-set eyes that Dominic has inherited, although when his mother's eyes are on him they are less critical. She gives me an even stiffer hug than Roger's. 'We're glad you're both here.'

Just as Roger did, she might be saying this, but an edge to her words suggests that she's far from *glad*. I give her a wide smile. I'll win this woman over if it's the last thing I do.

'Well, I wouldn't be anywhere else on our first married Christmas, would I?' I force a laugh as I gesture towards Dominic. However, Ann-Marie doesn't laugh back. Neither does anyone else. There's an awkward silence as I scratch about for something else to say. I really, really hope Sophie makes it. Her being here will make all the difference. 'Your hair looks lovely, Ann-Marie – have you just had it done?'

She pats at the coiffured waves that sit above her shoulders and the expression on her face finally softens. 'Yes, my hair-dresser was here first thing as it happens – thanks so much for noticing.' She shoots her husband a look that seems to say, *unlike you*. One brownie point to me, I think.

'Back in a moment,' Dominic says, as he heads along the hallway to the toilet, leaving me to make polite conversation with his parents.

'Is Sophie on her way – have you heard from her to say how long she'll be?' I ask, praying her arrival is imminent.

'No – she'll hopefully just be concentrating on the road.' Ann-Marie's manicured hands clasp together as she steps back. She's wearing red with a gold sprinkling – the most commonly requested colour from my customers this month. I can't imagine that she ventures out to a salon for her nails. She'll probably have someone coming here to do them. 'I won't rest until she gets here.' I get the impression that she and Sophie aren't especially close, but I understand her worry. It's really coming down out there.

'I'm sure she'll be here soon.' I wait for her to invite me further into the house, but we all remain facing each other in the hallway.

'It's forecast to get worse, I'm afraid,' Roger says, with a sweep of his hand towards the window.

The pause between us lingers for even longer this time, and the tension is tangible as I wait for someone else to fill it. I hope it's not going to be like this for the entire visit. Awkward pauses and me wondering what the hell to say.

'The tree looks fabulous,' I eventually remark. 'It must be lovely having a hallway large enough for a tree. Our hallway barely offers enough space for our shoes.' I laugh, but again, I'm the only one. At this rate, I'm going to quickly run out of the subjects I've listed in my head as discussion points.

'I'll leave you to get settled then.' Roger turns towards the room he calls his office. Sophie once told me that he practically lives in there. 'Ann-Marie will show you up to your room.'

'Shouldn't we wait for Dominic?' Really I'm wondering

why they haven't even offered us a drink yet. It's the first thing most people do – they put the kettle on. But no, not here.

Though perhaps it's best if I get freshened up in the en suite first. After all, I hadn't even checked my appearance before facing my in-laws. No doubt my mascara will have run and my hair will be frizzy from stopping at the motorway services, as well as from waiting for what felt like forever on their doorstep.

Dominic reappears along the hallway just as I'm starting to follow Ann-Marie up the winding staircase, passing windows with ornate vases sitting on their sills. I'd probably have to paint the nails of around five hundred women to replace one single item, so I take extra care with my rucksack.

I also avoid brushing against the walls or, to be more precise, knocking the artwork down. It crosses my mind to comment on it, if only for the sake of conversation, but whatever it is, I don't understand it, so I'm probably best staying quiet. Abstract, I think would be an appropriate word, but other than that, I haven't got a clue.

'So how have you been, Mum?' Dominic says as he trundles behind me and his mother. He's never very conversational with his parents, unless they're discussing business – only then does the conversation become more animated. It seems to be the main thing they all have in common.

'Oh, you know – busy, especially with all we're having to sort out right now.' She pauses at the top of the stairs and speaks over my head back to Dominic as though I'm not even here in between them.

'What are you having to sort out, Ann-Marie?' I might only be a nail technician, instead of a hot-shot lawyer like Dominic's ex-wife, Carla, but I am my own boss with a business that pays the bills. Surely we can find some common ground.

'Oh, there's too much to explain.' She dismisses my question with a wave of her hand as we follow her past several doors along the landing. My feet sink into the carpet as we arrive outside a door at the far end of it.

'Well, I've got all evening.' I laugh as she looks back at me. 'And I'm a good listener.'

'I'm sure you don't want to be bored with the details of my parents' business.' It's Dominic's turn to laugh. 'Not on Christmas Eve.'

'Quite,' Ann-Marie agrees. 'Anyway, here we are.'

'Aren't we in our usual room – the one with the en suite?' Dominic gestures to the room opposite the one Ann-Marie is waiting at. I stayed in it with him when we attended a barbecue here earlier this year – it's also the room we stayed in *last* Christmas when we were still engaged.

'Erm no, not this time, I'm afraid.' Ann-Marie sweeps past us and throws the door open to our intended room. 'Come in.' She beckons her arm and then flicks the light on. 'It's all made up for you and, well, it's not far to the *main* bathroom, is it?'

If only I had a family of my own that we could alternate Christmases with. There are another few years to go before spending it with my brother will become an option again. Instead, it looks like coming *here* each year might be my new norm.

According to Dominic, it's a foregone expectation that he and Sophie come here *every* year – something he seems to be happy enough with. At least he seemed happy enough until *now*.

'I'd rather we stayed in the room with the en suite if you don't mind, Mum.' Dominic remains in the doorway as I follow her in. It's a pretty room – cottagey and white. I've no complaint with it.

'Well, you're going to be in here this time.'

'Why? Sophie's not staying in our usual room, is she?'

'Actually' – an almost apologetic look crosses Ann-Marie's

face – 'I meant to text and let you know earlier, but I knew you'd be driving and I didn't want to disturb you.'

'Let us know what?' Dominic frowns.

'Sophie will be sharing the main bathroom with you.'

'So what's wrong with that room?' He points at it again. He clearly isn't going to let the subject go.

'Carla's staying in that room – she especially requested it, so I could hardly say no, could I?' Ann-Marie keeps her eyes forward as though she's avoiding looking at either of us.

Carla. My heart literally stops in my chest.

'What do you mean – Carla's staying in that room?' Dominic comes into the room after me, tilting his head to one side as he awaits his mother's reply.

'She's spending Christmas with us.' Ann-Marie's voice is as bright as I've heard it since we arrived. 'She can't get home because of the snowstorm, so of course we had to invite her here.'

'*Invite* her?' Dominic echoes, though he doesn't sound as annoyed about the situation as I'd expect an ex-husband to be.

'Well, like I've always told her, she's still one of the family, isn't she?'

THREE

Dominic lowers himself in the window seat as he looks at his mother. The colour has risen on his face, but his expression is impossible to read. I want him to speak up, to say something along the lines of how Carla ceased to be in their family the moment they got divorced, or, even better, how I'm their family now. But I know he won't. He never stands up to his parents.

The grooves in Ann-Marie's forehead deepen as she frowns. 'We can hardly leave the poor girl on her own and Natalie won't mind, will you?'

Her question takes me by surprise. As if she's asking *me* for my approval. 'Well, no, of course, I—'

'You wouldn't want to leave someone who can't get back to their own family stranded, would you, Natalie? Especially at Christmas.' Her tone is almost challenging me to disagree with her.

'Of course not, it's—'

'So, that's settled then.'

'But why does she get to stay in the en-suite room?' Dominic seems more bothered about that than anything else.

'It's where she feels most comfortable when she's here, that's all.'

'It must be awful for her, to not be able to get back to her own family,' I say. 'On Christmas Eve as well.'

I can do this. I have to rise above how unsettled I'm feeling. I've never had much to do with Carla before, but since she seems to get on with Ann-Marie so well, perhaps she can give me a few win-over-the-in-laws tips. It's not as if I've any choice other than to accept she's going to be here.

'She's stressed out enough,' Ann-Marie replies, 'with not being able to get herself back to York as she'd arranged. So we weren't going to add to her stress by making her sleep in an unfamiliar room as well.'

'I totally understand,' I say. 'And I don't mind where I sleep so long as I'm with Dominic.' I reach for his hand. It's true. I can put up with anything after the Christmases I spent with my ex, Kyle. It was always a lottery of what sort of mood he'd be in – it wasn't so much a case of whether he'd ruin the day because he always did, it was more to what degree he would ruin the day. In contrast with Dominic, Kyle didn't like to spend the festive period with anyone else, so I was solely at the mercy of his temper and his demands.

I know I won't have to deal with any of that with Dominic, but there can be no denying that having Carla sleeping at the other side of the landing is going to be seriously awkward. Every time one of us gets up to use the loo, she'll hear. And as for hopes of anything else occurring between Dominic and me, with Carla only a whisker away, there's going to be no chance.

'Will she be here for the *whole* of Christmas?' I try to keep my tone light, as though I'm only asking out of interest. 'Or might one of her own family be able to collect her at some point?' I emphasise the word 'own'.

If Ann-Marie notices this, she doesn't say anything. 'What do you think?' Her arm flails in the direction of the window.

Dominic twists in his seat to look out too, but still, he doesn't speak.

The snow appears to be falling faster, even in the short time since we arrived here. Normally the view from the windows of this house would be beautiful across its grounds, but this evening, all that can be seen out there is the relentless swirl of the snowstorm and the darkness.

'So when was this all decided?' Dominic looks at his mother.

'Earlier today – I called to wish Carla a happy Christmas, only to discover her planning to bed down at her office.'

'That's awful,' I say as I sink to the edge of the bed. 'It's a good job you rang her.'

Dominic gives me a funny look as if to say, *sterling perfor-mance, Nat.* But I do mean what I'm saying, ex-wife or not – no one should be stranded alone in an office over Christmas.

'It's not as if York's a million miles away though,' says Dominic. At least he's putting up some kind of argument for a change.

'Don't you listen to the news?' Ann-Marie rounds on him. 'All the trains have been cancelled. I could hardly abandon her, could I?'

'If she can't get home because of the weather, will she be able to get here?' I try to squash down the hope I'm feeling that she won't. No matter who or *what* she is, she's a fellow human being and has never done me any direct harm. The fact that she's drop-dead gorgeous and formerly married to my husband shouldn't even come into it.

'That's what she said to begin with. But she's managed to call in a favour with one of her clients. He's got a four-by-four and as he's returning from town up this way himself, he's going to drop her as close to here as he can.'

I definitely need to sort out my panda eyes and frizzy hair now. The last thing I want to risk is Dominic making unfavourable comparisons between us. It wouldn't be so bad if their marriage had been a cesspit of miserableness with an acrimonious break-up. But as far as I can gather, it was nothing of the sort. Dominic's never divulged the exact details, but it all seemed to be strangely civil. And even Sophie's been a closed shop when I've tried to pick her brains about what happened. Hopefully, I'll be able to prise it out of her over the next couple of days.

'Right – I'll leave you both to get unpacked, shall I?' Ann-Marie turns on her heel.

'Thank you.' I smile at her. 'And just for the record, I think it's a lovely room.'

'Give me a call if you need anything.' She closes the door behind her with a soft click.

I look at Dominic, expecting another reaction now his mother isn't here. But there's nothing. He probably doesn't know what to say and feels as awkward as I do.

'Well, that's a turn-up for the books,' I finally say. 'It's certainly going to be an interesting few days.'

'Whether I like it or not, Mum's always thought a lot of Carla.' He lets out a long breath. 'There's no way she'd have left her to spend Christmas in her office. There's no way she'd leave anyone.'

'It's OK, you don't have to explain.'

'I know it might be a bit uncomfortable for you at first, but—'

'Honestly, it's really OK,' I repeat. 'We're all adults and I'm sure we can make the best of things.'

'It amazes me how you can be so optimistic all the time.'

'It's better than the alternative,' I laugh. 'Besides, it's Christmas – who wants doom and gloom?'

'But you were looking forward to it being our first married Christmas together.'

'It still is, isn't it?' I rise from the bed and head towards him.

He puts his arm around me and I lean into him – we might be spending the festive period with his rather cold parents and ex-wife, but we're *together* and that's really all that matters.

I've only met Carla once, at last year's summer barbecue, and while she was pleasant enough, I could see in her clear blue eyes what she thought of me, the second wife-to-be. Second best, second rate, second place, the next best thing, et cetera, et cetera. So I just went out of my way to be extra nice to her while Sophie watched on with amusement.

'You're doing great.' She caught my arm as I went to refill my glass. 'She can be hard work, can Carla.'

'Your parents clearly think a lot of her.' It was more of a question than a statement. The difference in our backgrounds and lifestyles was a wide enough gap to close without also having to fight my way past Carla.

'It's her money they're impressed by,' she told me with a flick of her hand. 'In your case, once they get to know you, they'll be impressed simply because you're a hard-working, decent person and because you and my brother are happy together.'

Sophie will no doubt be shocked when she arrives to discover she's spending Christmas with her former sister-in-law as well as her current sister-in-law. But I'll be very glad to have an ally. Unlike her parents, she's made me feel welcome from the first time we met. However, she's remained fairly tight-lipped on what she thinks about Carla.

All I've found out from Sophie so far is that Dominic only walked away with a small – well, the word she used was *reasonable* – share of his and Carla's accrued wealth after their divorce, even after he'd done all he could to thrash out a better deal. Since then, Sophie told me, he's been forced to step up his game with his accountancy business. He freely admits to only tinkering with it until that point. When they were married, money flowed with ease from Carla's company and he didn't

really need to push things with his own business. I can believe
this – when I looked online, she's a partner in one of the biggest
and most well-known law firms in Yorkshire.

He shifts from beside me and strides across the carpet
towards his duffle bag. 'I don't know about you but I'm ready for
a drink,' he says with a grin and I resist the temptation to voice
my disgruntlement at not having been offered one already.
'Now we're here, we might as well get unpacked and then go
and get Christmas started.' He unzips his bag.

'I agree,' I say. A few drinks are sure to loosen his parents up
and will hopefully ease any tensions between me and Carla.
Who knows, if it wasn't for the fact we're ex-wife and current
wife, perhaps we could even get along.

'I can't believe Mum didn't let me know about Carla.' He
tugs clothes from his bag. 'Surely, she'd have other people
nearby she can stay with if she can't get home?'

'Your mum's invited her *here*, so all your whinging won't
change a thing. We just have to get on with it.'

'I suppose.' He grins at me as he slips a shirt onto a hanger.
'You're being really good about this. Most women would have a
meltdown.'

'I'm not *most women*.' I tilt my head and wait for the
compliment I'm certain he'll give me. It's not often that he
misses an opportunity.

'I know.' He threads his jeans through another coat hanger.
'Which is why I married you.'

I shouldn't need his reassurance, but I'm always happy to
hear it. After all, with my history, I wasn't exactly what
Dominic's parents wanted for him. However, Carla or no Carla,
I'm still certain I can change their perceptions about me during
our stay here, just like my brother said I'd be able to.

Despite my best intentions, my breath catches as the doorbell echoes through the house. Two sets of footsteps quicken
towards it.

'They're not leaving *Carla* waiting on the doorstep in the snow, are they?' Dominic mutters.

Though I'm inclined to agree, I don't want to add to the tension. 'It might be Sophie.'

'True.' His expression softens as he drops his bag on the bed. 'Let's go and see, shall we?'

'Let me sort my hair and face out, and then I'll be right with you,' I say. If it *is* Dominic's ex-wife at the door, I'm not going down there to greet her without dragging a brush through my hair and putting a bit of lipstick on. No way.

FOUR

'It's absolutely awful out there. I wasn't sure if I was ever going to make it here.' I watch from a shadowy part of the landing as Roger wraps Carla in a hug ten times more affectionate than the one he gave me on arrival. I know I shouldn't be making comparisons like this, but I can't help it.

Though, really, what I mean is the hug I gave *him*. I'd have got more response if I'd hugged an ironing board.

'I've had to walk – slide – up the last bit,' she continues. 'Even the four-by-four would have got stuck up the drive.'

'We'd have got you here somehow,' he replies. 'Wouldn't we, Ann-Marie?'

'Of course we would.' She busies herself with brushing snow from Carla's woollen coat. 'Here, let me hang that up.'

Dominic arrives at the foot of the stairs. 'So it looks like we're spending Christmas together.' His tone towards her is more pleasant than I'd have expected, given our conversation moments before.

'Who'd have thought it, eh?' She laughs.

For a moment, I'm torn between wanting to return and hide away in the bedroom we've been allocated, to remain here in the shadows where I can watch and listen or to get down those stairs and exert myself amongst everyone. I should have asked Dominic to wait for me – we should probably have gone down there together, presenting a united front. But it's too late now.

'I know – spending Christmas with my ex-wife,' Dominic laughs back as he stands in front of her.

'So, do I get a hug from you as well then? I've had one from your parents.'

I watch as they embrace. I should *definitely* have gone downstairs with him. It's not that I'm jealous – it's more that I don't think she'd have asked him for a hug if I'd been standing at his side.

'Even divorce can't keep us apart,' Carla laughs even louder, as does Ann-Marie.

She obviously has no idea I'm listening, otherwise she wouldn't be making such crass comments.

'I'm sure you can manage it without killing each other,' Roger says.

'It'll be challenging, but I'll do my best.'

'Now, now.' Ann-Marie returns from hanging her coat. 'I always forget how dry your sense of humour is, Carla.'

'Dry humour's the very best kind,' Roger laughs.

Try as I might to fit in with them, Dominic's family are in a completely different league to what I'm used to and there can be no doubt that Carla fits in far better with them than I have so far. But I can change things, *I can change things*. I just have to keep believing that.

I watch as she unwinds her scarf and then tugs off her gloves to blow on her fingers.

'Oh goodness, sorry – you must be freezing, dear – come and get warm in front of the fire in the main lounge.' Ann-Marie steps towards her and throws an arm around her shoulders. 'Dominic will take your bag up to your room. And Roger, fix Carla a drink, will you? What, will you have, dear, your usual?'

'Just a cup of tea will be fine, please. I need to warm up after that hike from the main road.'

So they've invited her in and are immediately offering drinks. Meanwhile, I'm still waiting for such pleasantries.

'What on earth are you doing?' I jump as Dominic appears in front of me; I didn't expect him to come up here *immediately*. He's carrying Carla's expensive-looking weekend bag, which is as perfect and stylish as she is. 'You don't need to hide up here on your own.'

'I know – I wasn't – it's just...' I follow him along to Carla's room as the corridor creaks beneath our feet, unable to give him any kind of logical explanation as to why I didn't come down straight away. I can't even explain it to myself. But I do know how awkward I feel now he's caught me spying on them all.

The doorbell echoes through the house again. 'That'll be your sister.' I perk up immediately. 'She's made it – thank goodness for that.'

I glance into Carla's room, my soul sinking at the sight of the fluffy towelling robe, cosy-looking slippers and soaps that have been laid out on the king-size bed. My mother-in-law has either gone to this trouble herself or she's instructed one of her staff to do it. Perhaps they assumed it was *me* staying in this room. I have to live in hope since the same treatment hasn't been replicated in *my* room.

Dominic places Carla's bag at the foot of the bed and strides back over to where I'm waiting in the doorway. 'Come downstairs, Natalie.' He catches my arm. 'There's absolutely nothing to be nervous about.'

'I'll be down shortly,' I reply. Now I've seen Carla, I'm going to get changed and make myself look more presentable, but I don't tell Dominic this.

'You're *not* hiding up here on your own on Christmas Eve – no way,' he insists.

'We could hide up here together?' I look at him hopefully. If only.

He laughs. 'I promise that I'll take you somewhere hot and exotic in the new year to make up for this.'

'You're on.' I slap his arm. 'Do I get to choose where we go?'

'Of course,' he replies. 'It'll be like a second honeymoon.'

Suddenly, I feel much more confident. I might not have Carla's beautiful complexion or perfect figure, but my husband loves me just as I am – frizzy hair and all.

'Come on – let's go down or they'll be wondering what we're doing up here. Sophie will think we're abandoning her.'

I sway in indecision for a few seconds before deciding that Dominic's right. Once we've all been around each other for half an hour or so, everything will be absolutely fine. And why should I need to dress up anyway – this is only my husband's family and ex-wife. It's not as if I'm at Buckingham Palace.

'Natalie!' Sophie bounds up the stairs towards me, dropping her bag on the landing between the two flights to hug me. 'Hi, stranger.'

'It's so good to see you.' I couldn't mean my words more. Having Sophie here will definitely redress the balance between us all.

'I thought I was never going to get here.' She leans against the wall. 'I had to abandon the car and walk along the driveway. Well, *slide* along the driveway.'

'Watch my art.' Ann-Marie's voice echoes from the hallway.

'Sorry, Mum.' Sophie straightens herself back up and pulls a face at me. 'I hear we've got company for the festive period. Are you OK with this?'

'I'm cool – really I am. It is what it is.'

She nods. 'After a glass of wine or ten, we'll all get on like a house on fire. And how's my favourite brother?'

'Your only brother.' Dominic rolls his eyes. 'And I thought you'd never ask.'

'I've come up to see Natalie, not you,' she laughs.

'I wasn't sure if you'd even get here,' he replies. 'Not with your driving skills.'

'How many times did it take you to pass your test, Dom?' She tilts her head to one side as she waits for his answer. 'And how many times have you been caught speeding.'

'That's only because—'

'Anyway, let's not go there now. I'm off to get a shower and warm up a bit. I'll see you downstairs shortly.'

I'm still smiling as I follow Dominic into the main lounge where his parents and Carla are waiting for us. Nothing and no one can possibly spoil our first married Christmas together.

FIVE

'You remember Natalie, don't you?'

Carla's perched on one side of the L-shaped sofa and Dominic's parents are on the other. The light from the lamp behind her forms almost a halo over the top of her blonde head. I suspect she won't even have to *think* about touching up her make-up – she's effortlessly pretty without it.

'Of course.' Carla places her tea onto the coaster on the table beside her and rises to her feet. I stare into her eyes wondering whether the reply she's just made is one filled with sarcasm – or something else.

'Hi.' I stretch out my hand. 'I'm sorry to hear you haven't been able to get back home to your family.' What else can I say? It's the truth. I'd feel sorry for anyone stranded in the snow, even as I wish she wasn't here.

'Apologies for gatecrashing your Christmas, Natalie.' She smiles as she squeezes my hand, but it's a smile that doesn't go anywhere near her eyes.

'Don't be silly. It's just lucky that Ann-Marie got in touch with you. Spending Christmas Eve alone in your office doesn't bear thinking about.'

I cast my eyes around the room as she sits back down, wondering where I'm supposed to sit. I don't particularly want to sit next to Carla, but if I don't, perhaps Dominic will, which would leave me having to pull up the footstool or bring an extra chair over. Either way, I'd be on the outskirts of their little gathering until Sophie comes downstairs, which is something I'd prefer to avoid.

'Have a seat,' chuckles Roger. 'You're making the place look untidy.'

I perch beside Carla, clasping my hands in my lap as I smile back at him and then at Ann-Marie. His words are probably meant as a joke but I still feel uncomfortable. They're all drinking tea but *still*, none has been offered to me. I catch Dominic's eye as I sink into the soft leather. 'Any chance of a drink before you sit down, hon?'

I might be imagining it, but I'm certain that Ann-Marie raises an eyebrow as if she can't believe I've been rude enough to ask.

'Anything for you.' He pushes the footstool closer to the sofa. 'What are you having?'

'A red wine please,' I reply. Maybe I should be asking for tea as well, but what the hell – it's Christmas Eve. Besides, I'm only following my brother's advice to *be myself*. And I want wine, not tea.

It looks to be Roger's turn to raise an eyebrow.

'Anyone else want one?' he asks, looking around.

'I'll have a wine as well,' Carla replies. 'Just a small one, mind.'

Roger nods, approvingly. 'You might as well just fetch a bottle in,' he says to Dominic. 'In fact, make it two. I imagine Sophie will be ready for a glass when she gets back down here if I know her.' At least Roger's backing me up which definitely feels like a small win.

The silence we sit in for a few moments is excruciating as we wait for Dominic to return. I rack my brains for something to say. 'The tree looks lovely, Ann-Marie,' I eventually come up with, even though I've already complimented her on the tree in the hallway, which is equally exquisite. 'Is it a real one?'

'Of course.' Her tone bears a note of indignation. 'We only ever have a real one. But I'm glad you like it.'

I glance at the neatly arranged presents beneath the tree. 'I must bring the gifts we've brought downstairs – though they're not quite as beautifully wrapped as all of those.'

'That will be nice, dear.' I don't think my mother-in-law could sound any less interested.

I stare at the fire, and we fall silent again. Silent, apart from Dominic as he tinkers around with bottles and glasses in the kitchen. What else do I have on my list to say?

'It must be lovely to have an open fire,' I pipe up again as I stare at the flames licking at the edges of the fireplace. 'We'll have to get one put in.' I think, almost unconsciously, that I'm reminding Carla that Dominic and I now live together. That he's gone on to make a life for himself, for the two of us, after her. If I were to explain this to myself, I think I'm trying to remind not only Carla, but also Ann-Marie and Roger of my right to be here.

'They can be a bit shoe-boxy, those terraced houses you're in,' Ann-Marie says. 'I'm quite surprised at Dominic for wanting to move somewhere like that, especially after where he lived before.' She glances at Carla as though trying to gauge her reaction.

Fury is starting to bubble within me. Not only has Ann-Marie pounced on an opportunity to criticise where I live, she's also been unable to resist referring to the house Carla and Dominic lived in together. Meanwhile, Carla's sitting as prim and proper as a princess in her side-saddle-type posture in her pencil skirt and sheer tights. She evidently doesn't feel awkward around Dominic's parents and doesn't seem to feel the same need to fill the silence as I do.

'Big houses still need cleaning and tidying,' she says. 'And, as we all know, neither of those things are Dominic's forte.'

'You've got maids, haven't you?' Ann-Marie raises an eyebrow.

'Just a cleaner,' Carla replies. 'And I don't know what I'd do without her, to be honest.'

Maids. Cleaners. I resist the urge to pull a face. It's just a reminder of yet another divide that exists between us all.

'Ah, there you are. I was beginning to think you'd got lost in that kitchen.' Roger smiles as Dominic returns to the room, clutching two bottles of red wine in one hand and six glasses by the stalks in the other.

'I do wish you wouldn't carry my glasses in that way.' Ann-Marie frowns at him. 'Do you know how much they're worth?'

I wish she hadn't mentioned that. I'm almost too frightened to touch anything in this house as it is. I'm renowned enough for my clumsiness without the added pressure of drinking from my mother-in-law's finest crystal. They sparkle beneath the glare of the overhead lighting as though daring me not to drop them.

Dominic rests them on the low table in front of us all.

'Be careful with that wine.' Ann-Marie purses her lips as she watches Dominic sharing the bottle between our five glasses.

My gaze roams over the cream carpet. Why on earth did I ask for *red* wine? Have I lost all leave of my faculties?

Go on, fill it up, I feel like saying to Dominic as he places the empty bottle next to the quarter-full wine glasses. But I'm having to be politeness personified. As I will have to be for the entire duration of our visit.

Be yourself, my brother said. Yeah right – fat chance.

'Cheers.' Roger holds his glass aloft and we all clink glasses with him. 'Here's to a very merry Christmas together and a prosperous new year.'

'Cheers.'

As we raise our glasses to our lips, Roger gives Carla a look I can't decipher.

SIX

'What's for dinner, Mum?' Dominic pulls the footstool to the other side of the coffee table and lowers himself onto it. 'I'm starving.' Out of everyone, he's sitting the closest to Carla, which I'm trying not to mind. But I can't help wishing he'd sat next to me, if only for the message it will give them all.

'You're *always* hungry.' Ann-Marie laughs. 'Anyway, you'll be pleased to know that Polly and Charmaine have prepared a delicious buffet for us.'

'Nice one.' He pats his belly. 'And what about tomorrow? Are they coming back?'

'I had to let them go early today, obviously, with the weather.' Ann-Marie points to the window, where all that can be seen are the huge snowflakes flecking the darkness, falling far heavier than they were when we arrived. She sighs deeply as she turns her attention back to us. 'But everything's all prepared for us.' Her face relaxes into a smile. 'It's just a matter of cooking everything, though we'll have to serve ourselves.'

I wish I could tell them that I've never known any other way, but I'm trying to respect their way of doing things. However, it isn't just talk of staff and cooks which is drawing the dividing line between us. We could be speaking a different language. They enunciate each consonant and elongate vowels which should be short and vice versa. I couldn't speak like they do if I tried. But then they probably couldn't speak like me either. Every time I open my mouth, I feel like a peasant, no matter how many times Dominic's told me that he loves my wholesome Yorkshire accent. It's only when I'm around people like this that I even become aware of it.

'I'm happy to lend a hand in the kitchen tomorrow.' I smile at Ann-Marie, in the hope of scoring a brownie point or three.

'Carla's already offered to help with the cooking,' she replies. 'And we'll rope Sophie in whether she likes it or not. She might think her catering days are behind her but she's not getting out of helping here.'

'Whatever possessed her to follow that line of business in the first place.' Roger shakes his head. 'After the education we gave her.'

'Let's leave that discussion for another time, shall we, dear?'

Sophie's work is clearly a bone of contention between them. Perhaps I should jump in with something and take the heat from her. 'I don't mind help—'

Ann-Marie turns her attention back to me. 'You can be in charge of the dishwasher and cleaning up if you don't mind.'

'Done,' I say, trying to sound positive as I try not to dwell on the fact that I've been given the lowliest of jobs. I can't help but consider the environment in that kitchen if it was just me Ann-Marie and Carla. I can only hope that Sophie will be in the kitchen with us as well. *Two's company, three's a crowd.*

We all fall silent again and I wonder if any of the others are trying to think of something to say as much as I am. Classical Christmas music is being played through the speakers in all four corners of the room. I'm unsure whether someone's only just turned it on or whether I just didn't hear it before. I seem only able to focus on one thing at the moment – namely my husband's ex-wife.

The music pauses and a voice announces the news on Classic FM.

'This is the Christmas Eve news at 6 p.m. where Britain has ground to a halt under a deluge of wintry conditions. The storm dubbed "The Icelandic Beast" has taken its worst hold in Scotland and Northern England, with people being advised not to leave their homes. Many homes throughout the far north of Scotland are without power. Emergency services are at breaking point, with NHS staff not able to get in or out of work and emergency vehicles unable to reach many of the calls that are coming in. All twenty-one of Britain's air ambulances have been grounded until visibility improves.'

'Blimey.' Dominic rests his glass on the table as the bulletin continues. 'The Icelandic Beast. It sounds like the name of a horror film.'

'You wouldn't want to need an ambulance tonight,' Roger says.

'Have you let your family know you're safe, Carla?' Ann-Marie peers at her over the top of her glass. She's barely taken the top off it, whereas I've nearly drunk mine. I'd better slow down.

'I've spoken to my brother,' she says, appearing to stiffen as she stares into her drink. Ann-Marie must have hit a nerve. 'He was going to let my parents know where I am.'

'No doubt it will have come as a shock to them,' I say. 'That you're here with your former in-laws.' As soon as the words are out, I'm aware that I've sounded a little critical.

Carla shrugs. 'My brother's aware that we're still in contact.'

I want to tell her that she doesn't know how lucky she is to have her brother in such close proximity, but that could pick the scab of a wound which is better left undisturbed.

'But, clearly,' she goes on, 'he'd much prefer I was in York with him.'

All falls silent again as I will Sophie to hurry up. She's out of the shower by the sounds of it, so, hopefully, it won't be too long before she joins us. There's an atmosphere in here which I can't put my finger on, but it's starting to make me uncomfortable. It's as if something's going on between everybody which, no doubt, I'll be the last person to know about.

'So, how's business?' Dominic swivels on his footstool to look at Carla.

'Never better,' she replies, her voice surprisingly sharp.

'Let's hope it stays that way for you.' Roger smiles. 'I truly think the coming twelve months are going to bring exciting opportunities for us all.'

Another silence lands over us. I'm not breaking it this time.

'Have you settled in with the accountancy firm you appointed?' Dominic finally says, seemingly happy to persist along this road of conversation.

'I can't believe you're talking shop on Christmas Eve.' I laugh, but it's forced. 'You said before that we weren't going to. So why don't we get that other bottle of wine cracked open?'

'Have you finished your drink *already*?' Carla's tone rises as she gives my empty glass a sideward glance.

Dominic frowns at me as if to say, *rein it in* and doesn't make any move towards opening the other bottle.

I sit for a moment, wondering what to do. I didn't mean to drink my wine so fast, but still, if no one's going to oblige me, I shall have to help myself. I wait a couple more minutes before reaching for the second bottle at Dominic's feet.

'Is anyone ready for a top-up?' I ask without looking at him.

'Not just now,' Carla mutters.

'Don't mind if I do.' I screw the cap off and the wine begins its satisfying glug into my glass. Until Carla knocks my arm as

I'm pouring, sending a stream of red wine all over the pristine oatmeal carpet. *Oh no!*

'My carpet!' Ann-Marie leaps from her seat as though a rat has just appeared in front of us. 'Oh my goodness – Roger – do something, will you?'

'I'm so sorry,' I gasp. 'But it wasn't my fault, it was—'

'Pour some white wine on it.' Carla's voice drowns mine out. 'That's supposed to neutralise it.'

'I'll fetch the carpet cleaner. As if we're having to get that thing out on Christmas Eve.' Then, as if realising the extent of his wife's distress, Roger rests a placatory hand on Ann-Marie's arm. 'Calm down, dear. It'll come out and even if it doesn't – it's only a carpet.' Roger continues to mutter away as he strides towards the door. 'It's hardly a life-or-death situation.'

I swing around to glare at Carla, waiting for her to apologise for knocking my arm. But she's too busy bending forward to dab at the streak of wine with tissues. As if *that's* going to do any good. As I glance at her face, I realise there'll be no apology from her. I'm torn between fury at Carla, whether her knocking me was an accident or not, and guilt that my need for a second glass of wine has put such a sour note on Christmas Eve.

Meanwhile, Ann-Marie seems so annoyed that she can't even look at me.

SEVEN

'I'm going to the loo,' I mumble as I rise to my feet.

I need to be on my own for a few moments to pull myself back together. Tears are burning at the back of my eyes, which is ridiculous. Anyone can have an accident, but I can't stand the way Ann-Marie is looking at me. I'm wobbly enough at the minute from missing my brother.

'Where are you going, Natalie?' Roger asks as I sweep past him and begin ascending the stairs.

'I'm just getting something from my room.' I turn my face to the wall so he can't see how upset I am. I'm overreacting, I know I am, and I'll be OK once I've had a breather.

As I get to the top of the stairs, I glance back, expecting Dominic to have come after me. But he hasn't. Evidently he didn't see what *really* happened. Or perhaps he's as annoyed at me as his mother seems to be.

Once safely in our room, I lean onto the dressing table, staring into the mirror as I battle to stop myself from crying. But it's no good. I can't stem the tears no matter how hard I try. They're flowing down my face faster than I can wipe them away. I wanted everything to be perfect this Christmas and it feels like it's going pear-shaped already and we're only a couple of hours in.

As I dab at the mascara running from my eyes, I have to concede that I'm no match for Carla – not with her ice-queen looks and considerable wealth. If I slipped back out of that front door right now, no one would even notice I'd gone, and if it wasn't for the weather, that's exactly what I'd do. Instead, I drag a brush through my tangled brown hair, though really, it's going to take a lot more than a hairbrush to make it look any better.

Right, stop it, Natalie, I say to myself.

This isn't like me at all. When my mum was alive, she once told me I'd been born sunny side up. And despite everything that life's thrown at me so far, I usually find the good in everything. Until I can't.

I can't face going back down there – not yet, anyway. I march over to my rucksack and pull out one of the bottles of wine we've brought with us. My eyes watered at the price in the supermarket, but Dominic said it's Ann-Marie's favourite. *She won't touch cheap plonk,* were his exact words. I resisted the urge to inform him that half of these winemakers invent the prices as they go along, and in any case, after a couple of glasses, no one would know a five-pound bottle of Cabernet from a hundred-pound bottle of Sauvignon.

I think this one was about fifty quid, but I don't care – I'm opening it. I wrench one of the water glasses that's been left on the bedside table and fill it to the brim, slopping it over the edge as there's a knocking at the door. *Please don't let it be Ann-Marie,* I think to myself as I screw the cap back on the wine. She'll think I've got a right drink problem.

'Come in.'

'Hey, what's up with you?' Sophie lets the door fall closed behind her and I breathe a sigh of relief that it's *her* and not someone else. She's a female version of Dominic, with her unruly dark waves and vibrant blue eyes. Like me, she dresses casually in jeans and jumpers as opposed to Carla's high-main-tenance ensemble. She's definitely more my kind of person. Which is probably why I get the impression that my in-laws favour Dominic over her.

'I've spilt red wine all over your mother's lounge carpet,' I sniff.

'Ah, her and her bloody obsession with the house.' Sophie strides towards me. 'Don't worry – she'll get over it.' She points at the other glass on the bedside table. 'Do you fancy some company with that?'

I reach for the other glass and pass it to her. 'She looked really annoyed,' I say, wanting to tell her how Carla knocked my arm but not wanting to make things any worse.

'Try not to take it personally. She likes everything to be just so, that's all. You should have tried growing up with her.' She laughs, and I can hear the bitterness in her voice.

Even though she and Dominic grew up in this sort of opulence, with cooks, cleaners and gardeners surrounding them, they're so much more down to earth than Ann-Marie and Roger. Which I'm thankful for. Perhaps without their parents around, they'd be closer, instead of being rivals all the time. Time will tell.

'I suppose I should get myself back down there shortly. It's going to look terrible that I've spilt red wine all over the place and then just run away. I've left your dad having to get the carpet cleaner on it.'

'You're alright up here for five minutes.' Sophie squeezes my arm. 'While you get yourself back together.' She glances towards the door and then back at me. 'Are you sure you're OK about Carla being here?'

'It doesn't sound like there was any other option.' I pour wine into Sophie's glass. 'Your mum stopped her from having to sleep on her own at her office.'

'Hmmm.' She frowns and looks away.

'What do you mean, *hmmm*? Do you know something I don't?'

'I don't want to talk out of turn here.' She takes a big sip from her glass. 'Bloody hell – that's nice wine.'

'It should be for fifty quid,' I reply. 'To be honest, I don't think it tastes any different than my usual plonk.' I smile, feeling far better about things since she came into the room. At least with her, I can be myself. 'Anyway, just tell me what you know. I promise I won't repeat what you say.'

'OK – well, not even a word to Dominic then. He doesn't need much of an excuse to have a pop at me as it is.'

It hasn't escaped my attention that my husband *still* hasn't come to check on me. But perhaps I should give him the benefit of the doubt. Maybe he's just busy helping Roger get the wine out of the carpet.

'I promise.'

'It's just that I drove past Mum last week – right as she was on her way out of Carla's offices.'

'Really?' Great. Ann-Marie specifically goes out of her way to visit her former daughter-in-law. She's never been to visit me. Not once.

'Mum was looking so pleased with herself, I nearly stopped to quiz her about it, but, to be honest, I'd rather keep out of any family drama.'

I want to say that Carla isn't really family anymore but that would just sound bitter. 'Has she mentioned anything since?' Really I want to ask her if she also thinks Ann-Marie's intentionally invited Carla here for Christmas.

Sophie shakes her head, her damp waves dancing with the movement.

'Carla and Dominic seem to get on well for a divorced couple – don't you think? Do you know what happened between them? Why they split up, I mean?' I cradle my glass in two hands as I look at her. 'I'm sorry to fire all these questions at you, it's just that he'll never talk about it.'

'He's never discussed it with me in any detail either. I think my parents know though.'

Of course they'll know. 'I've tried to prise it out of him several times. I've got to be honest – I'm intrigued to know what the story is.'

'Maybe you should ask her, if he won't spill?'

'Don't be daft. I'd look really insecure. Look, you won't tell Dominic I've been asking questions, will you? If he thinks I've been gossiping about him, he won't be happy. I know you're his sister, and—'

'Of course not. You can trust me a hundred per cent.'

'I'm so glad you're here, Sophie.' I reach for her hand. And I am. Christmas is an emotive enough time for me as it is. It's been years since I lost my parents but memories of them always bubble back at this time of year.

And I wish I was able to speak to my brother. Hayden would put me straight about the silly inferiority complex I have around Dominic's parents. He'd tell me in no uncertain terms to get my arse back down there and if the Elmers don't like me, and don't think I'm good enough for Dominic, then so what, who cares? Dominic loves me, which is all that matters.

So why hasn't he come after me?

EIGHT

The heat of the house rises to meet us as we descend the stairs. Feeling slightly spaced out after consuming nearly half of the bottle I opened in our room, I take care with my footing. Sophie giggles as she does the same.

'I think we need some food to soak this up.' She links arms with me as she glances down at the grandfather clock. 'It's nearly seven, so we must be dishing up soon.'

As we reach the bottom, conversation and laughter echo from the kitchen. Sophie gives me a sympathetic look.

'It's OK,' I tell her. 'We all have a past.'

Even if she cottons on to the irony of my words, she doesn't say anything.

Leaning against the doorway, we watch as Dominic flicks Carla's legs with a tea towel like they're a pair of kids. Carla's white-blonde hair swings out behind her as she dodges him.

'Children, children.' Ann-Marie's smile falters as she looks towards us. She folds her arms against her chest and I notice she's changed into a high-necked green blouse and linen trousers. I wonder if she's forgiven me for the wine stain yet.

Dominic straightens up as he sees me and hangs the tea

towel onto a hook beneath the island. 'You OK, Nat? We were just wondering where you were.'

'Of course,' I reply, brightly. And maybe after necking that expensive wine upstairs with my sister-in-law, I really am. But I don't believe for one minute that any of them have been wondering where I am. In fact, they seem perfectly happy without me.

'Have you been drinking *already?*' Ann-Marie gives her daughter a disapproving look.

'What makes you think that?'

'The red wine moustache is a bit of a giveaway.' Dominic laughs. 'Still an old soak then, sis. Perhaps that's why the business flopped, eh? Too much wine in you and not in the dish.'

'You never pass up a chance to have a dig at me, do you, Dom?'

I sense Sophie stiffen next to me. I've always sensed rivalry between the two of them but would have hoped that Dominic might be able to keep more of a lid on himself at Christmas.

'Come on, you two,' Carla says. 'Not on Christmas Eve.'

'We sorted the carpet,' Roger interjects. 'That cleaner worked like magic.'

'See – there's no harm done.' Sophie nudges me. 'How long will the food be, Mum?'

'It's coming – it's coming.' She smiles. 'It's like the old days – being nagged about when dinner will be ready.'

I smile. Hayden and I were just the same with our mother. She said we were like bottomless pits she could never fill.

'Is there anything I can help with, Ann-Marie?' I ask. No one else seems to be helping her.

'Oh yes, as it happens.' She sounds pleasantly surprised. 'Thanks for asking. You could wash those pans that the staff left – if you don't mind. There isn't enough room in the dishwasher for them.'

'No problem at all.' I'm actually glad to have something to

do, rather than to try and instigate conversation. Plus, it might sober me up.

As Carla leaves the room, Dominic sidles up beside me. 'You seem a bit off, Nat. Are you sure you're alright? We were only messing about before – with the tea towels, I mean.'

I glance around in time to notice Roger giving Ann-Marie a wide-eyed look behind his glasses as he jerks his head towards the door. 'Let's leave them to it, shall we?'

'Of course I'm alright.' I slide a pan into the sink as Sophie also follows them out. 'I just felt bad about your mum's carpet.' I nod in the direction of the lounge.

'Ah, don't worry. It's all sorted now. But are you *sure* you're alright about Carla being here?' He stands behind me and rests his hands on either side of my waist. 'We were honestly just messing about. It was actually my dad who started it.'

I scour the side of the pan. 'If you can't have a laugh on Christmas Eve, it's a poor do, isn't it?'

He lets go of me and steps around to my side, next to the draining board. 'You're great, you are.' His eyes crinkle in the corners as he smiles and I can't deny how wonderful it is these days to receive compliments, instead of the endless insults and name calling I knew when I lived with Kyle.

'Well, we can all see what it's like out there. No one's going anywhere for the foreseeable, so we might as well just focus on enjoying ourselves.'

'Are you *definitely* OK?' He pushes the sleeves of his Christmas jumper up his arm; he's clearly overheating with the exertion of all his running around the kitchen.

'Look I appreciate your concern. Other than missing my brother, I'm absolutely fine.'

Dominic doesn't reply – he probably doesn't know what to say. He never does when the subject of Hayden comes up. It's not exactly an easy topic of conversation, especially since Dominic still doesn't know the half of the situation.

My attention's caught by a sudden movement at the door, and while there seems to be no one there at first glance, there's a very long shadow being cast along the hallway. Not that our conversation is overly interesting, but someone's out there listening to us, I'm almost certain of it.

'Go and sit down, Nat.' Dominic whips the scourer from my hand. 'You're a guest, you shouldn't be washing up – I'll finish these.'

I wipe my hands on the tea towel he and Carla were larking about with and stretch my arms out to him. 'Come here, you.'

He tilts my chin towards his face. 'Like I said before, I'll make this up to you.'

Our eyes meet and I smile at him before nestling into his warmth.

'Don't mind me.' Carla's sudden reappearance is the catalyst for Dominic abruptly letting me go and stepping away from me. It *must* have been her eavesdropping. I eye him curiously. Clearly, he doesn't seem to want his ex catching us being close.

'I'm sorry – I thought it was my mum.' His expression is sheepish.

'So what if it was? We're married, aren't we?' I welcome the opportunity to assert this fact once again in front of Carla. 'We're not doing anything wrong.'

He doesn't reply, so I shrug and return to the sink. 'On second thoughts, I'll finish these pots myself, Dom. Doing as your mum asked might redeem me after my red wine incident.'

Plus I need to keep busy and distracted. With too much time to ponder and dwell, I'll either get very drunk or very down.

'Who wants a glass of something?' He strides over the beautiful stone floor to the fridge, which rattles with bottles as he pulls it open.

'Me,' Carla and I say in unison.

As I turn to face her, a look passes between us which could

almost be mistaken for solidarity. I can't deny that she looks shaken by *something* – it could be because she's still harbouring something for Dominic and it's been a shock to catch us in an embrace.

Or it could be something else.

NINE

'Right then, we'll wait for Dominic and Carla and then we'll sit and get stuck in.' Roger's changed into a checked shirt and blue chinos and is standing by the window of what they call the *drawing room*. He's grinning from ear to ear, evidently proud of the amazing spread which awaits us. As well he should be – it's quite something. The silver cutlery is laid out like it would be in a restaurant and the glasses look so expensive I don't know if I'll dare to touch them. The array of cold meats and the ornate way the salad is presented is like nothing I've ever seen before and almost looks too good to spoil by tucking into it.

My brother pops into my head for what feels like the millionth time today and I can imagine his reaction if he could see where I am right now – in a drawing room in this big, posh house. We'd probably have a right laugh about it.

I've been barely able to stop thinking about him since I got out of bed this morning and every time he enters my thoughts I'm hit with a sledgehammer of guilt about how things ended up. All Christmas, I'm going to be well fed, with plenty of wine and beer to drink, staying in beautiful surroundings and sleeping in a comfortable room with my new husband. I live an enviable life these days – which is more than can be said for poor Hayden. His festive period couldn't be any more different to mine. He's said that I deserve it after everything I went through when I was with Kyle, but I still find that impossible to believe.

I try to dismiss the image of his face from my head as I allow my gaze to sweep over the room. The sumptuous Christmas decorations have even been extended to the fox's head. Yes, there's a fox's head on the wall above the fire, an item of so-called decor which I find most disconcerting, though I can't seem to stop looking at it.

Sophie follows my gaze. 'Whenever I'm back here,' she says, 'I can't shake the sense of being watched by a variety of animals or birds of prey.'

I pull a face. 'Thankfully, there aren't any in our bedroom or I'd never get a wink of sleep.'

'I caught that one myself.' Roger looks proud as he points to the fox.

I'd love to tell him how barbaric I think these items of pretentious decoration are, as well as the practice of obtaining them, but really, I've just got to accept that we inhabit very different worlds. However, as Hayden has often reminded me, it doesn't make them any better than me just because I live in a modest house, have to shop around for deals and am forced to make larger purchases on credit.

Dominic used to bang on about how all this wealth will be shared between him and Sophie one day, though he's not gone on about it quite so much lately. Since the Elmers' 'troubles' began, their inheritance doesn't seem to be quite as guaranteed anymore.

I look away from the fox and its beady eyes, but then I notice its reflection shining onto the surface of the grand piano in the corner. Sophie and I were raucously playing 'Chopsticks' on it when we were here for the last summer barbecue only to get short shrift from Ann-Marie, along with, *have you any idea how much that piano cost?*

'Help yourself, Natalie.' Ann-Marie holds a plate in my direction, but her attention seems to be fixed on whatever's going on beyond this room. Following her gaze, I notice what looks like a heated exchange occurring in the hallway between Carla and Dominic.

'What's going on out there?' Without waiting for a reply and before I can stop myself, I'm already heading to the door and glaring from one of them to the other. 'What's the problem with you two?'

'Nothing.' But Carla avoids my gaze as she brushes past me and heads towards Ann-Marie in the drawing room. Roger hands her a plate as she sits down.

'It didn't look like it was nothing to me.'

'I was just setting Dominic straight about something, that's all.' She picks up a slice of quiche and places it gently onto her plate.

'*What* exactly?' Ann-Marie's expression is a cross between curiosity and hope. I'm getting the impression that all my mother-in-law's Christmases would roll into one if Dominic and Carla were to get back together.

When we get the respite of going to bed tonight and are finally alone in our room, I'm not going to let up until I get the full story from Dominic about why they split. I've got a right to know what happened between them and when I think about it, I could kick myself for accepting his wishy-washy version of events in the first place.

Even though I never told him the full story about the end of my relationship either.

'We were just talking shop.' Dominic comes into the room. 'That's all.'

'Let's leave that sort of talk now, shall we? It's Christmas

Eve,' Roger says as Ann-Marie shoots him a look. 'We all know the score and it's not as if anyone's going anywhere for the foreseeable, is it?' He looks from Dominic to Carla. 'Which means it will all keep for another day.'

'But *I* don't know the score,' I say, suddenly not caring how pushy I might sound. 'Nor do I know what will keep for another day. What are you on about?'

'You don't *need* to know either.' Carla begins piling salad onto her plate.

I glare back at her. Us being around each other is eerily reminiscent of the part Kyle's ex played when I was with him. They always remained in touch and he would frequently draw comparisons between the two of us. Of course, she was more fun, better in bed, kept a nicer house, et cetera, et cetera. I knew Kyle was only ever trying to wind me up, but it still got to me. Every. Single. Time. Dominic doesn't really bring Carla up, but I still have a sense of history repeating itself, though in this case it's almost worse as I'm having to actually *face* the woman.

'Why's everyone so serious?' Sophie transfers some ham to her plate. 'Is it Christmas Eve or are we at a wake?'

'Somehow we've all got on to talking about work.' Roger pulls a face.

'Get those glasses filled up,' Sophie says as she flicks her hair back behind her shoulder. 'Can we not agree that we spend a full forty-eight hours with no shop talk?'

'Suits me.' Carla sniffs as she rests her plate on the table. She's bagged the seat in between Ann-Marie and Dominic. Anyone can see that she's made a beeline to ensure she's sitting next to him.

I want to know what they were *really* having 'words' about in the hallway. Maybe she's jealous of me and has made some kind of advance towards him. At least I know he'll have put her straight. At least I hope he will.

Our plates are laden but I'm waiting for someone else to start eating first. 'Shall we stand.' I'm taken aback by the instruction from Ann-Marie but do as I'm told, regardless. She nods at Sophie.

'For what we are about to receive,' she begins. 'May the Lord make us truly thankful. Amen.'

I shuffle from foot to foot. It's not that I object to the tradition of saying grace, it's more that Ann-Marie and Roger are people who don't seem to have a godly bone in their bodies – not really.

'It's such a shame we're probably not going to be able to get to the Christmas service tomorrow,' Ann-Marie says, as we all sit down again, her words suggesting that she needs to reaffirm that, really, she does know the real meaning of Christmas.

'We'll just have to watch the service here on the TV.' Roger delves his fork into the coleslaw.

'According to the earlier news report,' Carla chips in, 'there won't be many services being held tomorrow anyway, so you'll be lucky to find one even to watch.'

'If there are no live services, perhaps channels will be forced to broadcast pre-recorded ones.'

I can't think of anything worse than being forced to sit in front of the TV with them for an hour tomorrow morning – singing carols. I generally only sing when I'm alone in the car or the shower – and certainly not in front of my husband's ex-wife.

'Well, we'll have a lovely day, whatever happens. It doesn't matter what it's doing outside – we have everything we need in here, don't we?' Ann-Marie smiles around the table at us all. I'm unsure whether she's trying to convince us or herself. 'It's just lovely to have you here with us, Carla – every cloud, or snowstorm' – she chuckles – 'has a silver lining – as they say.'

'Hear, hear.' Roger raises his glass.

I try to catch Dominic's eye. I wonder if the same thing's

going through his head as through mine. They should be raising a glass to us. It's our first Christmas as Mr and Mrs Elmer.

Yet, as I'm thinking this, the realisation that I'm not the *first* Mrs Elmer sitting here dawns on me. And by the looks on the faces of my in-laws, they'd prefer it if I wasn't sitting here at all.

TEN

'This quiche is delicious, Ann-Marie. You must give me the recipe.'

'Thank you, dear. I will.' She rests her wine glass in front of her plate as she smiles back at me. Perhaps if Carla wasn't here, Ann-Marie might have been easier to make conversation with. I keep feeling like it's one step forward, two steps back, but I'm determined to keep trying.

'Which one of your minions made it for you, Mum?' Sophie laughs. 'Honestly, Natalie, she's always doing this. We all know full well who slaves away in the kitchen here and it's not Mum.'

Dominic and Roger laugh.

'Actually, the quiche recipe has been in the family for years. As has the raspberry cheesecake recipe with the nutty base that we're having for dessert.'

'Nutty base?' I begin. 'I'm sorry, but I won't be able to have—'

'Have you sorted a special portion for Natalie, Mum? Without nuts?'

I shoot Dominic a grateful look. It's heart-warming when he

looks out for me, although I can't help but feel disappointed that his mother needs reminding.

'Yes, don't worry – I remembered.'

'So you've got a nut allergy, have you?' Carla swirls noodles from her salad around her fork. She's barely spoken to me directly, so I'm taken aback for a moment that she suddenly has.

'Erm, yes...'

'It's presumably not a serious one then, since there's nuts in the house.'

Sophie snorts. 'What are you saying about our family?'

Everyone laughs.

'It's serious enough – but only if I actually ingest them.' I pat the strap of my shoulder bag on the chair. 'So I've always got my EpiPen nearby.'

'Ah, right.'

It's the first time she's appeared genuinely interested in something I've got to say.

'Wow, just look at it out there.' We all follow Sophie's gaze to the window.

'It makes you glad to be inside where it's warm and cosy, doesn't it?'

Nobody answers me, so I continue.

'It looks so pretty, I think, especially on Christmas Eve – it's just a shame it causes so much chaos.' I glance back to Carla. 'Will you be able to make up for missing it with your family?'

'How do you mean?' Carla's voice has an edge as though I've overstepped the mark with my question.

'Like – by having a second Christmas Day or something. I expect they'll all miss you spending it with them.'

'Yes, well, I guess I'm spending the day with the next best thing to them, aren't I?' She rests her fork down and allows her hand to brush over Dominic's before reaching for her wine glass. 'My *second* family.'

'And don't you forget it,' Roger says. 'To family.' He holds his glass in the air for a second toast.

'To family,' we all echo and I try to load as much positivity as I possibly can into my voice.

'I've got a feeling that the new year is going to be an excellent one – even for you, Sophie.'

I glance at my sister-in-law as her face falls. The catering business she started up went to the wall earlier this year and, from the quip Roger's just made at her expense, he's got little sympathy for his daughter and doesn't even seem to care about being so insensitive in front of everyone. I'll have to check with her later that she's OK.

'What are you doing for work these days, Soph?' Carla looks at her.

'I thought we weren't going to talk about work on Christmas Eve,' Sophie replies.

'That means she isn't doing anything much.' Dominic laughs. 'If she had anything going on, she'd be chewing our ears off about it.'

'When I can get a word in edgeways,' Sophie retorts. 'After all, we know it's almost always all about *you* in this house.'

Gosh, if this first meal together is anything to go by, this visit is going to drag by.

'I'll clear the table a little for you, shall I?' Sliding my plate on top of Dominic's, I reach for one of the serving plates that have been emptied.

'That would be lovely, dear – thank you. While you're doing that, Roger can start bringing dessert in. Natalie's cheesecake is on the white plate, dear,' she says to him before looking back to me. 'I've made sure the ice cream doesn't contain any traces of nuts either.'

'Thank you. I'm sorry to have put you to any trouble.'

'It's no trouble at all.'

Ann-Marie's already stacked a few plates, so balancing what I've already got with them, I head for the door.

As I pass Carla at the end of the table, she swings around with her plate, catching my arm and taking me so much by surprise that the largest and heaviest serving plate slips from my grasp. Time seems to stand still as it collides with the corner of the table. I watch in horror as it smashes into several pieces on the wooden floor. A feeling of déjà vu steals over me as I relive the same emotions as with the wine earlier.

'Oh my goodness – that was my mother's plate!' Ann-Marie shrieks as she jumps from her chair and rushes around the table. Dropping to her knees, she exclaims, 'She used to use it for the Sunday roast.'

'I'm so sorry, Ann-Marie,' I say as I rest the remainder of what I was carrying back on the table. 'I'll replace it, of course I will.' As I also drop to the floor, I begin gathering its gilded edges, attempting to contemplate how much it could cost to replace. A week's wages, no doubt.

Dominic joins us on the floor and also begins collecting the larger pieces. 'Don't worry, love.' He nudges my arm.

'It's only a plate,' Sophie says. 'Don't be giving poor Natalie a hard time.'

'It's an *irreplaceable* plate, not that I'd expect *you* to understand.' Ann-Marie's face tightens as she wrings her hands in her lap and looks up at her daughter. 'You've never known the value of anything that's important. They don't even make these anymore – it was a Churchill.'

Like that's supposed to mean anything to me. As far as I'm concerned, it was just a heavy plate with a fancy pattern. But there can be no denying that it's one of my mother-in-law's prized possessions that I've managed to smash – or should I say, that Carla's managed to smash.

'It's not worth ruining Christmas Eve over though, is it, Mum?'

'I'll fetch the dustpan and brush,' Carla says as she rises from her chair and steps over me.

'Do you know where it is?' Ann-Marie asks.

'I should do by now.' Carla laughs as she makes her way to the door. 'I've been here often enough.'

'It wouldn't be so bad if it hadn't been my mother's,' Ann-Marie wails as Carla leaves the room. 'I'm sorry, Natalie – I know that must be difficult for you to understand but—'

I rise back to my full height. 'What do you mean?' Like I even need to ask. But enough is enough, and no matter how wobbly I'm feeling, I'm going to have to start sticking up for myself.

'Oh, Mum.' Sophie rests her knife and fork on her plate. 'I can't believe you just said that.'

'I only meant that obviously, you grew up without your mother, did—'

'Mum!' Dominic jumps to his feet. 'That's quite enough on that subject now, don't you think?'

'I'll take the plates through,' I mutter as I grab the rest of what I was carrying and make it towards the door before the tears start again. I can't believe what I've done to Ann-Marie's plate. And I can't believe she deems it acceptable to bring up the loss of my mother on Christmas Eve.

I turn my face away from Carla as we pass in the hallway.

'Natalie, I—'

'Don't even speak to me,' I hiss as I arrive at the kitchen door and slam it behind me with my foot. I've been trying to be friendly towards her and to make the best of an awkward situation, but I can't shake the suspicion that she's caused my two 'accidents' on purpose. She's definitely trying to cause trouble for me.

ELEVEN

Dumping the plates onto the island, I head over to the exterior door through the utility room, unlock it and pull it open. It's heavier than it looks and I stand for a few moments, the freezing air cooling my angst as I stare out into the darkness.

It's impossible to see anything out there apart from the heavily falling snowflakes which show absolutely no sign of abating. We've been here for around four hours now and the snow looks to have deepened three times over to what it was like when we first arrived.

'Are you alright, Natalie?'

I swing around to face Roger.

'Yes. I'm just so sorry about the plate. And the wine before. Thanks for coming to check on me.'

'Well, really, I'm just doing as I'm told and fetching these desserts.'

'And I've been sent on ice cream duty.' Dominic comes in behind him, balancing the pieces of broken plate on the dustpan. 'Hey, what are you doing out there? Mum'll have a fit at all the heat being let out. *We're not paying to heat the garden.*' He mimics her voice.

'I'm just having a moment,' I reply. 'I'll be OK. Just give me a couple of minutes and then I'll be right back in.'

'Do you want to talk about it?'

'Honestly, I'm fine. I'm just getting a breath of fresh air.'

'Was it the mention of your mum that's upset you? Sophie wanted to come after you, but I told her that I'd check on you.'

I nod without turning back to him as fresh tears spring to my eyes. I'm all over the place tonight, but I can't go back in there until I've pulled myself together. 'You go back in – I won't be long, I promise.'

I turn around to notice Dominic and Roger as they catch each other's eye. Then respectively grabbing what they've been sent in for, they leave the room again. I wish Dominic had let Sophie come. She'd have been far more sympathetic.

As I close the back door against the frozen air, the hum of voices drifts from the drawing room. Gently, I pull the kitchen door towards me and head back out into the hallway. They've closed the door, which is strange.

I tiptoe along the hallway to listen outside. *Eavesdroppers never hear any good about themselves.* My mother's voice resounds in my head. I didn't want to think about her today, but since Ann-Marie's brought her up, no doubt she'll spend the rest of Christmas on repeat inside my brain like she did last year.

'I made it perfectly clear *why*,' Carla says. 'Do we really need to keep going over this?'

'You can't deny that it's in all our interests to take things forward,' Roger says. 'As quickly as possible.'

'You mean *your* interests,' Carla replies. 'You can't just get me here and bamboozle me like this – it's not fair.'

'For goodness' sake, I thought we weren't going to talk about this,' Sophie says.

'We're just hoping for things to go back to how they were.' It's Dominic's voice now.

What is he referring to – it can't be his former marriage, surely? Oh God, I can't go through any more grief – not after everything that's already happened.

'It's not as straightforward as that,' Carla says. 'You can't just expect me to come running back.'

He *must* be referring to their marriage.

'Resorting to this way of doing things isn't filling us with glee either, Carla,' says Ann-Marie. 'But you must be able to see what'll happen if you were to decide to go the other way. It would be so easy just to change things here and now.'

Doing *what* things? Changing *what* things?

'I can't – I still need to think about it all.'

'You've had long enough to think. We need to act now,' Dominic says.

'It's Christmas.' Sophie's voice is flat. 'There's nothing anybody can do until after it's over – not officially – so let's just try to muddle on for now, can we?'

'But you're considering it, are you, Carla?' It's Roger's voice now.

I lean against the wall. *Are* they all talking about Dominic and Carla getting back together? I can't make head nor tail of it. I'm sick of being on the outskirts of everything. It was just the same in Kyle's family.

'I haven't got a lot of choice in the matter, have I?' Whatever it is, she doesn't sound too happy about it.

'Natalie could come back in here at any moment.' It's Dominic's voice now. 'So can I suggest we change the subject?'

Dominic, you've got so much explaining to do when we're on our own later.

'Perhaps I'd better go and see how she's getting on and apologise for being so uptight about the plate.' Ann-Marie's tone is begrudging as she seems to resign herself to coming to check on me.

'Good idea.'

At the scraping of what must be Ann-Marie's chair across the floor, I dart back to the kitchen. As she walks in, I fill a glass with water, trying to look as nonchalant as possible. I'm dying to ask her what they've just been talking about, but she's hardly likely to admit that they're all trying to coax Carla into returning to Dominic and that she'd be only too pleased to permanently snap the Natalie branch off their family tree – if that's what they were all on about.

'I'm sorry for what I said before, dear.' She reaches for my arm. 'I didn't mean to be so insensitive. As Sophie's so rightly pointed out to me – this time of year must be difficult enough for you already.' I'm unsure at first, but perhaps there is the slightest hint of sympathy in her voice.

'You could say that – but it's fine – I know you didn't mean anything bad by it.'

'Are you going to come in and join us for dessert?' She tilts her head to the side as she awaits my reply.

'Yes.' I force a smile at her. 'I'm looking forward to it.'

'Oooh, this looks fab, Mum.' Sophie pours cream over her cheesecake. 'I couldn't have made it better myself.'

'Which is why your business flopped.' Dominic grins and I shoot him a look. He really is going too far with this.

'I agree, Ann-Marie.' Carla waves her spoon around. 'It's the best cheesecake I ever tasted.'

Ann-Marie might not have cooked the food with her own fair hands but she still seems to bask in the praise.

'It was one of their grandmother's recipes.' She rubs her hands together. 'Right, shall I have cream or ice cream?'

'You could have both, like me.' I hover the spoon over my plate.

'Do you remember that cheesecake *we* once tried to make?' Carla nudges Dominic. 'The one that was an absolute disaster?'

Why is she talking about times when they were married in front of me? I can tell she's trying to upset me by the way she looks at me so slyly from the corner of her eye. She knows exactly what she's doing but I'm not going to rise to it.

'It sounds like he's improved since then,' I tell her. 'He's cooked some lovely meals since we've been together.'

'Do you do much cooking, Natalie?' Sophie smiles at me. 'I think we're all still awaiting a dinner invite to Chez Elmer, aren't we?'

'Yeah, I love cooking,' I reply. 'We'll have to get something in the diary soon.' Even if it's about time they came over to our house, the thought of trying to impress Ann-Marie fills me with dread. No doubt she'll pick fault with absolutely everything.

'That sounds lovely,' says Ann-Marie. However, her expression conveys otherwise. 'Anyway, I hope we're going to keep with our Christmas Eve tradition this year.'

'Oh no,' Dominic groans. 'She's getting the photos out.'

'Another evening of the Dominic show then.' Sophie rolls her eyes. 'Since they're all of him.'

'There's plenty of you, dear.' Ann-Marie taps her hand.

'We both know that isn't true, don't we? You've got three times as many pictures of him as you have of me.' Her tone is light but there's a trace of bitterness within it.

'I've got a name, you know.' Dominic frowns at his sister.

'Do we really have to get the photos out, Dad? It's not going to be much fun for Natalie, is it?'

'You all love it really,' says Roger, as he finishes his dessert. 'Especially now that we can do them as a slideshow on the TV. I'll go and get it all set up, shall I?'

'I hope you've still got lots of me.' Carla smiles, rising from her chair. 'I'll come and help you.'

I'm almost certain there'll be none of me in their perfect slideshow. I've already looked around for the wedding photo of us which I framed and gifted for them, but it's nowhere to be seen.

TWELVE

'If you'll just excuse me, I've got a couple of phone calls I need to make.'

'Now?' Dominic asks as I get to my feet.

I can't bring myself to look at him. I just need to get out of here. One hour of feigning interest at those dratted photographs has been quite enough.

'Are you alright, Natalie?' Ann-Marie calls after me as I close the door behind me and head for the safety of my room. Thank goodness I have somewhere I can escape to.

There's a sudden tapping at the door.

'Come in,' I say, hoping to see Sophie. But it's Ann-Marie. And I haven't even had the chance to move the wine glasses from earlier. However, if she's noticed them, she doesn't say anything.

'It's only me,' she says. 'I thought I'd check in and apologise for upsetting you – again.' She pulls a face.

'You haven't upset me – it's just – you know.' I fold my arms as I sit deeper into the bed. There's no escaping the position I'm suddenly in. I'm just going to have to face it.

'The photographs?' she asks. 'It's just our silly family tradition to go through them on Christmas Eve.'

'It's not silly at all, it's just…' My words trail off. 'You weren't showing them all of Carla *last* Christmas when I was here.'

'Oh Natalie, we're just trying to keep you all happy. There were a few of you in there, weren't there?' She squeezes my shoulder. 'From your wedding day?'

'Two.' I sniff. 'Look, it doesn't matter. I'm sorry if I've been hypersensitive today.'

Though I know full well that I haven't. There weren't just umpteen pictures of Dominic and Carla, but Carla on her own as well.

'You haven't been at all.' She sits beside me on the bed. 'But you have to understand that even though you're around now, we did think a lot of Carla – we still do. She was so much more than our daughter-in-law and now—'

'And now I'm your daughter-in-law – whether you like it or not.' Tears spring to my eyes again as the words spill out of me. 'And it was Carla's fault that I spilt that wine and smashed that plate – I didn't like to say so at the time, but—'

'Look, Natalie.' She leans forward and pats my arm. 'Carla wouldn't behave like that, no matter what you might be thinking of her. I know she's Dominic's ex-wife, but honestly—'

'So you're saying you don't believe me?'

She looks straight into my eyes. 'I've been a terrible hostess, Natalie, and I'm so sorry. I've been so wrapped up in my own concerns that I haven't been nearly as hospitable to you as I should have been.'

I want to say, *You've been incredibly hospitable with Carla* but I've probably said enough already. Instead, I wait for Ann-Marie to continue.

'We're under a lot of pressure – Roger and I.' She draws her arm back and rubs her hands together like she's wringing out an old dishcloth. 'It's all very complicated and – well, you've probably heard all about it from Dominic already.'

'He's told me bits and pieces. About the problems you've been having with your business.'

Problems with your business is the understatement of the century.

'What people must be thinking of us is the worst thing about it all, but then...' She looks down at the carpet. 'You're no stranger to fending off people's reactions either, are you?'

So we're going down this road then. 'You're talking about the newspaper article from almost three years ago presumably?' Here we go. The elephant in the room has risen from its slumber. I knew it would sooner or later.

'Word travelled fast that you and Dominic were marrying – so, as you can imagine, we had lots of explaining to do amongst our friends and clients last year when we discovered Dominic was marrying you.' She folds her arms across her middle as though trying to protect herself. 'But now, with what's going on with us, we seem to be sinking fast. So many people have turned their backs on us. Friends and colleagues we've known for years.'

'You find out who truly matters when push comes to shove,' I say, shocked at how much I sound like my mother. She always said it would come to me one day. 'I certainly did.'

'What actually happened, Natalie?' Her voice is gentle and she looks genuinely interested.

'It's more or less like you read it in the paper.' I reply. This is as much as she needs to know. It's quite enough as it is. 'Only they hugely sensationalised it – as they always do.'

She looks uncertain for a moment, as though she's deliberating whether to say whatever it is she's planned out in her mind.

'What is it, Ann-Marie?' Maybe I should be letting it go but I want to know, I *need* to know what she's thinking.

'You must be able to understand why we've had our reservations about you marrying our son. There was all the awfulness on social media too.'

I want to tell her that as long as Dominic's happy, she should be happy. Instead, I say, 'I did read some of it at the time – until I became so upset and afraid that I could barely venture from my door.'

'At least it's all in the past now.'

I want to say, *apart from the fact that* you've *brought it up* but I clamp my lips together.

'It's never too far from my mind though.' I try to meet her gaze but she looks away.

'Anyway, it's getting late, so I'll leave you to rest, shall I?'

This suits me fine. I've discussed my past with her as far as I want to for one night.

She pats my hand again as she rises from the bed. 'I've got a few things still to prepare before our big day tomorrow so I'd better be getting on.'

I lie back on the bed and close my eyes. Kyle fills my thoughts, which is no surprise. I've thought about him far more today than I normally do and can't shake the memory of a Christmas Eve I spent at *his* parents' house.

'I didn't like what you were saying about me before,' he said as we were getting ready for bed.

'What do you mean?'

'The Jekyll and Hyde comment. The difference between how I am at work and at home.'

'It's true though. And it's not *me* who gets the best of you.'

He slammed his palm onto the bed. 'You never resist an opportunity, do you? This is why I make us keep ourselves to ourselves. You shouldn't be bad-mouthing me to *anyone*, especially my family.'

'I wasn't. I was joking. I—' In that moment, I knew I should have kept my mouth shut. I knew all about his temper flares, but had still dared to challenge him.

'We should never have come here.'

'Please, Kyle. Pack it in – your parents will hear us. Please don't spoil Christmas for us.' I tugged my nightie over my head.

'And as if that wasn't enough...' He swung around to face me, anger flashing from his eyes. 'What were you thinking of telling my mother that I won't let you go out to work?'

'But it's true. And if you won't listen to me, perhaps you'll lis—'

'Keep away from me.' Kyle tugged the duvet to his side as I tried to climb into bed beside him. 'I don't want to sleep with you.'

'So where I am supposed to sleep then?' I tried to tug it back. 'I can't exactly go downstairs. Your parents are still up.' I briefly toyed with the idea of telling Kyle's parents that he was trying to oust me from the bedroom, but he'd have only denied it and I'd have looked stupid.

'Just not next to me. You can sleep down there.' He threw my pillows onto the carpet beside the bed.

'But I'll freeze. Please, Kyle. You're being ridiculous.'

But that was how I spent Christmas Eve. Sobbing silently, lying on the carpet beside the bed on which my bully of a husband softly snored until his parents retired and I could sneak onto the sofa. Looking back, I can hardly believe I allowed him to treat me so badly, but my self-esteem was so low, I probably thought that the floor was exactly where I belonged that night. I know I won't be sleeping on the floor tonight, but I can't help but feel that my first Christmas married to Dominic isn't going to plan.

· · ·

'I'm really sorry about earlier.' Dominic closes the door behind him and stares at me. 'I don't blame you for being so upset.' His voice is loaded with sympathy, which brings fresh tears to my eyes.

'I just wish we could go home.' I swipe at my eyes before the tears have a chance to spill from them.

'Well, we can't.' He sits on the edge of the bed and pulls his socks off before unbuckling his jeans and sliding them off as well. 'Until this weather improves, no one's going *anywhere.*'

'I can't believe they made me sit through that.' I shake my head. 'Why would I want to see pictures of your first wedding day and holidays from when you were still married to Carla?'

'At least my dad apologised,' he replies. 'And you got to see all the embarrassing ones of Sophie and I when we were kids too.' He tugs his jumper over his head and lifts the duvet back. 'Anyway, you don't need to worry about Carla.'

'It's just—'

'Let's get some sleep, Nat.' He slides into bed and draws the duvet over himself.

'I wish I could.'

'Why can't you?'

'Because my head's going around and around. Can I ask you something?'

'Ask away.'

'I want to know what you were all talking about earlier – when you thought I was in the kitchen.'

'When? What?' He stiffens, which suggests I've shocked him by asking him about this.

'You were in the drawing room – all talking about Carla running back. And then something was said about how nothing can be done until Christmas is over.'

'Oh, that? It's—'

'Don't try to pull the wool over my eyes here. I then heard

you shushing everyone and saying, *Natalie will be back in a minute*. What's going on, Dom?'

'It's just all the *stuff* my parents are dealing with at the moment. The tax and the court stuff – you know all about it.'

'So why did you say, *Natalie will be back in a minute?*'

'Because you've got enough to deal with without getting caught up in my family's woes. Anyway, I'm knackered, love, after that horrid drive earlier; are you turning your lamp off?'

'I really don't think I'll be able to sleep.'

'Just try – cuddle up to me and you'll be asleep in no time.' He kisses the top of my head and turns away from me. I had such high hopes of how we might spend our first married Christmas Eve once we'd got to bed, but there's no chance of that.

'Your mum came in to see me earlier.' I reach from the bed to click the lamp off. It's a strange kind of darkness when everything outside has been whitened by the snow.

'Yeah – I asked her to put her head in.' He turns back over to face me. 'Was everything OK?'

'She brought my past up. But when I tried to properly address it with her, she just shut up shop,' I say, lying on my back and staring up at the ceiling.

'It *was* rather a lot for them to get their heads around at the time – especially when they first found out.'

'But they're judging me on an article without giving me the chance to explain my side of things.' I turn my head to look at him but all I can make out is the square outline of his jaw. 'And as for that picture of me and Hayden they printed...' I close my eyes in an effort to somehow shut it out of where it's appeared in my mind's eye. 'If only I could have it all taken down off the internet – I'm never going to stop trying.'

'If anyone should have been scared off by the article' – he reaches for my hand across the duvet – 'it's me. So stop worrying about what my parents might be thinking.'

I can't decide whether his reference to being 'scared off' is meant to comfort me or worry me, but I'll let it go for now. Things are bad enough as it is. 'I just feel like I'm no match for Carla in their eyes. I know it's stupid but I can't shake it.'

'You just do you, Nat. Anyway, I'm off to sleep.' He turns away again.

After a few minutes, his breathing has settled into a soft, rhythmic snore.

Feeling suddenly wide awake, I swing my legs over the side of the bed and head for the door. I'll visit the bathroom and then I'll try to settle. I'll draw a line under all the tension of today and start afresh tomorrow.

As I creep along the landing, Carla's room is in silence and there's a low hum of conversation emitting from either Ann-Marie's or Roger's room. According to Dominic, they've slept apart for years but must have things to discuss now that everyone else has gone to bed. I pause outside but they must be at the furthest side of the room – too far away for me to make out what they're talking about.

As I clean my teeth, I stare into the mirror.

'You're alright, Nat,' I say to myself as I rinse my tooth-brush. 'You can do this.'

And I can. I'll win them all over if it's the last thing I do.

It's no good. I really can't sleep. Ann-Marie's earlier words won't stop swirling around my mind. The *reservations* she said she and Roger have had about me. Perhaps if I was a mother myself, I might be able to imagine how she's feeling.

I sit up slowly and carefully to avoid waking Dominic, then without stopping to talk myself out of it, I type *Natalie Miller Yorkshire* into Google and there it is; I'm still top of the search. I only ever read the article once – straight after my suspended sentence was handed down to me nearly three years ago. But now, like picking the scab from a wound, I'm going to read it again. If only to try to see the situation through the lens of my mother-in-law and all the other people in her circle who know about it.

Is what was written about me and my brother really as damming as I remember?

THIRTEEN

TEN-YEAR SENTENCE FOR BROTHER-IN-LAW KILLING

A brother and sister have today been convicted of killing a twenty-eight-year-old man in York.

The decomposing body of Kyle James Parkes was found dumped in bushes along a remote edge of Danefield Park by a member of the public.

Following an investigation by Yorkshire's Murder Inquiry Team, Hayden John Miller, aged thirty-four, and his sister Natalie Ann Miller, aged twenty-eight, who had initially reported her partner missing, were eventually arrested.

Miller admitted stabbing Parkes in a frenzied attack after what he described as a domestic violence incident in which he insisted his sister was a victim. What he did, he maintained throughout their trial, was in protection of Natalie Miller rather than what the prosecution had alleged, a financially motivated attack. They claimed that Miller owed his brother-in-law a substantial amount of money that he was having diffi-

culty repaying and it was this that had initially fuelled the violence between them.

In the hours that followed the killing, the pair set about covering up Miller's actions, including the sending of text messages to Mr Parkes's phone and the concealing of his body.

The pair denied and lied about their involvement in Mr Parkes's killing but the CPS presented compelling evidence which proved that Hayden Miller was responsible for Mr Parkes's death, and that while it was claimed that Natalie Miller wasn't there when her brother attacked her partner, CCTV evidence at the entrance to the park showed that she was jointly responsible for helping to conceal his body.

When sentencing the pair at Yorkshire Crown Court, Judge Peter Smythson said, 'What's striking about this case was that in the first four days after you killed him, you both just went about your business, calmly covering what you had done without any hint that you knew where he was all along. And throughout this process, no regret for your actions has been demonstrated, only a chilling self-interest in your own preservation. While it is accepted that your actions were not premeditated, what followed the brutal stabbing of this man was a deliberate attempt to run away from what you had done to him.'

Speaking for the defence, Jonathan Jones stated that Miss Miller suffered behind closed doors for several years, while her brother could only helplessly watch on from afar. He said the unfortunate events of 24 March were an explosive culmination of several years of unresolved trauma between the couple.

Miller, he maintained, was merely protecting his sister, who had already been threatened by the deceased with a knife. To punish her as well, he claimed, demonstrated the fragility of a system which should exist to protect her.

This was refuted by the prosecution, who said there was

never any evidence of Kyle Parkes perpetrating domestic abuse. There were no police records or witness accounts – instead, the deceased was described as a stalwart of the community, respected by his teaching colleagues and the parents of the children he taught. The prosecution alleged that the domestic violence story had been fabricated by Natalie Miller as a way to protect her brother.

Miller was found guilty of manslaughter and, along with his sister, was also found guilty of perverting the course of justice and preventing a lawful and decent burial.

For Hayden Miller, Judge Smythson handed down sentences of ten years, four years and two years to be served concurrently and in the case of Natalie Miller, sentences of two years and eighteen months were passed, and suspended for two years. Natalie Miller was also ordered to complete three hundred hours of unpaid work as reparation towards genuine domestic violence sufferers.

Domestic violence campaigners lined the streets outside the court and took to social media after what they deemed to be a gross misjustice.

Jones, speaking for the Millers, has confirmed the sentences will be appealed.

But those appeals came to absolutely nothing. I carried out my unpaid work, which I'd thankfully completed well before I met Dominic, and my poor brother still has three years to serve before he completes two-thirds of his sentence and is eligible for parole.

All for defending me.

I stare once again at the back of my sleeping husband's head. I'm thankful that Dominic accepted my version of events, however, sooner or later, I'm going to *have* to tell him the full story.

.   .   .

Re-reading that article was a *big* mistake. If I couldn't get to sleep before, I *really* can't get to sleep now. Every time I close my eyes, I see Kyle's sneering face from the many times he had me walled up, pinned down, or was just saying something nasty at my expense. Then, of course, the final time – when he thought he could get away with threatening me with a knife.

Hayden and I were scapegoated. Who were the police ever going to sympathise with? My brother with a list as long as each of my arms for juvenile crime, or my partner, a salt-of-the-earth primary school teacher, regular fundraiser and all-around good egg.

Until he was at home with me, that is.

I've never been more isolated and more alone. In the time we were together, he systematically cut me off from everyone. Once, when out for a walk, I got chatting to a woman who sat beside me on the park bench and I just let rip about what was going on at home.

'People think he's a decent guy,' I told her. 'But he's awful to me.'

Shock was etched across her face as she cleared her throat. 'So why are you still there?'

'I'm scared to leave,' I admitted. 'He's warned me of all sorts of things if I try.'

'There are places out there that can help you,' she said. 'You don't have to stay with him.'

We'd talked at length for over an hour until she announced that she needed to collect her son from school. As soon as I discovered the school she was referring to, I knew I was in for it in spite of her promises never to repeat what I'd told her.

Two days later, Kyle stormed in after work and, without saying a word, he marched across the kitchen and slapped my face so hard that it knocked my head into the cupboard.

'That's for going around and spreading lies about me,' he

yelled. 'Someone's reported me to the head. It's a bloody good job I've been able to convince them of your instability and propensity to seek attention.'

'You've lied, in other words.'

He slapped me again, so hard that I saw stars.

I slid down the cupboard to the floor. 'Get away from me.' What I should have done was run out into the street while my face was red-raw from his slaps but he'd never let me past. And who'd believe me anyway?

It's no good. I need to move myself. Sitting up, I swing my legs to the floor and reach for my dressing gown. I need to get out of this room before I drive myself insane.

As I get out on the landing, Roger's snoring vibrates from behind one of the doors. No wonder Ann-Marie has a separate bedroom from him. I tiptoe down the stairs and head for the kitchen. A chamomile tea might settle me down.

I jump as Carla pops out from next to the office door. 'What are you doing?' I ask her. She looks decidedly shifty.

'I'm just looking for something I left down here,' she replies. 'My, um, phone charger.'

'In *there*?' I whisper, pointing at the office door.

'I thought there might be a charger in the office, but it's locked.'

'What are you *really* up to?'

'Look, Natalie, I know we haven't got off to the best start but you should know—'

'Just leave it, will you? I've honestly had enough for one day.'

As I reach the kitchen door, I look back to see Carla heading up the stairs, wrapped in the fluffy robe Ann-Marie laid out for her.

I click the kitchen door behind me, cursing myself for not putting socks on before I came down here. As I pad across the kitchen to the kettle, the stone floor is freezing beneath my bare feet.

I pull the blind to one side, hoping that the snowfall might have eased, but it's just as heavy as it was earlier. If not more so.

There's no way any of us will be leaving any time soon.

FOURTEEN

At some point after I headed back up to bed, I must have fallen asleep for when I wake, daylight's streaming through the window. I reach across the bed for Dominic but he's already gone. Checking my watch, I realise I've slept much later than I normally would, which should hardly come as a surprise after the time I finally got to sleep.

I need a shower and to wash my hair. Carla will, no doubt, be breezing around looking her usual gorgeous self, while I... I sit up straight and catch sight of myself in the mirror. Ugh. My hair's on end, the bags under my eyes could fit a week's shopping in them and I've got lines up and down the side of my face. I don't usually feel this bad about myself and I need to get a grip of it today. *If you don't love yourself, no one else will.* It's Mum again.

Putting my dressing gown on, I head for the door, hearing Dominic's voice as soon as I open it. *And* Carla's. But rather than drifting up from downstairs, their voices are coming from the room opposite.

He's in her room.

'We're going round and round in circles here, Dom,' Carla says.

How dare she call him Dom? That's *my* name for him.

'How about we just muddle through today and then revisit things tomorrow?' His voice is as placatory.

What things? What are they talking about now?

'Nothing can change how I feel, you know.'

I can't discern what Carla's talking about from her tone of voice. Does she mean how she feels about *Dominic*? Bloody hell, I thought their former relationship was dead and buried before our arrival here yesterday. Now I'm really not sure.

'I know you're probably thinking that I'm only in here to discuss one thing but—'

She cuts him off mid-sentence. 'You shouldn't be in here *at all* – I don't care what your mother thinks or says – if Natalie were to catch you...' Her voice becomes louder as if she's stepping towards her door to show Dominic out.

I slink back into our room. What the hell's going on between them? From what I've seen over the last day, it seems like Carla's *never* truly gone away. She's certainly more part of this family than I've ever been.

I sink to the bed. After all the misery I lived through with Kyle, meeting Dominic felt like all my Christmases and birthdays rolled into one – at least to begin with.

So I'm going to fight for him. I sit up straight. If Carla thinks I'm just going to roll over and die, she's got another think coming.

I feel far better as I head down the stairs. I've curled my hair, put some make-up on and I'm wearing my new dress. As soon as I tried it on in the store, I knew I had to have it. I'm not normally a 'dress' kind of person but this one fits in all the right places and even Dominic said that it brings out the colour of my eyes.

I take a deep breath as I reach the second flight. The conversation I overheard before was probably nothing. I trust my husband. He's never done anything for me not to trust him.

Anyway, it's Christmas morning. I need to plant a smile on my face and make the best of things.

I wish Christmases were as they used to be before my parents died – when we made paper chains and helped Mum bake mince pies and hide coins in the Christmas pudding. In the days before my brother went off the rails after we were separated and were fostered out. We didn't have anything like the sumptuous lifestyle of this family but there was a *feeling* of Christmas in our home at least – a sense of joy and a reason for celebration.

Christmas Carols are drifting from the TV in the lounge and the house is filled with the scent of a roasting turkey and open fires but I'm not feeling Christmassy in the slightest here. By the sounds of it, Roger has managed to find a televised church service to watch in the lounge.

Ann-Marie's and Carla's voices echo from the kitchen – I'll go in there soon and offer my help with the food preparations.

As I reach the bottom of the stairs, Dominic's on his way along the hallway as the kitchen door falls closed behind him. 'Carla said you were up and about in the night.' He smiles as he catches hold of my hand. 'So I thought I'd leave you to sleep in this morning.'

'Thanks, hon.' My voice is strained. 'And I'm glad I've caught you on your own – I need to ask you something.'

'This sounds ominous.'

'It's just that I heard you in Carla's room before.'

'Oh, it was just business.' He answers quickly but there's no denying that he looks taken aback at my directness.

'What do you mean, *business*? What sort of business?'

'Sorry to interrupt.' Carla appears behind him. 'But are we going to get these presents opened, or what?'

'Merry Christmas.' Sophie rushes out of the lounge towards me.

'Thank you – you too.' As I hug her back, I look over her shoulder. 'Merry Christmas to you all too.' I nod towards my in-laws, then Carla, who's now sitting in front of the tree.

'We've been waiting for you,' says Ann-Marie as she passes me. At least she's smiling. She's certainly a tough nut to crack and I never quite know where I am with her.

'I brought our gifts down and added them to the others while you were in the bathroom,' Dominic says.

I take my place in the circle on the carpet, surprised to see six piles of presents. If Carla wasn't expected here this Christmas, which she shouldn't have been, why are there presents under the tree for her? The only sensible explanation is that it's been planned all along. Even without the excuse of the snow, I'm sure they'd have come up with another excuse to use.

Ann-Marie picks a present up. 'Who's going to open a present first?'

I recall from last year, the Elmers' ritual of going around in a circle, each opening one gift at a time. It's a far cry from my childhood Christmases when my brother and I couldn't get the wrapping paper off our presents quickly enough.

'I'm sorry I haven't got anything for any of you.' Carla crosses her legs carefully in her thigh-skimming tartan dress and woolly tights. She looks bright and fresh and Christmassy and I can totally understand what initially attracted Dominic to her.

'You go first then.' Roger points at Ann-Marie. She's holding the present I've bought her – I can tell from the gift wrap that I paid the assistant extra to do for me. I've spent a small fortune on the gifts for this family, more than I'd *ever* normally spend on Hayden. At Christmas, we were more bothered about getting together for dinner and a few drinks than we were about fancy presents.

'Oh, it's a bowl.' She sounds almost disappointed as she sets it on the carpet in front of her. 'Though it's nice to get something so, erm, functional. Thank you, dear.'

'It's a Waterford bowl,' I tell her, loading as much enthusiasm as I can into my voice. 'To match your glasses.'

'My turn.' Roger rips into his gift, again with our gift wrapping on it. 'It's a wallet,' he exclaims.

'You can put that with all your others,' Ann-Marie chuckles. 'Go on, Natalie, open one of yours next.'

I check the label. *To Natalie, from Ann-Marie and Roger.* There's no *love* from but that's clearly their way – with me, at least. At least Ann-Marie's gone into a shop with me at the forefront of her mind and I'm intrigued to find out what she's bought for me. I rip the paper from it.

'Thank you,' I say, placing the toiletries set behind me. 'They're lovely.' Blimey – I can't believe she's presented me with a box of smellies.

'Your turn, Carla.'

To give her at least *some* credit, Carla looks very uncomfortable as the paper falls away to reveal a Pandora charm. 'Erm, well this is lovely,' she exclaims, holding it up and twirling it between her fingers so it sparkles in the lights of the Christmas tree.

'I thought of you as soon as I saw it. Now it's your turn, Sophie.' She smiles at her daughter, just as my phone begins to ring.

'I'm sorry – I need to take this.' I grab my phone from the carpet in front of me and dart to the door. I don't care what they think of me rushing off. It's Christmas Day and I want to speak to my brother. He might not be able to call me back later.

This is a call from a person in a UK prison. If you do not wish to speak to them, please hang up now. All calls will be recorded.

'Hayden,' I say as I rush up the stairs. 'Happy Christmas – I'm sorry – I know it isn't, but I've got to say it.'

'Not really – it's just another day here really – only we're banged up even *more* than we usually would be.'

Something inside me sags at his words. 'You'd think it would be the other way around,' I reply. 'Do you think you'll get a reasonable Christmas dinner for a change?'

He chuckles. 'You've got to be joking.'

'I'm so sorry, Hayden.' I click the bedroom door behind me. 'Really I am.'

'Anyway, I've only another two of these to go and then I'll be back eating turkey with you. I've got to look on the bright side, haven't I?'

'I didn't know there was one – and you know how dreadful I already feel about you being where you are so there's no point trying to make light of it.' No matter how often we have this conversation, I never feel any less guilty.

'I'm surviving – there's not a lot of choice really.'

'Seriously, what you did for me—' I sink to the bed as I try to picture my brother's face on the other end of the phone. If the last time I visited him is anything to go by, he'll be unshaven, pale from not getting any fresh air and still badly in need of a haircut.

'Let's not go there, sis – not today, eh? I haven't got much phone credit left but I thought I'd use the last of it up on you.'

'I'm honoured.' I laugh. 'No seriously – it's good to talk to you – things have been pretty strained here.'

'At your in-laws'?'

'Yep. It doesn't help that Dominic's first wife is spending Christmas here with us because of the weather.'

'It's pretty wild out there. We haven't even been allowed out for exercise today. Are you getting on OK?'

'Not really. I've tried to be friendly and all that – you know me. But it's not working.'

'How do she and Dominic get on?'

'A little too well for my liking, but I'm trying to rise above that.'

'It's about time I met this new husband of yours, don't you think? Though he can't be any worse than the last bloke you were with.' There's a bitter edge to his words.

'He doesn't know the full story yet, Hayden.'

'What do you mean?'

'About what happened.'

'But he's seen the article, hasn't he?'

'The whole bloody world has seen that damn article. But look, yes, I'll talk to him about visiting next time I come – he's led a pretty sheltered life.' A vision of Dominic being scanned and patted down by the security guards enters my mind. 'I can't really imagine him putting himself through the security rigma-role in the visitors' centre.'

'Oh bloody hell – it's just beeped. I've got even less time than I thought I had. I'll ring you after next Saturday when I—'

But he's cut off before he finishes his sentence. I'd give anything for things to be different and to be spending the festive period with him instead of knowing he's stuck inside the concrete walls of his tiny cell on Christmas bloody Day. Again.

All because of me.

FIFTEEN

I was made out to be cold, callous and capable of inventing a domestic violence story as a way of saving my brother's skin in the aftermath of Kyle's death. But I'll never, ever forget what Hayden did for me and I'm overwhelmed with guilt each time I allow myself to linger for too long on it.

After he'd been sent to prison, the theories and speculation reached fever pitch on social media. Some of the comments will be etched in my memory forever.

'I always knew there was something cold about her. You can see it in her eyes.'

'That poor man. What an awful end. They didn't even afford him the dignity of being properly laid to rest.'

'It should have been her that died, not a good man like him. Why the hell is she still walking free?'

'Do we really want her sort living among us?'

Dominic already knew who I was when he responded to a Facebook post I'd put up in the nearby village group looking for an estate agent when I was searching for somewhere new to live. It was close enough to my old home so I wouldn't feel completely displaced, but far enough away to make a fresh start away from the accusing stares and finger-pointing. I'd had enough.

'You'll probably already recognise me from the papers,' I said when he asked if we already knew each other from somewhere.

'I do,' he replied. 'But it's got nothing to do with you looking around this place.'

'So don't you want me to just leave then?'

'I'm here to show you around, that's all.' He kept his back to me as we walked to the door, keys jangling. Perhaps he didn't want to look at me, given my conviction. Or maybe he just wanted to convey his nonchalance about the situation.

'Is Elmer Lettings *your* company?' I followed him into the terraced house which I fervently hoped would soon become my home.

'No – but it will be one day.' His chest swelled with pride as he said that and I can remember thinking how lovely it must be to feel that sort of pride in yourself. 'Right now, I'm just looking after things for my parents while they're away.'

The house was empty, it was in a new area and it was more than adequate. If it had been only *half* as good as it was, I'd have *still* wanted it.

'I'll take it.' I swung around from looking out of the lounge window to face him. 'How soon can I move in?'

'Well, my parents don't usually allow tenants to move in straight away,' he replied. 'Not until all the checks are back...' He sounded hesitant but at least he wasn't saying there was no chance for me, like other prospective landlords had.

'You already know my history – so you know I'm not going to pass any police checks, but like I said to you on the phone, I'm happy to pay the first six months upfront.' I'd sensed it would be easier to win him around than his parents, so I wasn't going to let go until he'd accepted me for that flat.

It had wiped out my savings, but I had to get away from my

previous home. In the months following our sentencing, I'd had a brick through my window, my front door daubed with red paint and nasty messages posted through my letterbox. With Kyle being a primary school teacher, he was very well known and loved in the small market town where he taught and we lived, so the awful backlash towards me was almost inevitable.

'I should probably let my parents have the final say.' Dominic still looked hesitant. 'After all, I don't want them to think their company won't be in good hands when it eventually passes to me. But I'll put in a good word for you when they get back, I promise.'

'I really, really need to move – like *yesterday*.' I gave him my most beseeching expression.

It had been almost two years since Kyle's death and nothing had got any easier. The ghosts in the house we'd lived in pursued me night and day and I was constantly looking over my shoulder in fear of reprisals from the other locals.

Dominic looked at me like no one had for a long time – as though he was *really* seeing me.

'You don't know how much you'd be helping me,' I persisted.

'Well, I'll probably get it in the neck, but I guess that once you're in here, you're in, aren't you? There won't be much they can do about it.'

'I could kiss you,' I declared, then blushed at what I'd just said to this sharply dressed, good-looking man who, judging by the way his shoes shone and the plum-in-his-mouth lilt to his words, was clearly in a very different league to me – particularly given the circumstances I'd ended up in.

'How about you buy me a drink to say thank you instead?' He tilted his head to the side as he awaited my response.

'Really?' I could hardly believe what I was hearing. In the space of a minute, I'd bagged myself somewhere new to live and, so it seemed, a date.

'I know what it's like to have everyone talking about you,' he replied. 'I'm going through a pretty acrimonious divorce as we speak. To be honest, going out for a drink would provide some much-needed distraction.'

Well-dressed, good-looking and *single*. Wow – things were massively looking up.

If we'd met in any other circumstances, Dominic might not have looked twice at me, but he said he'd seen something in me that he'd never seen in anyone else. Something that intrigued him. So it could be said that we were both in the right place at the right time.

I pushed all my doubts about getting into another relationship to the back of my mind. After my nightmarish experience with Kyle, I'd sworn myself off men forever, but it was clear from that first drink we went for that Dominic was just as interested in me as I was in him. I also hoped that our being together might fend off the necessity for his parents to want to run their usual vetting checks on me as a new tenant. Perhaps they'd just trust their son's judgement. But there was no such luck.

'I'm sorry, but Mum's got a real bee in her bonnet about this,' Dominic told me when he came around one evening after work when I was just three weeks into the tenancy. 'She's digging into you more than she normally would.'

'So she's done *all* the checks?' I hadn't even met the woman and knew at that moment that I'd have to work harder than ever to win her over when we finally got to meet.

'She insisted on it. It's my fault, really.' He hitched his trousers up as he lowered himself onto my new sofa. 'As soon as I told her to leave it, she went hell for leather, starting with social media.'

'Oh bloody hell. I've tried to get some of all that hate taken down but most of it's still up there for the world to see.

Including your parents.' It had broken my heart to read it all – especially the comments that were being made about my brother. The thought of my new boyfriend's parents reading it all before even meeting me was horrendous.

'I don't think my dad will be too bothered. He just does as he's told.'

'Will they want me to leave here?' I swept my arms around the lounge. I'd bought new pictures and cushions for my long-overdue new start.

'You're already in, so it's too late for them to do anything about it until the lease is up.' He reached for my hand then, which reassured me.

That was true at least. In the eyes of the law, I'd paid my money and had a tenancy agreement.

And by the time that was up, Dominic had moved in with me and we'd begun to plan our future.

When his mother made noises about needing to put a new roof on the house I was renting, Dominic said I could move in with him. And I've never looked back.

Until now.

I never did find out exactly what Dominic meant when he said, *I know what it's like to have everyone talking.* He kept all his private papers locked in his briefcase and would always be more interested in talking about *me* when our conversations used to veer back to the past.

Even stalking Carla on social media left me none the wiser. I was dying to know why they'd split up. I wanted the insight – I needed to know so I wouldn't make the same mistakes – whatever they might be.

Dominic's explanation for their split was *financial differences*, but from the way he always clammed up when the subject of exes and former relationships was raised, I suspected things ran a lot deeper than he was letting on.

And I've got a feeling that this Christmas is when I'm going to learn the full story.

SIXTEEN

'Can I come in?' Sophie's cheery voice echoes from the landing.

'Of course you can.'

'Was it an important call before? I've never seen you move as fast.' She laughs as the door closes behind her.

'It was my brother.' My voice dips as I picture him in his prison-issue clothes. The longer he's in there, the harder it becomes. I always thought it would be the other way.

'The one who—'

'I've only got the one brother.' My voice is sharp, but I'm still reeling from my brief conversation with him.

'Oh right – sorry, I didn't mean to pry.'

'You're not – it's fine. I'm fine. It's just – hard, you know. Anyway' – I try to load cheer I'm no longer feeling into my voice – 'it would have been much, much harder if *you* hadn't been here this Christmas.'

'Well, I *am* here. And I've got your back, don't forget that.'

'What did you think about Carla's present?'

'How do you mean?'

'It might just be me but I'm thinking this situation has been planned all along.'

'Do you mean Carla spending Christmas with us?'

'Yeah – your mum *already* had presents for Carla under the tree. She *must* have been expecting her.'

'Maybe it's got something to do with when I saw Mum leaving Carla's offices. If they *have* invited her here, it'll only be to butter her up. They want her to buy more shares in their company, don't they?'

This is news to me. Dominic's certainly omitted this part, but I won't let on how much or how little I know to Sophie. I just want to find out what *she* knows. 'They must be more desperate than I knew about if they're putting all their faith in their son's ex-wife to save the day?'

'You do know about the size of their tax bill, don't you?'

'I know it's big but Dominic's been evasive when we've discussed it.'

'It's seven-figure big.' She pulls a face.

I take a deep breath as I sweep my gaze over the room and it falls on the oil painting on the far wall. I didn't realise it was that much. Perhaps if they sold some of the art they've collected, they could raise whatever they're short of, but obviously, I can't say this to Sophie.

'When are they in court for that other thing?'

'What other thing?' She eyes me with what looks like suspicion.

'Dominic told me about the dodgy boiler in one of the houses they let out.'

'He did? The *whole* story?'

'I know the tenant died in there. Why – is there even more to it?' My mind drifts back to the reference Ann-Marie made last night to her 'business issues'. There's only her who could make light of what happened like she has.

Sophie swallows. 'Do you really want to know?'

'Of course. I'm part of this family now, aren't I?'

'Alright – listen. This is the other reason why they're

buttering Carla up so much. Her firm's supposed to be acting for them.'

'I didn't know *that* – Dominic never said.' My shoulders sag with disappointment, yet relief. Disappointment that he hasn't told me *everything* and relief that at least I know what all the whispering's been about now. It also confirms why they're so keen to court favour with Carla.

I knew Ann-Marie and Roger would be facing massive legal fees, as well as having to pay damages to their dead tenant's family, but I had no idea *Carla* was so heavily involved.

'Rumour has it though' – Sophie sits on the bed beside me – 'that Carla's company haven't been as efficient in dealing with Mum and Dad's case as their reputation suggests. The negligence case has been dragging on for over two years.'

I've already googled the legal firm which Carla and her brother first started a decade ago. Since then, they've grown into one of the biggest firms in the North.

'What do you mean?'

'Lost letters, late letters, lots of miscommunications – that sort of thing.'

'The tax thing's more recent though, isn't it?'

She nods. 'Yeah – that's only come to light this year.'

'Could your parents lose The Elms as well?'

'It's certainly looking that way. But Carla can afford to bail them out ten times over if they can keep her on side.'

I look around the room again, at the beams and the beautiful rustic furniture. The light reflecting from the snow bathes the room in a soft glow. The house has apparently been in their family for several generations. The threat of losing the place must be breaking Ann-Marie's heart. Having said that, it must cost a fortune to run. Two people don't need all this.

'What if they can't? Keep her *on side*, I mean?'

'Oh, they will – they've got something on *her* as well.'

'Like what?'

'The whole thing is a stinking, toxic mess.' Sophie stares out of the window. 'Just like everything always is with my family.'

It's the first time I've ever heard Sophie talk like this. 'Are *you* OK?' I ask. 'It's a lot for you to cope with. And I heard your dad last night – when he had a dig about your business. It can't be easy for you.'

'Oh, that.' Her face falls even more. 'Yeah, he never resists an opportunity to rub it all in,' she replies. 'To be honest, I don't think they'd have even noticed if I'd never arrived here yesterday.'

'No – that's not true.'

'It really is. If I were some hotshot like Carla, they might pay more attention to me.'

'Well, I'm not a hotshot either – I paint nails for a living. So – what *have* they got on Carla?'

'Look, I'm sorry – I've probably said way too much as it is.' She rises from the bed, looking suddenly anxious to get away.

'Like I said, you can trust me.'

'It's my parents' problem. To be honest, I just want to keep out of it. I've spent my whole life taking care of myself and keeping out of their way and there's no reason why that should change now.'

I smile gently at her as she leaves the room. They're certainly a family with issues that they don't seem to want to discuss around me. Slowly but surely, I'm piecing extra bits together and, eventually, I'll have the full story.

There's no denying that there's an almighty parallel between me and my in-laws – perhaps this is why they avoid me so much – my *history* probably holds a mirror up to what they're dealing with. After their company's negligence, I'm not the only person with someone's death on their hands.

But I've still got so many questions whirring around my head – why did Dominic and Carla split up? Does she want him back – is that partly why she's still around? And what barrel do the family have her over? It's clearly one that's substantial enough for her to have agreed to spend Christmas with her former husband and in-laws instead of her own family. It certainly sounds like she'd have been here this Christmas no matter what – the snow has simply provided the perfect cover story.

SEVENTEEN

I lie back on the bed, deliberating what to do next. I should return downstairs but I can't really face having to paint on a false smile of gratitude when I open the rest of my presents. I just want to be on my own for a while. Plus, after the rubbish sleep I had last night, a wave of exhaustion is sweeping over me. Maybe I'll just close my eyes for ten minutes. It's not as if anyone will even notice I've gone. The only problem is that every time my subconscious takes over, I'm flooded with visons and memories I'd rather leave in the past...

My brother begged me for as long as I can remember to leave Kyle, once even paying the bond on a flat for me to move into to get away from him, but like an idiot, I still went back to him.

'I promised Mum I'd look after you,' Hayden reminded me, over and over again. 'But how can I while you're with that maniac?'

Kyle did have a decent side to him, though, as time went on, he showed it less frequently. When we first met at the gym, we'd been almost happy for a while, a little co-dependent perhaps, but in my naivety, I thought that the two of us not needing anyone else besides each other was really romantic. And I was happy that he wanted to take control of things. After losing my parents at such a young age and spending my teens in foster care, it felt good to have someone who not only wanted to *be* with me but wanted to take *care* of me.

But Kyle and the other most important person in my life, Hayden, detested each other. When Hayden came around, Kyle would remain in the other room or he'd answer the door and tell him I wasn't in.

'As long as you're with *him*, I can't come to your house anymore,' Hayden eventually said. 'He's a complete bastard and I can't bear how he treats you. I can't be around it anymore.'

'He just prefers to have me to himself,' I explained. 'He's got no siblings, so he just doesn't grasp how close you and me are.'

'That's his problem.'

'He's just jealous, that's all.'

'Jealous of your brother.' Hayden shook his head. 'And you're willing to accept it, is that what you're telling me?'

Kyle got his way for a while and Hayden, true to his word, backed off. At first, we agreed for me to visit him instead or to meet for lunch or a coffee. But Kyle became even more controlling, and it got increasingly difficult to leave the house without the third degree. He set 'track my phone' from his own iPhone, so I'd turn mine off when I went out through the day, but that caused a ton of trouble. He'd charge my phone himself overnight so I could never use the excuse that it had run out of battery.

We became locked in a claustrophobic circle of rowing, then making up, or him accusing, me conforming or placating until, eventually, my self-worth was so eroded, I didn't think I could ever come back from it. I lived for the nicer side of him, the one he'd showed me in the beginning and the one he still showed occasionally. But *only* occasionally.

'Have you looked in a mirror lately?' was one of his most frequent insults. 'Have you seen the state of yourself?'

My tears seemed to inflate his sense of power.

We never married; he didn't believe in all that – however, he *desperately* wanted children.

'He'll be just like me,' he said during one of his 'nicer' episodes when we were out for dinner. 'I've always wanted a son – someone to take everywhere I go and to carry my name on.'

'What if it's a girl?' I thought that I'd best humour him even though I had no intention of getting pregnant with his child.

'Then she'd be *your* department and we'd keep trying until we get *my* boy.'

Month after month, it didn't happen and this became one of the catalysts for his temper. But how could I have brought a child into the hell I was living in? Which is why I secretly continued to swallow my contraceptive pill every day. Until, one day, I was busy cooking dinner and, unbeknown to me, Kyle was conducting one of his many checks through my things and found the foil strip of my pills which I'd hidden in the lining of my handbag.

'What the hell are these?' Kyle thrust the pills under my nose as I chopped vegetables. I'd heard somewhere that when your partner's acting in a threatening way, it's wise to get clear of the kitchen – well away from dangers like knives and boiling water but it was too late for me to move.

'They-they must be an old pack,' I stammered as I shrank away from him. We'd been getting on for a couple of days, which had lulled me into a false sense of security. *How could I have left my bag unattended?*

However, I'd been missing my brother unbearably and not seeing him as much was bringing me to my senses about Kyle. I knew I had to leave him, but as he'd warned me so many times, wherever I went, he would always come after me – another reason why I stayed so long. Nor did I have the money and I didn't feel like I could ask my brother again although I am sure he would have helped if I had swallowed my pride. Kyle insisted that the money I earned from doing nails was paid into our joint account so the only time I could squirrel a little away towards my freedom fund was if someone paid me in cash. He never found *that*.

He held the strip of pills towards the light and read out the expiry date – two years away. 'Liar.' He spun me around to face him by my shoulder and bellowed into my face. '*It's an old packet*. Try again, why don't you?'

'Please, Kyle,' I begged, trying to step back, but I was already up against the counter. 'You've got to believe me. They've honestly been there for ages.'

'If you can lie to me so blatantly about something so impor-tant to me,' he shouted, 'what the hell else are you lying about?'

'Nothing.' I tried to sidestep him but he followed.

'Why don't you want a kid with me? That's what I want to know.'

His teaching colleagues were all having babies and I knew he was looking forward to taking a good stretch of parental leave, especially since we'd be allowed to share the time between us. Mums at his school told him at parents' evening what an amazing dad he'd make and, obviously, this went to his head.

'I-I just don't think it's the right time.' I shrank back as much as it's possible to shrink back from someone when your back is against a kitchen counter.

'So I was right then, you lying cow? And you wonder why I can't trust you outside the house when I can't even trust you *inside* it. I should find someone else, Natalie, someone who'll give me what I want.'

'Yes, maybe you should.' My voice was small but assertive enough to rile him even further.

'Is that what you want?' He grabbed me by the throat before bending me backwards over the counter. Then he started to squeeze.

'Get off me. Please get off me.'

As I gurgled within his grasp, I grappled around until my hand fell on the only thing that could possibly help me at that moment – the knife I'd been using to chop vegetables.

As I dug it into his shoulder blade, he cried out in pain. But at least he let go of my neck. Blood spurted from him as I drew it back out of his flesh, barely able to believe what I'd done. But he came at me again so it was my turn to cry out as I drove the knife into his back for a second time. More of his blood splattered over me and although I knew I was going to be done for, I also knew I couldn't risk him being able to get back up again. Nor, in that moment, did I want him to be able to.

As he dropped to the floor on all fours, howling in pain, I completely lost all control. I wrenched the knife from his flesh again before stabbing it into him for a third time, grunting with the exertion, and then again and again and again until I was completely spent.

Smeared in his blood, I suddenly realised what I was doing and staggered back, horrified at what I'd done to him. Now flat on his stomach against the floor, the white shirt I'd only ironed the day before was punctured with at least a dozen stab wounds. I crept back to him, recoiling at the connection with his skin as I felt for a pulse. Looking back, I don't know why I was bothering – *no one* could have survived what I'd just inflicted.

As I expected, there was no pulse. As I cried out in fear, the only thing I could think of doing was to call my brother.

Hayden threw up in the sink when he first saw Kyle laid out on the floor – the knife was still skewered in his back and there was blood *everywhere*.

'What the hell have you done, Natalie?' he finally whispered.

'He-he was going to choke me,' I replied as I slumped back to the floor beside Kyle's body. 'It was self-defence.'

'But how many times have you stabbed him?'

He coughed and turned to the sink to carry on retching.

When he got himself back together again, he lifted his head and said, 'Oh my God, Natalie. There's self-defence and there's—'

He never actually said the word *murder*, but I knew what he meant.

EIGHTEEN

'All those months of his bullying,' I explained to Hayden, 'and his abuse just ran through my mind like a film reel – it's as though I went into some kind of trance. Once I started with that knife, I just couldn't stop.'

'Have you been drinking?' He filled a glass with water and looked back down at Kyle. 'Oh my God, Natalie. What the hell are we going to do?'

'I don't know. I'm sorry – I'm just so sorry, Hayden – I couldn't take it anymore.' Whilst avoiding looking at Kyle, I looked at him as he wiped his mouth.

'The problem is that you've stabbed him so many times.' He looked at Kyle's body before scrunching his eyes together. 'How can we possibly argue that you acted in self-defence?'

'*We?*' I asked. He'd used the word twice. He was going to help me – he was *really* going to help me.

'Well, I'm not going to let you face this on your own, am I?' He dropped down beside me and passed me the water. 'You're my little sister.'

'Even after what I've done?' I pointed at Kyle, still in the belief that I'd wake up at any moment, in a cold sweat at the nightmare I'd just had.

But no, it was for real.

'If Kyle had been a nice guy, if there were any traces of a *nice guy* within him, I'd obviously feel differently, but after what I've witnessed—'

Reality washed over me as I realised that I really shouldn't be involving my brother. 'I'm so sorry, Hayden, I shouldn't have rung you – this is my mess—'

'I'm going to help you – of course I am.'

'You should just leave here now, Hayden. This is all my problem – I've done this and I can't possibly involve you.'

He didn't seem to be listening to me. 'If we don't get our thinking caps on sharpish, you'll get life in prison for this – look at the state of him.'

What I'd done suddenly became real. I didn't even consider prison. I didn't consider *anything*. 'I wouldn't last five minutes in prison.' My breath was coming even faster than before. 'Look how things were in that children's home we were in – they'd have made mincemeat of me if it wasn't for you.' The blown-up canvas of Kyle's graduation day above the kitchen table suddenly caught my eye. 'His superhero reputation isn't going to help me either, is it? I can imagine the headlines, *depraved woman with a foster care background brutally stabs pillar-of-the-community primary school teacher.*'

'You're probably right,' he said.

'Prison's nothing less than I deserve though, is it?' I looked back at my handiwork. 'Look at what I've done – it's little wonder he hated me so much. I deserve to be locked away forever, I deserve to rot in hell, I—'

'Natalie.' Hayden took my shoulders in each of his hands. 'Get a bloody grip, for God's sake. We're going to sort this, OK? Me and you, side by side, like we always have been. I'm here now, aren't I? Which makes me part of it all whether I like it or not.'

'How can we possibly *sort it*? As soon as the police take one look at him – that's it. I'm history.'

Hayden rose back to his feet and looked thoughtful for a moment. 'Just let me think.'

'I don't see what else I can do other than turn myself in.'

'Right – we're going to get him out of here,' Hayden said after a moment. 'That's what we're going to do.'

'But how? We can't—'

'There's some wasteland – right at the edge of Danefield Park – it's all overgrown and no one ever goes in there.'

'So how come *you* know about it?'

'That dog I used to have got lost around there once. Anyway, there's a stretch of thick hedge we'll be able to get him under. We'll surround him with logs and all that and he'll just rot away.'

'Just like that.' In my delirious state, I actually felt a spark of hope at what my brother was proposing. Maybe I *could* avoid being found out and sent to prison.

'It's the best plan I've got. The only plan, as it happens.'

'But assuming by some miracle we get him there with no one seeing us, what'll we tell people? His work – his—'

'That he's gone off somewhere and we don't know where he is. It happens all the time. People do just disappear – they go off on their own, don't they? The police have files full of them.'

'You make it sound so easy. I really don't think—'

'The hardest part's going to be us getting him into the back of my car without being seen and then—' He looked around. 'Getting this place thoroughly cleaned up before we report him missing in a couple of days. We'll need to bleach the place to within an inch of its life, as well as the car. Plus' – he gestured at his bloodied knees and then at me – 'everything we're wearing and everything we use to clean will need to be burned.'

With my brother helping me, I started to believe we *could* pull it off. Hayden stuck by me like glue in the days following Kyle's 'disappearance'. We tried to cover our tracks for a day or so, sending and receiving text messages from his phone in different locations and using his bank card. Then, in front of Kyle's family, the police and the media, I attempted to act like someone whose partner had gone missing, but on day four, his body was found.

As I probably always knew it would be. People don't get away with murder.

Especially people like me.

Guilt plagued me and the nightmares were relentless. Each night I'd wake myself up, drenched in a cold sweat as I relived what had happened.

'Get off me! Please get off me.'

'He was going to choke me.'

'It was self-defence.'

'I couldn't stop.'

'I'm sorry. I'm just so sorry.'

'Natalie, what's going on? What's all the shouting about?' The firm grip shaking at my shoulder forces me back into consciousness as I squint against the light at Dominic, who's silhouetted in the window behind him.

I jump as I'm woken. 'Eh? I must have fallen asleep.' My heart's hammering in my chest as I start to come around and realise that I'm here now and not still there.

'You're soaked through.' He looks down at me and then looks away.

'What was I saying?'

Dominic stands from the bed, keeping his back to me. 'You'd better get a shower. I'll wait downstairs.'

'But what was I saying?'
This is the problem. What the hell *was* I saying?

NINETEEN

'Natalie?' Sophie's calling me from the bottom of the stairs. 'Are you alright? Dinner won't be long.'

I rub at my hair with a towel, knowing I'll have to show my face down there *eventually*. If Dominic had pieced anything together from my earlier shouting as I dreamt, I'm sure someone would have been up here to turf me out on my ear by now. I can't imagine Sophie would still want to check on me if she knew what I'd once been capable of.

'Natalie?' Her voice is growing closer. She must be on her way up.

Her concern brings tears to my eyes. I shuffle off the bed and head towards the door.

'I'll be down in a few minutes,' I call into the landing. 'I've just got out of the shower.'

'Right, before we start eating, I want to say something.'

'Here we go.' Sophie nudges me.

'There have been more than enough squabbles and whispering in corners since you all arrived yesterday.' Roger rubs the carving knife against the serving fork as he presides over the turkey at the end of the table. 'I know it's hardly a conventional situation' – he looks from me to Carla facing each other across the table – 'but let's just make the best of things and enjoy a civilised festive meal, shall we?'

'I haven't been squabbling and whispering in corners.' Sophie's voice carries an edge of indignance as she looks at her father.

I catch Dominic's eye and he holds my gaze for a moment. I'd love to know for certain what I was shouting about before, but we probably won't get the chance to speak again until later.

If people genuinely understood the misery I was living in and the threat I was constantly under, surely they wouldn't keep judging me as severely as they have so far.

'Help yourselves.' Ann-Marie gestures to the serving bowls along the centre of the table. 'Would everyone like champagne with their meal?'

I'm the first to hold my glass out. This *civilised* meal will be far easier to get through with as much alcohol in my system as humanly possible.

'To family.' Roger holds his glass in the air. 'No matter how unconventional we may be. May we always stick together and keep each other's secrets.' He winks at Carla.

I watch for her reaction and she looks away in the other direction – at Dominic.

'I remember, Dom' – Carla spoons carrots onto her plate – 'the time you burnt carrots so badly we had to throw away the pan.'

Ann-Marie laughs. 'Cooking never was your forte, was it, dear?'

Carla glances at me over the burning candle between us. 'Can you pass me the salt please?'

I stab at a piece of broccoli.

'You need to wait until we've said grace.' Ann-Marie scowls at me.

Here she is, on court bail, waiting to be sentenced for *manslaughter*, while thinking it's perfectly acceptable to look down her nose at me for not saying grace before eating. Yesterday I tried to be positive about being here, but today it's all faded away.

At least I had just cause for what I did to Kyle. But in her case, she was just lazy, selfish and negligent.

'Perhaps you'd like to say grace for us all, Natalie.'

'Erm – I don't think so. I don't go in for all that.'

'Of course you don't,' Roger replies. 'Carla, would you do the honours instead please?'

Whilst I wonder what on earth Roger meant by that, Carla rests her glass beside her plate. 'For what we are about to receive, may the Lord make us truly thankful.'

'Amen,' everyone choruses. Everyone, other than me.

The meal is excruciating. I pick at my food while Sophie makes most of the efforts at conversation.

'So, what'll we do this evening?' she asks. 'Will it be a games night, like we normally have?'

Dominic pulls a face. 'I'd prefer if we just watched a film or something. What does everyone else think?'

'Suits me,' I say. And it's true. I can just sit in the dark and feel sorry for myself. The only thing that could make me feel better at this moment is my husband's trust and support.

'This is lovely, Mum,' Sophie says.

'Yes, it is,' I say as I pick at my vegetables. It wouldn't be so bad if there was some music on in here to swallow up the awkward silences when no one is speaking.

'You're eating like a sparrow,' Ann-Marie remarks. 'Would you like some more turkey?'

'No, I'm fine,' I reply, bristling at Ann-Marie's cutting remark. 'I'm saving room for dessert.'

There's a sudden bleeping and Sophie's eyes flit to the phone at the side of her plate. Her face softens as she stifles a smile. It can only mean one thing.

'Who's the lucky man then?' I nudge her.

'Shh.' She scowls at me.

'You've got a boyfriend?' Ann-Marie arches an eyebrow. 'You never said.'

No wonder Sophie's irritated. Clearly, she didn't want her mother to know and it seems that I've inadvertently rumbled her.

'You never asked,' she replies. 'You never do. You've always been more interested in your *golden child* there.'

'Me?' Dominic's voice rises. 'What are you on about?'

Sophie's phone beeps again.

'What's that thing doing at the dinner table anyway?' Roger's expression hardens.

'You're not telling *him*, are you?' Sophie nods towards Dominic's phone, also resting at the side of his plate. 'It's always been one rule for me and another for him.'

'That's not true,' Dominic retorts.

'Yes it is,' she bites back. 'Just because I'm the eldest and not the one who'll carry the name on, and—'

'That's enough, Sophie.' Ann-Marie frowns. 'It's Christmas Day.'

I catch Dominic's eye again and he seems to smile at me, although it's a smile that doesn't really reach his eyes. He's always said that I'm the only person that 'gets him' and it's true. He's the only person that 'gets me' too.

I've never had a more serious Christmas dinner in my life. I think back to my childhood, to a time of pulling crackers, telling bad jokes and the obligatory wearing of party hats, and I smile to myself.

Life might have gone badly wrong for me since then but no one can take away my memories.

'Penny for them?' Sophie says. 'What are you secretly smiling about?'

'I'm just thinking of the bad cracker jokes from when I was a kid,' I reply. 'Don't you guys do crackers at Christmas?'

'They're a tacky waste of money,' Roger replies and I resist the urge to laugh at his response. My previous misery suddenly seems to have been replaced by some kind of warped mania.

'What's for dessert, Mum?' Dominic asks.

'Torte,' replies Ann-Marie.

'Torte?' I echo. I'm dying to ask whether a *torte* is just a posh tart but I'd probably be the only person laughing at my own joke. So I stuff a potato in my mouth to contain myself instead.

'Yes, it's chocolate and walnut. And there'll be the choice of fresh cream or ice cream.'

'Mmm. I'll have both then,' says Sophie.

'You've got a piece without any walnut, Natalie. It's chocolate and orange – is that OK?'

'Perfect,' I reply. 'Thanks.'

'Oh' – Ann-Marie flicks her hand – 'I really can't take the credit. It was all down to Polly and Charmaine.'

'This is definitely the one with no nuts, isn't it?'

Ann-Marie sweeps her gaze around the table. 'Yes, yours is the only piece on a white plate – the rest of us have black plates.'

'*Bon appetit.*' Roger spoons a piece of torte into his mouth and I do the same.

The atmosphere seems to have changed throughout the course of the meal, thankfully. Everyone seems more relaxed – it must be something to do with the champagne.

I turn the delicious torte around and around in my mouth before swallowing it.

'This is really lovely,' I say as I raise a second spoonful from the plate.

'Thank you, dear.'

As I savour it in my mouth, I suddenly become aware of the telltale numbness which spells trouble for me. But as I try to spit the torte back onto my plate, it's already taken hold of my lips and tongue.

'Natalie! What on earth—'

'She must be reacting to something on her plate.' Dominic leaps to his feet and dashes around the table to me. 'Where's your pen?'

I've already wrenched my handbag onto my knee and am fumbling to get it open. But I've gone really light-headed. Shit. I need to find that pen – and quickly. I pass the bag to Dominic.

'Where is it?' He drops to his knees at the side of my chair as he riffles through the contents.

'Should we be doing something?' Ann-Marie cries. 'Shall I call for an ambulance?'

'There's no point, dear.' Roger's voice sounds far away. 'It's not as if one would be able to get through the snow.'

I slide from my chair and onto the floor. 'I. Don't. Feel. So. Good.' As I land beside Dominic, I raise my fingers to my lips which are swelling fast. 'Please.' I reach for the bag.

He tips it up and there's a crash as the contents scatter on the floor and he starts rummaging through them.

'It's not here, Nat.' I'm struggling to focus but I see something in his eyes which I've never seen before. Panic, I think. 'Where the hell is it?'

'Should. Be. There.' I'm already struggling to get my words out and know from experience that I've only got five to ten minutes before I'm *really* in trouble. 'Sophie.' I manage to gasp out my sister-in-law's name and point up at the ceiling as her face appears above where I'm lying. 'Bag... upstairs.'

'I thought you only had them in this bag,' Dominic says. 'I'll run up for them!'

'I'm on it.' Sophie jumps past him, banging the door behind her. Her footsteps thunder up the stairs.

'Just try to stay calm, dear.' Ann-Marie's face appears above me now. 'She'll be back in a moment. You'll be as right as rain.'

'Feel. Sick.' I try to swallow, but my throat feels like I've swallowed a melon. 'Help. Me.'

'Just keep still. Your EpiPen should be on its way. Have you *definitely* got one in your other bag?' Dominic asks.

I try to nod. They're all crowding around me now, even Carla, and their faces could well be the last thing I ever see if Sophie doesn't hurry up. I try to breathe through my nose, but it's just as much of a struggle. I feel like I've got about two minutes before I can't breathe anymore. My heart already feels as though it's going to pop out of my chest. This is awful – and probably the worst reaction I've ever had. But then, I've never been without my EpiPen before. I've normally got two in my handbag, one in the car and two in another bag wherever I am. Mum drilled the importance of always having them nearby into me when I was young, and I'm certain I had at least one in the handbag I brought down with me.

Suddenly, the drawing-room door slams into the wall and Sophie bursts back in.

'I've got it. What do I do? Tell me what to do.'

I point at my leg.

'Through your clothes?'

It takes all I've got just to nod back at her. I'm really struggling to get any air in now.

'Press it as it goes in,' Roger tells her. 'We once had to practise this on oranges on a course I was on.'

Without wasting any time, Sophie plunges the pen into my skin and relief washes through me along with the lifesaving drug she's administered.

Within a few minutes, the swelling in my lips and throat begins to subside and my breathing feels less laboured.

'Thank you.' I grasp Sophie's hand. She hasn't moved from my side since she administered the EpiPen. 'You've probably saved my life.'

'*Really?*'

'Really.' The thought unsettles me, though it's not something I want to dwell on. I shuffle backwards and raise my legs up against the chair I was sitting on. 'I just need to stay like this for a while,' I say to Ann-Marie, who's also kneeling beside me. I'll no doubt be an odd sight in their drawing room laid out here on my back with my legs draped up and over a dining chair. Dominic's busy returning all my stuff to my handbag, while Carla just stands there, like she has throughout my entire ordeal. 'Where the hell did my EpiPens go?' I turn my head towards him. 'I'm certain that I had two of them in there.'

He shakes his head as he closes the zip on my bag without looking at me. 'Won't you need checking over after that?'

'Like your dad said,' says Ann-Marie, 'no one's coming or going anywhere in that snow – it's coming down heavy again – just look at it.' The room's definitely darkened since I first came in here. Something darkens inside me too. I know full well that without Sophie's quick action, I'd be in serious trouble and there'd be no way an ambulance would have been able to get to me in time.

'You're just going to have to rest up then, aren't you?' Dominic says. 'Maybe you should go for a lie-down.'

'She'll be as right as rain for Boxing Day tomorrow,' Sophie adds.

It dawns on me that Carla seems to have mysteriously disappeared from the room.

Perhaps she knows something about my missing EpiPens.

TWENTY

'Do you think you're alright to move now?' Dominic gets to his feet as I open my eyes. I must have drifted off. I just feel so weak, not to mention, exhausted.

'How long have I been here?'

'About twenty minutes since your EpiPen.'

'I should be fine now. I'm starting to feel numb on this hard floor.'

'I'm always telling Roger we need a carpet in here.' Ann-Marie's voice is surprisingly light, given the circumstances.

'What, so your daughter-in-law has a soft landing when she has an anaphylactic shock?' I force a laugh out, though what's just happened is far from amusing. I really thought I'd had it for a few moments. Dominic, Ann-Marie and Sophie haven't left my side since I went into shock, so they obviously felt the same.

'I'll find out where Carla's got to, shall I?' There's the scrape of a chair and a squeak of the door as Roger leaves the room.

'Will you help me get up?' I hold my hand in Dominic's direction and allow him to help me into a sitting position.

'How are you feeling?' It's the first time Ann-Marie's been so attentive towards me. It's a shame it's taken a near-death experience to make her warm to me. Could it be guilt? Could she be responsible for the so-called mix-up?

'I'm feeling much better, thank you. Hopefully, I swallowed a piece with hardly any nuts in.'

'I thought you'd made sure of Natalie's piece, Mum?' Sophie turns to her mother. 'Those staff of yours need a rocket putting up them, if you ask me – Natalie's slice was even on a different coloured plate, wasn't it?'

'I'm so sorry.' Ann-Marie sinks to a seat. 'I should have double-checked and triple-checked. But with all that's been going on lately, perhaps I've taken my eye off the ball.'

'It's OK, Mum.' Sophie rests her hand over her mother's.

It nearly wasn't, I want to say. But obviously I don't.

'Look, I know you're upset, but resting up is hardly the end of the world.' Dominic draws the curtains against the snow as I lie back against my pillows.

I blink back even more tears. I haven't cried so much over Christmas since – well, I can't even let my mind wander back to that time. 'Can you have a good look around for my pens? Perhaps they've dropped out in the car?'

'Have you seen it out there? I'll check tomorrow.' Dominic shakes his head as he gestures at the window. 'Besides, you're alright now, aren't you?'

'Do you think someone might have switched the plates over, Dominic? Your mum was adamant that my nut-free portion was on the white plate.'

We both probably know who I'm referring to when I say *someone*.

'Nah. A mistake's been made, that's all. It'll be the staff, like Sophie said.'

I nod. However, the more I think about what happened, the more unsettled I feel. Everyone's been far too quick to blame 'the staff'. 'But what about my EpiPens? It's all too much of a coincidence if you ask me.'

'What is?'

'That the cake gets mixed up *and* my EpiPens go missing at the same time. Someone did it on purpose, Dominic. And you know what I'm thinking, don't you?'

'Just get some rest. I'll be back in a couple of hours.'

'I just want you to stay with me *now*.'

'Dominic,' Carla calls from the landing. 'Are you in there?'

'What is it?' he calls back.

'Your dad's putting a film on.'

'I'm coming now.' He looks back at me. 'I won't be long.'

I close my eyes as he leaves the room. I can't believe he's just leaving me on my own after what happened – especially since I wanted him to stay. I want to talk about it too. *Where did Carla disappear to before?* I'm convinced that she's as responsible for switching the desserts around as she was for the spilling of the red wine and the plate breakage yesterday, especially since she made herself scarce immediately after I ate that torte.

But I've no proof whatsoever that it was her and if I start throwing accusations around, it will only make me look spiteful and paranoid. As Ann-Marie said before, mistakes do happen, though she admits that it was unlike her staff not to pay extreme attention to detail, especially with something as serious as a nut allergy.

I try to read for a while but I can't concentrate. All I can hear is gunshots and shouting from the room below. I wonder what they're watching – it certainly doesn't sound like my kind of film. More importantly, I wonder where they're sitting. No doubt Carla will have sidled up next to Dominic on the sofa. I can almost see her with a smug expression on her face. Perhaps she'd do *anything* to get Dominic back. Does that include hurting me?

Her voice suddenly floats across the landing. Who's she talking to? Is it Dominic again?

I throw my covers off and tiptoe towards the door. I can hear her quite clearly from here and there only seems to be *her* voice – she must be on the phone.

'Yeah, well, it's three against one, isn't it?'

What's that supposed to mean?

'Nope, she's got absolutely *no* idea.'

She must be referring to *me*.

'I agree. I don't want to go that far, but, to be honest, I might not have a lot of choice.'

Go *what* far? Hasn't she already caused me enough damage?

'You've got to trust me on this. Somehow I'll get us out of it, no matter what it takes.'

Who's she talking to? What's she on about? Get out of what?

'I know. I should never have allowed myself to be dragged in so deep. But you know, what is it they say? *Everything happens for a reason.*'

Since I've been here, I keep overhearing snippets of conversation, but they're all in riddles. I'll have to try grilling Sophie again for information and see if she's willing to shed any more light on anything. Wine seems to help. She was forthcoming about having seen her mother coming from Carla's office earlier this week, so it's worth asking her.

Hi Sophie. Thanks again for all you did to help me earlier. Can you pop up and see me when you have five minutes? I could use some company.

Her 'read' receipt doesn't flash up like it normally does. Perhaps she's turned in already. Or maybe she's just glued to the film.

I lie back on my pillows, trying to steady my anxious breathing, but the constant boom-boom-boom echoing from the surround-sound speakers downstairs only intensifies my racing thoughts and pulsing heart rate. I've no chance of sleeping, that much is certain. So I reach for my Kindle and force myself to read again.

There's a sudden tapping at the door.

'Come in,' I say, hoping to see Sophie. But it's Ann-Marie.

'I'm on my way to bed, but I thought I'd check in and see how you are after what happened before.'

'Thank you,' I reply. 'I'm alright now. A bit concerned over where my EpiPens might have got to, but thank God I had some up here.' I point at my bag.

'Might these be what you're looking for?' She holds up two pens.

'Where did you find them?'

'They must have fallen from your bag when you rushed to take that phone call earlier.'

'Oh, right, OK.' I want to tell her that they were zipped into a compartment inside, but I don't wish to sound like I disbelieve her. Anyway, whatever happened to them, I'm OK, but I was extremely fortunate.

'If Sophie hadn't acted as quickly as she did,' says Ann-Marie, 'it could have been a very different story.'

I don't need her to remind me. I am extremely grateful to Sophie. The untimely death of my parents and the fallout from my relationship with Kyle has made me appreciate each new day I am blessed with.

'Is Dominic coming to bed shortly?' I glance towards the door.

'I think he might have dropped off on the sofa,' she replies. 'His dad'll give him a shake before he comes up.'

As I watch Ann-Marie retreat to the door, a strange feeling washes over me. She was the one who told me the cake was on a white plate. She's now also the one who miraculously found my missing EpiPens. What if it's her, and *not* Carla, who's guilty of what happened to me earlier? I know I'm not the daughter-in-law she wanted.

Perhaps Ann-Marie will secretly do whatever it takes to get Dominic and Carla back together.

Which probably means getting rid of me.

TWENTY-ONE

I wake with a start as Dominic snores beside me. Great. He's come up to bed and we haven't even had the chance to talk.

I stare at the shadows on the walls, willing myself to be able to go back to sleep, but it's no good – I'm wide awake again. I'll have to do what I did last night – try to knock myself out with a chamomile tea. I just hope I don't bump into Carla again this time. I don't think I could stop myself from accusing her.

Thankfully, there's no one around when I get downstairs. As I wait for the kettle, I allow my gaze to roam over the kitchen, hoping to spot a discarded pair of slippers for my freezing feet. However, my attention rests on what looks like a camera in the corner of the room. With the amount of money that will exist within The Elms, it doesn't come as a surprise that a security system would be installed. I'm surprised I haven't noticed it before, though I've not really spent much time in the kitchen. Also, this is the first time I've had a really good look around. However, what is of more interest to me is that it also covers the island in the centre of the kitchen. This is where the dessert plates were left earlier and is also where I left my handbag unattended for a short time when I was setting the table.

I peer more closely at the camera. There, in large, black lettering on the side, is the word *Teko*. It looks like a camera that would record the room's activity – it seems to be more than just a movement sensor. If it is, its footage could be hooked up to the Elmers' phones or computers, which obviously I can't get access to, but then again, the camera system *could* just be linked up to their TV.

Stepping back out into the hallway, I notice there's another camera up in the corner there, and a further one in the drawing room. I try the door to Roger's office, but it's locked. What could be behind that door that needs to be locked away? I wonder if Carla might have the answer since she was trying to get in there last night.

All I need to discover is *where* all of the cameras connect to and then I might be able to find out whether those plates *were* switched, as well as whether anyone went into my handbag and took my EpiPens.

I return to the kitchen for my drink and then head to the lounge. Another Teko camera is in the corner facing the door. Dropping to my knees, I gently open the doors to the cabinet on which the TV rests, reassured by the continued vibration from upstairs of Roger's snoring. At least that's one less person to come down here and catch me snooping around. Dominic looked as though he was out for the count as well.

Bingo. There it is. A Teko console complete with a remote resting on top of it. All I need to do is—

'What *are* you doing, Natalie?'

I slop my drink all over my leg at the sound of Ann-Marie's voice behind me.

'Ouch! You made me jump.' I rub at my leg with the sleeve of my dressing gown.

'It's a good job we didn't set the alarm down here. Are you OK?'

'I was, erm, I just couldn't sleep. I thought I'd make a drink.'

'What is it you're looking in *there* for, exactly?'

I turn to face where she stands with her hands on her hips in her floral dressing gown. She's wearing a similar expression to what she might have if she'd caught a burglar in here.

'I was just going to put the TV on for a bit. It helps when I'm at home. I suffer from insomnia quite a bit, you see.'

'If you don't mind, I'd rather you headed back up,' she says. 'I honestly thought we had intruders when I heard all the doors opening and closing down here.' The way she's looking at me makes me wonder whether she knew what I was really up to down here.

'I, erm, totally forgot which room was the lounge,' I tell her. 'I think I'm still a bit spaced out after what happened earlier.'

'All the more reason for you to try to get back to sleep then.' She holds the door wider as if to say, *now, please.*

'Yes, you're probably right – I'll take my tea back up with me.'

'Goodnight – again,' she says as I pass her in the doorway. 'I'll see you in the morning.'

'Yeah, goodnight.' She might have thwarted my plans to get to that camera footage this time, but I *will* get to it.

I stretch my arm out in the search for my phone. Damn – I've slept even later than yesterday. I turn over, hoping to find my husband still slumbering at my side. But he's gone. Probably long gone.

In the end last night, I poured the last glass of red wine from the bottle I'd previously opened with Sophie in a bid to properly knock myself out and fall back to sleep after being caught in the lounge by Ann-Marie.

Shit! I must have fallen asleep with the glass in my hand. Red wine is *all over* the pristine white duvet cover, the sheet and the pillowcase. I don't believe it! It must have still been dark when Dominic got up and left the room. Surely he'd have alerted me to the mess I've managed to make if he'd seen it?

So another job for me today, as well as making progress with the cameras, is to suss out a way of changing the bed and getting this bedding into the wash *without* Ann-Marie noticing. I doubt she'll spend a lot of time in her utility room though – not when she's got her staff to do her laundry for her.

If they're all out of the way, I can get it washed, dried and back on the bed before tonight – easily.

I strip the bedding and stuff it all into my rucksack. Then I nearly jump out of my skin as Sophie pokes her head around the door.

'I'm sorry I didn't come to talk to you last night. I fell asleep. To be honest, I was whacked after all the wine I drank yesterday.'

'It's fine – I just felt like some company. But I fell asleep as well, so it's all good.'

I'm not going to tell her that, really, I wanted to pick her brains more. That was *before* I found the security camera. Once I get a look at the footage, I should have my answers.

'How are you after what happened yesterday?' She comes deeper into the room and allows the door to fall closed behind her.

'A bit shaken still, but without what you did—'

'I only did what anyone would do.'

I want to say that I didn't see anyone else jumping up to find my EpiPen but I don't.

'So what's going on here then?' She gestures at the bed.

'A slight spillage. I'm hoping to get to the utility room without being spotted.'

'Honestly, Mum's not that much of an ogre. I'll stick them all in the washer for you if you want?'

'It's OK – I'll do it after I've had a shower.' I smile at her. 'But thanks.'

As I head down the stairs and glance into the lounge, the back of Ann-Marie's head is visible above one of the armchairs, so checking those security cameras is still a no-go for me. Eventually, I'll prove what happened to my EpiPens and find out who's responsible for swapping those desserts around. I still believe it was Carla's handiwork, but it could just as easily be Ann-Marie's.

I should say good morning to her, but I don't want to draw attention to myself. I just want to get these sheets into the wash.

Male voices echo from behind the office door, which accounts for the whereabouts of Roger and Dominic. I peek into the drawing room, but there's no sign of Carla – she's either at the other side of the lounge where I can't see her, or she's upstairs in her room. I doubt she'll be in the kitchen on her own.

But she is. Sitting at the island, nursing a coffee, she jumps as I walk in.

'Where are *you* going?' She eyes my rucksack 'You're not exactly going to get far in this weather.'

'I've got a few bits to put in the washing machine,' I tell her as I head over to the utility room.

'That looks like more than a few bits.' She jumps off her stool and follows me. 'What are you really up to?'

'I'm putting some sheets in the wash, alright? I spilt some wine.' I don't even know why I'm bothering to reply to her. Who the hell is she to give me the third degree?

'Again?' She raises an eyebrow.

'Just leave it, will you? At least you succeeded in getting rid of me for the evening, even if that was less than what you really wanted.'

I know I should be waiting until I've seen the camera footage for proof, but the words are out before I can stop myself. *I know it was her.* Really, I should be trying my best not to rile her. Who knows what else she might be capable of doing to me?

'What are you talking about?'

'Well, *someone's* responsible for what happened to me yesterday.'

'Sorry, Natalie.' She leans against the doorframe. 'But trying to bump someone off isn't my style. You're barking up the wrong tree here.'

'What's that supposed to mean?'

'You need to look closer to home – that's what I mean.'

'You *all* knew, *you* included, about my nut allergy. Someone swapped those plates around and someone took my EpiPens out of my bag.'

'It wasn't me, Natalie,' she says and as I raise my eyes to meet hers, I actually think I believe her.

'So who was it then?'

'You need to be careful, Natalie.' She lowers her voice. 'In fact, we both do.'

'What are you on about?'

'Yeah, what are you on about?' Dominic appears behind Carla, making her jump.

'Leave me alone,' she mutters as she pushes past him and marches from the kitchen.

'What the hell's going on with you two?' I stare after her, then at him. How bizarre. One minute they're as thick as thieves, the next, they seem to hate each other.

He leans into the doorframe. 'She's just uptight about all this business stuff with my parents.' He glances over his shoulder. 'And with me having previously done her company's accounting, I know things she'd rather I didn't, that's all.'

'So...' I lean forward and stuff our sheets into the washing machine. 'Does what you know have something to do with these shares you're all forcing her to shell out for? Needing her to shell out for, should I say?'

'What's Carla been saying to you? Apart from what I've just heard, I mean?'

I'm not going to answer that. Not until I've had the chance to grill Carla about what she meant. 'Do you know how to work this washer?' I stand away from the washer and glance out of the window. The snow's falling again, though not as heavily as last night.

He bends to fiddle with the dials. 'What are you doing here, anyway?'

'I spilt some wine.'

'You've become pretty accident-prone since we arrived here.' His face breaks into a smile of sorts. 'Even more than usual.'

'Why didn't you wake me this morning?'

'It sounded like you'd had another bad night. Mum said she found you down here.'

'I haven't been sleeping well,' I begin. 'And after yesterday—'

'Take no notice of my ex-wife,' he says as he pushes the button on the machine.

'Why are you going on about *her*?'

'If the truth be known, Natalie' – he looks me straight in the eye – 'Carla's made it clear that she wants to get back with me.' He jerks his head in the direction she walked away in. 'In fact, she wants to make us starting again part of the criteria for buying the shares in our company.'

'But you're married to me now!' A soapy fragrance fills the air as water begins hissing into the machine. I knew it. What Carla said before about being careful was some kind of smoke-screen to throw me off what she's truly after. *Getting back with*

Dominic. I tried to give her the benefit of the doubt when we first arrived. I even felt sorry for her.

'It's difficult though, isn't it?' He leans against the washer. 'My parents would like nothing more than to see Carla and me get back together, but as I've told them a million times, it's not going to happen.'

'What's going on?' Ann-Marie calls from the kitchen. 'What are you doing in there?'

I push past Dominic and out of the utility room.

'What on earth's the matter with Carla?' She looks from me to Dominic. 'Who's been upsetting her again?'

'Again?' I ask.

'It's nothing.' Ann-Marie dismisses my question with a wave of her hand.

What she means is that it's nothing to do with me.

'Natalie knows all about the investment money we want from Carla,' Dominic says, his voice flat.

'How?'

He shrugs.

'How?' She reframes her question in my direction.

'I'm here, aren't I? I'm bound to pick things up.' I won't tell her that her own daughter has been my main source of information all along. I'll just keep that as a bullet in my gun in case I need it.

'Let's just forget all that for the time being, shall we?' Her voice softens. 'We're serving a continental brunch in the drawing room.'

TWENTY-TWO

I pick at a croissant. I'm probably feeling about as hungry as Carla seems to be. She's doing exactly the same thing.

'What's up with you both?' Sophie laughs. 'You'll be in danger of offending my mum if you're not careful.'

'I'm feeling a bit off it,' I reply. 'Perhaps after last night – I always feel nauseous for a day or two after a reaction.' This isn't a complete lie. But it's more everything that's going on which is unsettling my stomach.

'Oh you poor thing.' Sophie shoots me a sympathetic look. 'Well, you don't have to force yourself to eat if you're not hungry, does she, Mum?'

'Of course not.'

'Does anyone mind if I head to the lounge and sit in front of the TV while you all finish?'

'Actually—' Roger begins.

'That's absolutely fine.' Ann-Marie smiles. 'You go and make yourself comfortable.'

. . .

I click the door to the lounge behind me and speed across the carpet to the TV cabinet, rummaging through the remote controls until I find the one with the Teko logo again. My breath's coming fast as I point it at the TV, but nothing happens. What I'll probably have to do is change the input mode. Hopefully, it's as simple as that – anything more technical and I might be in trouble here.

With a hammering heart, I check back over my shoulder and then hunt around for the TV remote control, my heart beating faster with every moment that passes. Thankfully, it's a Samsung, a make of TV that I'm accustomed to, so I know what to do to change the source feed.

Bingo. The screen immediately fills with an image of them all still sitting at the table in the drawing room. They're probably pleased I've left them to it – if I felt like an outcast on Christmas Eve, I do even more *now*.

As the next image flashes into the office, I hit the stop button on the remote and then press rewind. Wow, this is really it – it was easier than I thought. So long as nobody comes in here and catches me.

I wind back through Ann-Marie staring at the TV earlier, then to Roger and Dominic speaking in the office. I continue back through the hours of stillness overnight, apart from when I got up to make a chamomile tea before being caught by Ann-Marie. It's going to take another minute or so to reach the moment I'm searching for, so still clutching the remote, I creep over to the door. I'm ready to change the channel back at any moment if I need to. All I have to do is hit source and then TV. Hopefully, I can be quick enough.

I glance back to the screen, which is now filled with the dinner scene from yesterday, and then it flashes to the kitchen.

This is it, I wind back further, landing on the scene where we were all in the dining room eating Christmas dinner, going forward and back until I find what I'm looking for.

Then I see it. First, at quadruple speed and then in slow motion. As I rewind the scene in question, I blink hard, unable to believe my eyes as a chill creeps up my spine.

Perhaps I could be mistaken.

I press play again, and pull my phone out, ready to record the evidence for safekeeping.

I rub my eyes just in case they are really deceiving me. But no. They're not. Tears burn at the back of them as I press record on my phone.

TWENTY-THREE

There, in all its black and white glory, Dominic loiters next to my bag before taking what looks like my pens out of it. Carla rushes over to him, looking like she's saying something to him, but he swats her away like a fly.

From the look on her face though, she could have been trying to find out what he was doing, rather than having anything to do with my anaphylactic shock herself. It's definitely not *her* who goes into my bag.

It was *Dominic*. Oh. My. God.

But why? I thought he loved me. My husband, who slid a white gold band onto my finger, while promising to love me forever, only months ago, has tried to kill me. Or perhaps his parents are somehow involved. Maybe they've put him up to it.

As I wrestle with the urge to charge into the other room and confront him, I realise I need to keep watching this footage. It's the only way I'll be able to learn more. And recording it.

Next, as Carla leaves the kitchen, Dominic throws the slice of torte that was originally meant for me into the bin, before taking another one from the fridge and placing it onto the plate, glancing around himself as he does this. He's either unaware of the cameras or has forgotten about them.

Beyond where the island is in the centre of the kitchen, I can't tell whether anyone else is in there with him. Whether anyone else knew the extent of what he did to me.

'I warned you that you needed to be careful.'

I nearly jump out of my skin at the sudden voice behind me and hit the pause button on my phone. I didn't even hear Carla come in. I swing around to face her as she closes the door. Out of the options of people it could be, I'm actually glad it's her.

'How long have you been standing there?'

'Long enough to see what I need to see. It's OK,' she says, her voice soft. 'I've left them all arguing amongst themselves. I told them I needed a few minutes to come to the decision they're waiting for me to make.'

'It was *him.*' My voice is a whisper. I point at the TV screen. 'My pens – the nuts – I can't believe it.'

She steps closer to me, gingerly at first, as though she's worried I might strike out at her. Then she perches on the arm of the sofa nearest to where I'm standing. 'At the time, I saw him taking something from your bag, but I wasn't sure what it was.'

'I can't believe what he's tried to do to me.'

'I had no idea he was also swapping the dessert plates over.' She tosses her hair behind one shoulder as she stares at me. 'I'd have intervened if I'd known.'

Her voice and her face are genuine. I believe her.

What a nightmare. I glance towards the window where the snow is still falling beyond it. The sky is heavy with even more and it's starting to look as though I'll never get out of here. I just want to leave – I don't know *where* or what I'll do after this, but I definitely need to get away from my husband.

This is all down to my shouting out in my sleep yesterday morning. The timing of what he's done is too much of a coincidence for it not to be.

'Was he trying to actually kill me, do you think?'

'It certainly looks that way.'

'Throwing the pens away was bad enough.' I swallow. 'But swapping the desserts—'

'Get it turned off before one of them comes in here.' She points at the TV and then glances back at the door.

'I can't let them know that I've found out about this – not while I'm still here with them.'

'Have you made a copy of the video?' She nods towards my phone.

'Of course I have.' I hold my phone aloft. 'But look – how do I know I can trust you with all this?'

'You just can, alright? You have to.' Her voice is almost a whisper as she reaches for my arm and squeezes it. 'I know this might feel weird but we need to stick together for as long as we're here.'

With a shaking thumb, I press play on my phone and then re-run the footage, making sure I've captured the whole of what I needed to. This might be my only chance. Then I turn back to Carla. She's told me this much already – perhaps she'll be willing to tell me even more now.

'I've been thinking you wanted him back since we all got here.'

'Never in a million years.' She looks at me directly in the eye. 'I meant what I said before, Natalie. We're both in trouble if we don't get away from this lot.'

I don't know how, but her use of my name helps me to trust her slightly more. However, I still can't take it all in.

'He was supposed to love me.' Tears fill my eyes. I don't think it's hit me yet. I should be furious with what he's tried to do to me, but right now I just feel like my heart's been ripped out. I can hardly believe what I've seen and without watching that footage with my own eyes, no one would ever have convinced me that Dominic could be capable.

'As you're starting to find out, deep down, he's a very nasty piece of work. Hang on a second, they've gone really quiet in there.' She rises from the arm of the chair, creeps back to the door and listens. As I watch her, I feel like I'm in some kind of trance. As if we're suddenly in the same league. Us against them. 'It's OK, I've just heard Ann-Marie's voice again.'

'Why did you and Dominic split up, Carla?'

She takes a deep breath. 'I probably fell into a similar trap to what you did.'

'What do you mean?'

'Well, he was lovely with me in the beginning,' she replies. 'Until he started to turn.'

'In what way?' My heart drops even further.

'He was jealous of my company's success – that was the main thing, at least to begin with. He couldn't bear that I was doing so much better than him.'

'We certainly don't have that problem – I paint nails for a living.' I'm surprised Carla can even compare her experience with mine. She and I are like chalk and cheese in every way.

'He became really, really controlling,' she continues. 'Has he been like that with you?'

'Not really,' I reply. 'I honestly thought things were OK between us. We've only been married for five minutes.'

'I paid for *everything* in our relationship.' She twirls at the end of her hair as though she's nervous. 'Our wedding, our home, our entire lifestyle – he hated things being that way but he was forced to accept it. He wanted the nice life, but he was clearly emasculated that it was my firm's money funding it.' She pauses for a moment as though checking that I really want to hear what she's telling me.

'Go on.'

'He became nastier and nastier as the months went by.' She looks down at the floor. 'He seemed to think that because he'd been our accountant since the early days of mine and my brother's business, that gave him some sort of rights to become a director.'

'How do you mean, he became nastier?'

'When me and my brother wouldn't bow to him wanting to be a director, he tried everything to force me to change my mind. To begin with, he said he'd leave me if I didn't make him a director – obviously, I laughed at that one.'

'Then what happened?'

Her face darkens. 'He had no plans whatsoever to split up with me, really, so he became violent instead.'

'He was *hitting* you?' I can hardly equate the man I've known so far with this person she's describing. But after what I've seen with my own eyes on that video, nothing should shock me about him now.

'Not hitting exactly, but, you know, pushing me around, holding me against walls, grabbing me, that sort of thing.'

Violence. No matter how it's dressed up, it's still violence – I should know. I stare at her while at the same time starting to find parallels between myself and this seemingly cool-as-a-cucumber, self-assured woman.

'It was an absolute nightmare – I couldn't even tell my brother the extent of what was going on.'

After everything that happened with Kyle and the fact that *my* brother was also involved in my own violent relationship is the most eerie of coincidences between us.

'Why not?' I exaggerated when I said I was feeling sick before but now I'm starting to feel sick for real. Carla *must* know something about the situation I was in.

'It would have made the whole situation even worse if I'd asked for help – my brother would have probably killed him.'

'But you seem to get on now – you and Dominic – I've seen you. No one would ever suspect he'd been violent to you in the past.'

'Things have moved on,' she replies. 'Are you sure you want to hear this?'

TWENTY-FOUR

I should just leave and take my chances. If I have to crawl through that snow to the nearest police station to get help, I don't care. Perhaps one of the neighbours will notice me and take me in if I tell them I'm fleeing my violent husband and his family.

Violent husband. Until a few minutes ago, I thought I knew all his faults. Yes, he could be abrupt at times, but I didn't have him down as someone who would ever hurt me.

'Why are you even here, Carla – spending Christmas with them?'

'Do you think I'd have *chosen* to spend Christmas like this? With *them?*' She wrings her hands together, her bracelets rattling with the movement.

'That's what I don't understand.'

'They're blackmailing me.' I have a sudden recollection of my conversation with Sophie. *They've got something on her*, she told me. She was telling the truth.

'What could they possibly be able to blackmail you with? You're the CEO of a law firm, aren't you?'

'It's my position that means they're able to blackmail me.'

'But surely you'd have the power and the know-how to sue the lot of them into the next century?'

There's a scrape of a chair from the other room. Carla and I look at each other and I rush to the TV, pressing the off button on both remotes as I get there. Then I throw them back to where I got them from and swing the door shut with my foot.

'Carla?' Ann-Marie's voice echoes through the hallway. I fling myself onto the sofa, after all, I'm supposed to be in here because I'm not feeling a hundred per cent. So while it might raise an eyebrow that Carla and I are being civil to one another, me being in here in the first place shouldn't warrant any questions.

'I'll be there in a minute,' Carla calls back. 'I'm just looking for something.'

'In here?' Ann-Marie pokes her head in. 'You've been ages.'

'I just wanted to find that lovely gift you gave me. I can't remember where I put it.'

I keep my eyes fixed on the floor – I don't want to give anything away that could make them suspect Carla's confided in me. After all, they think we despise each other.

'It's over there.' Ann-Marie points to the Welsh dresser in the corner. 'How come the door was closed anyway?' She looks over to me. 'It was propped open before.'

'So I could hear the TV and so it wouldn't disturb your meal.'

'How very thoughtful.' She nods in its direction. 'So why isn't it on then?'

'Oh gosh – perhaps I sat on the remote.' I feel around where I'm sitting, knowing full well that I've hurled it back into the TV cabinet. I'm not even sure that I've returned the source channel to where it needs to be either. If Ann-Marie suddenly decides to turn the TV on for herself, I could be done for. The colour's rising in my face – my cheeks are literally burning.

Just as I'm fit to burst with anxiety beneath the scrutiny of

Ann-Marie's gaze, she returns her attention to Carla. 'Are you coming back in, or what? We're waiting to serve coffee.'

'I'll just pop to the loo and then I'll be right with you,' she replies. 'I'll be along in a few minutes.'

'Alright.'

I glance in Ann-Marie's direction to make sure she's heading back to the others, but no, she's still standing there, watching as Carla strides across the room towards the Welsh dresser. I just want her to go. I want Carla to tell me what they've been blackmailing her over.

'Like I said, I won't be long.'

'Is everything alright in here?' Suspicion is written all over Ann-Marie's face.

'Of course.' Carla offers Ann-Marie what's probably her brightest smile. 'Why wouldn't it be?'

'No reason. We'll wait for you before we start coffee then.' Ann-Marie eventually allows the door to fall closed and I let out a long breath of relief.

'Natalie, I urgently need you to cover for me,' Carla hisses as Ann-Marie's footsteps click away back through the hallway. 'If you can do this one thing for me, I'll tell you the full story afterwards.'

'Cover for you! What do you mean?'

'I've got the chance to get into Roger's office.' She jerks her head in its direction. 'He's left the key, here on the dresser.' She holds it aloft. 'But I need to be quick – this might be my only chance.'

'Why do you want to get in there?'

'Can you just keep an eye on them all while I get what I need out of there – then I'll meet you in the kitchen.'

'What do you need?'

'I'll tell you everything when I've found it.' Panic is etched across her face as she drops the key into her pocket.

'Can't you tell me now? If something goes wrong or if they catch you getting in there, you might not get the chance.'

'You've seen what Ann-Marie's acting like,' she replies. 'They're all getting impatient.'

'Impatient for what?'

'If you can stall them for me, I'll tell you the full story afterwards, I promise.'

As if my husband's ex-wife is so dependent on me all of a sudden. When I think back to how I felt about her only a quarter of an hour ago, I can't believe how the situation has turned.

'They're not going to be happy when it's me who joins them for coffee.'

I can just imagine their faces, *oh, it's you.*

'I'll be as quick as I can,' Carla says. 'I've got a good idea of where to look, then, like I said, we'll speak as soon as we can both get away from them.'

TWENTY-FIVE

I take a deep breath before pushing the door into the dining room. The hum of conversation immediately pauses and everyone turns to look at me. They're definitely wearing their *oh, it's you* faces. All apart from Sophie, who smiles at me.

'Are you feeling any better?'

'Yes thanks.' I smile back. 'It must have been the lovely smell of coffee that's done it.' I point at the jug in the centre of the table.

'Where's Carla?' She gestures at the door.

'She's still in the loo,' I reply. 'She said her stomach was feeling a bit off and to carry on without her.' My own stomach knots at the realisation that they're hardly going to just leave her to it – it's going to be up to me to stop them checking on her.

'I'd better go and see if she's alright.' Ann-Marie starts to get up.

'I'd leave her alone for a few minutes,' I reply. 'You know what it's like when you're feeling like she is.'

'How come you two are best mates all of a sudden?' Dominic frowns.

'I'm just looking out for someone who's feeling unwell.' I

give him my best wide-eyed look as I retake my seat at the table, all the while trying to quell the anger swirling around me at what he tried to do to me. 'Like I would for anyone.'

'One minute you're scarpering to the lounge, saying you don't feel well' – his frown deepens – 'then the next you come back in here, saying it's Carla who's ill.' He sits up straighter in his seat. 'What's going on, Natalie?'

Dominic's eyes are cold as he looks at me. They've been this way since yesterday, or maybe they've *always* been this way. I was so lonely when we first got together that I think I only saw what I wanted to see. Part of me can't believe that I'm going to be returning to those days. Endless evenings, the walk past pubs and restaurants, knowing I can't go in because I'd be sitting on my own...

'That's women for you.' Roger shakes his head as fills a cup from the jug and passes it to me. I'm grateful he's spoken up, albeit as derogatory as ever. 'Show me one of them who knows what she thinks and feels and I'll show you a flying horse.'

'Alright, Dad.' Sophie shakes her head.

'We can't just leave her out there.' Ann-Marie is still on the edge of her seat, clearly wrestling with herself about whether or not to check in the toilet.

'She told me she wouldn't be long,' I say. My stomach's doing somersaults. I'm presuming that whatever Carla's gone to find has something to do with whatever they're blackmailing her with. I only hope she can find it and can then get us out of here.

'Let's have coffee, Mum, and if she's not back out of the loo by then, one of us can check on her.' But as Sophie passes her mother the milk jug, a dull thud echoes from the office.

I cough as loudly as I can to try to cover it up and then say, 'What kind of coffee is this, Ann-Marie? It smells really very—'

'What the hell was that?' Wiping his mouth on a napkin, Roger jumps to his feet.

Dominic gets to the door before him. 'She's in the bloody

office.' He swings around to face me. 'Why did you tell us she was in the toilet?'

'That's where she said she was going.' I don't know how I'm managing to be civil to him after what I've found out on that video. For now, I've got to be, but not for much longer. I'm just praying that Carla's had the chance to find whatever it was she was looking for and can come up with a good cover story for why she's in there.

'Who left the door unlocked?' Roger bellows.

'Just get in there, will you?' screeches Ann-Marie.

Roger charges past her, elbowing Dominic out of his way as he goes.

Dominic looks sheepish as he darts after his father, followed by Sophie and then by me. As we collectively lurch across the hallway, there's no mistaking what the low rumble emitting from behind the door is. The sound of shredding paper.

Roger throws the door open. 'No! Stop!'

A lever arch file is wide open on the desk next to Carla as she glances over at us with a look of glee on her face, continuing to feed pages into the shredder.

Dominic lunges over to her and grabs hold of the sheets that are half in and half out of the machine. 'You little bitch,' he yells, sounding just like his father. 'What the hell do you think you're doing?'

The shredder makes a wheezing noise as Dominic attempts to tug the pages back out.

'And that's the last of them.' She points at the desk. 'So you can take your threats of what'll happen if I don't buy back my shares into your shitty company and shove them right back up your arses.'

'Surely you haven't...' Roger's in front of them both within a second, reaching into the empty file and snatching the remnants of paper that Dominic's clutching out of his hand.

'It's over, Roger.' Carla smiles. 'There's *nothing* you can do to me now. We all know what my brother did was wrong, but the way you've had us both over a barrel for all this time is far worse than anything he ever did.'

'He fiddled the system.' Ann-Marie spits the words out as she lets the door fall closed behind her. 'The two of you should be in prison.'

'It actually wasn't me,' Carla replies. 'As you very well know.'

'It was *your* bloody company,' Roger shouts. 'I'm warning you, Carla, you cough up that money we need or I'll—'

'You'll *what*?' She steps closer to him. 'I'm not scared of you anymore. *Any* of you.' The look she gives Dominic says it all – it's loaded with hatred and contempt. And to think I was scared that she wanted him back. It shows what a poor judge of character I've been.

I glance at Sophie, trying to catch her eye, but she doesn't look back. It's difficult to know what might be going through her head.

'I should have shopped you to the Legal Aid Board when I had the chance.' Dominic's mouth curls into a sneer. 'All those years, I knew what your corrupt brother had done and—'

'He was young and stupid and you *knew* that.' She shouts into his face. 'You also knew how bitterly he regretted making the claims he did. But we were getting the company off—'

'Nothing can excuse robbing money from taxpayers though, can it?' Ann-Marie's voice bears a desperate edge I've never heard in her before. 'However, you can still make amends and make this go away.'

'Your family won't get another penny out of my company.' Carla turns on her. 'It's over, Ann-Marie – you don't know how long I've been waiting to get my hands on that file.'

'Surely you had copies of it all?' Dominic says, turning to Roger.

The look on his father's face says it all. He clearly thought that what he had was safe under his lock and key.

'How can you treat us like this?' Ann-Marie continues. 'We've looked after you like family. We've—'

'Do you want to know how your son *looked after me* before I left him – the violent, controlling—'

'That's enough.' Roger's face is pinched and white. 'You've caused quite enough damage as it is. All we're asking is that you reinstate your shares in our company.'

'Without your help, Carla,' Ann-Marie says, 'you *know* what we're facing. Prison *and* financial ruin.'

'You *deserve* prison and financial ruin,' she snaps back. 'After your *utter* negligence. You might sit here in your ivory tower, but that poor man *you two* killed was a human being – a more decent one than the lot of you put together. Someone with a future and a family.'

I think they've all forgotten I'm in the room. I stand in the corner, observing the angry words ping-ponging around them all like a pinball machine. It's the same feeling as when I was a child and didn't want to be sent to bed – stay quiet for long enough and they'll eventually forget you're even there.

Carla marches across the room and some other pages on the desk flutter in the waft she's created. She faces Roger. 'Get out of my way, will you?'

'Where do you think you're going?' Roger doesn't move.

'I'm going upstairs for my things. And then I'm leaving.'

She meets my gaze and her unspoken message seems to be inviting me to join her. All I know is that if she does manage to leave, I'm going with her.

However, as a cursory glance at the window tells me, with the snow still falling as it is, both Carla and I need to be careful. Unless this weather suddenly releases its grip, I don't think we can get away from here.

And who knows what this family who are on the verge of losing *everything* could be capable of?

TWENTY-SIX

'Not so fast, young lady.' Ann-Marie corners Carla in the hallway. 'We haven't finished with all this yet.'

'I've got nothing more to say to you.'

I guess she wouldn't have. Carla's done what she came to do – she's shredded the evidence they've been lording over her. But the Elmer family are not about to let her get away, that much is obvious. And where I'm going to factor into all this is anyone's guess.

'I'd like a word with you in private if you don't mind.' Ann-Marie grips Carla's shoulder and attempts to shove her towards the kitchen.

'There's *nothing* you can do or say that can change my mind, Ann-Marie. Dominic and I are divorced and I'm cutting all ties with the lot of you from now on.' Carla jabs her finger in the air. 'And that's the end of it.'

She tries to shake free of Ann-Marie's grip on her shoulder, but with Roger and Dominic right behind her, she's not going anywhere. Who knows where this is going to end? Sophie's standing by the front door, as if she's guarding the entrance in case Carla tries to get out that way. Surely not though? I can't imagine Sophie would have supported how her family have been blackmailing Carla.

'You're in *my* house. So, it's the end when I say it's the end – do you understand?' Roger's tone is calm, yet menacing. I've never warmed to this man and with very good reason. Carla and I could be in real trouble here. And after what I've seen on the video recording, I've got every right to be worried.

But Sophie's here and I'm sure she'll intervene if things get any more out of hand. Even if I'm not entirely sure anymore how much I can trust her.

'Let me get to my room, Ann-Marie.'

'You're not going *anywhere* until this is sorted. It doesn't even need to be the shares anymore – we can clear this up simply by you transferring the necessary money to our account.' Ann-Marie tries to turn her back in the direction of the office. 'Then you can leave as soon as this weather eases, we can all get back to business, and there doesn't have to be any more unpleasantness between us.'

'Your family's had more than enough of my money.' As Carla tries to force herself through the three-person-strong wall, I try to visualise whether our bedrooms have inside locks, but I don't think they do. Maybe we'll have to barricade ourselves in one of the bathrooms. However, judging by the fury on all their faces, they'd probably kick the door in to get at us. There's only Sophie who seems to be staying calm.

Suddenly, Dominic barges forward and slams Carla into the kitchen door.

'Get away from me.' Her voice is a wheeze – the impact of her back against the wood seems to have winded her.

'Dominic! Stop!' I lunge in their direction, but Roger blocks my path. I can't believe what he's doing to her.

I feel in my pocket for my phone. Shit! I must have left it in the lounge after I filmed the footage. How could I have been so stupid?

Thankfully, Carla manages to spin herself around, seemingly catching Dominic off guard. She takes the chance to jab her knee sharply between his legs, watching then as he staggers back, leaving her able to push the door into the kitchen.

'Get out of here,' I yell after her. 'Get out the back door.' I only hope it's open, or if it isn't, that they've left the key in the lock. It was there the other night.

But Roger and Ann-Marie dart straight after her.

'What an absolute bitch.' Dominic grimaces in pain as he crouches against the wall clutching at his crotch. 'What's wrong with you?' It's as if he only just realises that I'm still here. 'Are you just going to stand there gawping at me?'

I push into the kitchen, where Roger's gripping Carla's arm as though his life depends on it. She's tugging away from him, this way and that, to no avail.

'We just need that bank trans—' He jerks his arm away from her. 'You vicious little—' Beneath the edge of his shirtsleeve, she's clearly managed to draw blood with her fingernails. But she's got herself free again. Hopefully, this time, she'll be able to get out of that door. And I'll be going straight after her.

She lurches towards the back door into the garden – if *garden*'s the right word for the two acres out there.

She's made it.

Ann-Marie and Roger are straight after her again. I head after them. I'll get away around the other side of the house and meet Carla at the front. Even in slippers, youth is on our side and we should be faster than the Elmers.

But then, as I reach the door, Dominic barges past me, lunging at Carla, and bringing her crashing face down into the snow where he forces his weight onto the back of her neck for several seconds.

'No, stop!' I cry, lunging in their direction before I'm pulled back by Sophie.

'Stay out of it,' she urges. 'This isn't your fight.'

'But I can't just stand back while they—'

'Get off me!' Carla shrieks, lashing out with her hands and feet in all directions. She tugs at Dominic's ankle, causing him to lose his balance in the snow and slip to the floor. It's long enough for her to be able to stagger back to her feet and make another attempt at getting away. But how far she can get wearing jeans, a jumper and slippers in the thick snow is anyone's guess. Though surely she'll be able to make it to the nearest neighbouring property and call for some help.

Shit, he's got her again. And Roger too. It's up to *me* to go for help while they're preoccupied with Carla. I run back inside and towards the kitchen door, ready to head out the front way. At least I might have the time to grab my coat and boots as I'm passing.

However, Sophie appears in the kitchen doorway.

'Let me through.'

'I've told you to stay out of this.'

'Then let me through.' I attempt to force my way past her. I probably shouldn't leave Carla at their mercy like this, but one of us needs to get out of here and get some help. I don't know how far I'll get, but I've got to try.

'Get off me – get your bloody hands off me.' They've forced her back into the kitchen. I can't leave her now – I'm just going to have to try to calm this down and then we'll both leave later when they're sleeping or something. She's covered in snow and make-up is running down her cheeks as she wrestles to get free of Dominic. 'Please just stop this – things have gone far enough now.'

Ann-Marie grabs the stalk of the S-blade from the blender off the draining board and holds it in front of Carla's face. 'What's going to happen now is that *you're* going to get back in that office and transfer that money to us. Do you hear me?'

I hold my breath. I've seen how effortlessly those blender

blades liquidise fruit and ice for Dominic's morning smoothies – that thing could do a hell of a lot of damage.

Carla knows it too, for her voice trembles as she stares back at Ann-Marie. 'You can threaten me with what the hell you want – but you won't be getting another penny out of me.'

'I'd think very carefully about that if I were you,' she replies.

'Ann-Marie.' I sidle around the side of them while trying to keep out of arm's length of my mother-in-law. I certainly don't want to be on the receiving end of that thing. 'This has gone far enough.' I can't quite believe she'll inflict any damage to Carla – Ann-Marie is many things, but surely she won't want to make things any worse for herself. She's already risking a prison stretch as it is. But if she attacks Carla with that blade, they'll probably throw away the key.

'She's right, Mum.' Sophie steps to my side and it's a surprise to see her finally standing up to her mother. 'Why don't we all try to calm down.'

Carla laughs but I can hear the fear in it. 'Come on, Ann-Marie, we both know you wouldn't do anything to me with that thing. Put it down for God's sake.'

'Then do as she says.' Dominic looks to be tightening his grip on her arm.

'Let her go.' Ann-Marie nods at her son. 'This is between me and her now.' She turns to Carla. 'I've welcomed you into our family, I've treated you as a daughter, we've trusted you with *everything* and *this* is how you repay us?' Her voice rises.

'You *forced* me to come here this Christmas.'

'And you only came because you were biding your time to get inside Roger's office. Who told you where those papers were, anyway?'

'It was obvious where they'd be.'

'Ah, come on. It would have taken ages to find the right drawer, the correct file. You were only in there for a few minutes.' Her tone and her face harden. 'I asked, who told you?'

'Nobody.'

'Please, Ann-Marie.' Perhaps there's only me who can see the intent in her eyes as she brandishes the blade towards Carla. I know what the desperation not to be sent to prison feels like, but if she maims Carla, or worse, then the boiler issue and their tax bill will be the least of their problems.

The face-off between them continues as though they're daring one another to make the next move. But one of them can't defend herself against the other. Carla's going to be pretty helpless against that thing if Ann-Marie starts lashing out. However, I really don't believe she will. She's simply trying to scare Carla into doing what she wants.

'So what's it going to be then?' Roger stands beside his wife. 'Are you going to sort us out with that money, or what?'

'She won't do anything with— Oww—' Carla cries out as Dominic grabs her hair from behind. She shrieks again as he pulls at it, jerking her head backwards with the force.

'You'll listen to my mother,' he snarls. 'You'll put this right, or else.'

'Just let her go,' I shout. 'This has gone too far.'

'Whose side are you actually on?' Roger looks at me as though I'm vermin that's crawled in from outside. 'I always knew there was something off about *you*.'

'You're calling *me* off?' I could laugh but the situation's far from funny. Carla's being held literally at knifepoint, Dominic's already tried to kill me, though he's unaware that I know yet, and they've made it perfectly clear that *neither* of us is going anywhere. I'm still not clear where Sophie is in all this. She seems to be reasonably neutral, so why won't she just let me leave?

Ann-Marie's still not taking her eyes away from Carla. 'All I care about is getting our money.' She brings the blade closer to Carla's face. I still don't believe she's going to use it.

'It's. Not. Your. Money,' Carla hisses through gritted teeth.

If I was in her position right now, I'd just do whatever they're demanding. Before they died, my parents always told Hayden and me that if someone were to threaten us with a blade or other weapon, we should just hand over whatever was being demanded of us. Unfortunately, they didn't survive long enough to ever know the irony of their words.

Ann-Marie's holding the blade an inch away from Carla's face and I can't believe Carla's even risking her using it. One move and she'll be permanently disfigured – at best. 'Do what they're telling you, Carla,' I shriek. 'No amount of money's worth you getting hurt.'

'She's right,' Sophie says.

Carla glances at Sophie and then back to Ann-Marie. 'As if I'm going to let this bitter old has-been get the better of me.'

'You nasty little bitch.' As she spits the words out, Ann-Marie swipes upwards with the blade, and Carla's arm flails out to protect her face. As I jump towards them, the blade carves a curved line into her skin as sharply as a knife through butter.

Fear catches in my throat as blood spurts everywhere. 'Nooo.'

Carla presses onto her arm. But within a split second, blood's pumping from in between her fingers.

I hold my breath as everything seems to go into slow motion. Ann-Marie's stabbed her – she's *really* stabbed her – and in a pretty bad place by the looks of it. She's going to bleed to death – and probably quite quickly.

'Help me.' Carla staggers back against the counter, her bulging eyes imploring me. 'Please! Please don't let me die!'

'Oh my God.' Sophie's hand flies to her throat.

But I can't move – it's the blood. I'm not seeing Carla – instead, I'm seeing Kyle. I'm not hearing her anguished cries for help – I'm hearing *his*. It's as if I've gone into shock just like I did when *he* was dying. And now Carla's going to die too, no matter what *anyone* does to try to help her. From the amount of blood that's spurting all over the place, Ann-Marie must have sliced into one of her main arteries.

She slides down the cupboard to the floor, her face as white as the crisp linen still whirring in the washing machine behind us. There's absolutely nothing I can do other than get myself out of here.

For if I don't, it's likely to be *my* turn next.

TWENTY-SEVEN

In the chaos that follows, I make it back to the hallway, but there's no sign of my coat or boots. I'm just going to have to make a run for it, dressed as I am. Gasping for breath, I grapple with the door handle. I doubt I can save Carla now, but I can still save myself. It crosses my mind to run back for my phone, but that will waste precious seconds. Seconds I don't have.

'Natalie.' Dominic hurls himself between me and the door and pushes me back. 'You can't go out there.'

'Please just let me go, Dom.' By using the shortened name I've always called him, surely I can evoke *something* within him. After all, he must have thought something of me *once*.

I twist the handle again but it's locked – I can't believe this. *It's bloody locked.*

'My dad's ringing for help for Carla. Just come and sit down.' He points towards the lounge.

'*Come and sit down!* Your mother's just slashed your ex-wife's arm, she's through there bleeding to death and all you can say is *come and sit down*.'

'Everything's going to be alright.' He tugs at me.

'How do I know it's not going to be *me* next?' I glance

around, stalling for time. *Where's the key? Where's the bloody key?*

'I wouldn't let *anyone* hurt you – you should know that, Nat. Please, you've just got to trust me here.'

I could almost laugh. *Trust him?* But he has no idea that I've seen the footage of what he tried to do to me.

'How can you be so calm? Your ex-wife's at death's door in that kitchen.' I point towards it. 'You need to get back in there and help her.'

'It was a moment of madness.' Sophie joins in trying to usher me away from the door and into the lounge. 'Mum had no intention of things going this far.'

'Just get off me, will you?' I tug my arm away from her. 'I'm quite capable of walking on my own.' I want to get in there *without* them so I can get to my phone.

'Mum's in absolute bits,' Sophie continues, 'but she's doing her best to bandage Carla up until the ambulance gets here.'

'So help's definitely on its way?' I glance down at myself, bile rising in my throat as I see how drenched in Carla's blood I am. Anyone would think I'd sliced her myself.

'Of course it is.'

'Even if you're telling the truth, you know as well as I do that *nothing* can get here.'

'It's stopped snowing now, look.' Dominic points to the hallway window. I follow the direction of his finger, the outside world grounding me somehow, yet also bringing home the enormity of what's just happened. 'They should be able to get the air ambulance up – it's clear enough now.'

All fight seeps out of me as I look from one of them to the other. They're not going to let me go, so I'll have to stay and play along with things until I can break free and tell the truth about what's happened. At least someone's called for help. Though I can't imagine any help could possibly arrive in time to save Carla.

'I can't believe what she's done to her.' I lean against the wall, feeling unsteady. *Or what you've done*, I want to say to Dominic. I stare at him, trying to read his expression. After what I saw him do on that camera, I know how unsafe I am in this house.

I'm trying to convince myself that Ann-Marie really *did* act in a moment of madness. She's not going to do the same to me – after all, what could possibly be gained by that? It's not as if *I've* got any money or status – which is all they wanted Carla for.

However, knowing that she's lost *any* chance of obtaining the money she wanted, Ann-Marie will be feeling even more desperate about her situation than she was before.

Not to mention, unhinged.

She emerges from the kitchen, followed by her husband.

'What's going on?' I try to peer to the side of her before the door closes. 'Surely you shouldn't leave Carla alone until the air ambulance gets here.'

'Who said anything about an air ambulance?'

'You said—' I swing around to face Sophie.

'I thought he was—'

'There's nothing anyone can do,' Dominic says. He's as splattered in her blood as I am, having been in the vicinity of what Ann-Marie did. 'You know as well as I do that she's going to bleed to death on that floor.'

'She looks like she's gone already,' Roger says, his voice as soft as I've ever heard it. I stare at the passive expression on his face. They claimed she was their family, yet he's acting so clinical and seems so unmoved by what his wife has done to her.

'Oh my God – I thought you'd tried to bandage her.' I'm clutching at straws here. They had no interest in trying to help her. And now they're just going to let her die on their kitchen floor. And what the hell am *I* going to do?

'Stay out of there.' Roger catches my arm as I attempt to pass him.

'I'm involved in all this whether you like it or not.' I look around at my audience. 'I don't care whose wife she *was* or what she's done, I'm not just going to let her die through there. Not without at least *trying* to help her.'

'It's too late for that now.' Ann-Marie slides against the hallway wall into a crouch on the floor.

'Mum, are you alright?' Sophie darts towards her.

'I just can't believe what I've done. It's all over for us – it's all over for *me*.'

I stare at her. 'Is that all you care about? *Yourself!*'

'I shouldn't have done it,' she wails.

'Then, please, let me get in there and help her. We might still have a chance of saving her.'

'I'm done for,' she wails even louder. 'Me and my stupid temper. What have I done?'

'Pull yourself together, for God's sake,' Roger snaps.

'The cameras,' Ann-Marie cries as her gaze is averted above me. 'We need to wipe them – quickly – get rid of the proof of what I did.'

I glance at Dominic, trying to gauge his reaction at the mention of the cameras, but he seems unmoved. I guess that what he tried to do to me yesterday won't be at the forefront of his mind right now.

'You're right.' Roger turns on his heel and heads towards the lounge. He runs across the room and drops to his knees in front of the TV.

'What about Carla?' I sob. 'We can't just leave her like that.'

'Stand there.' Dominic points towards the doorway of the lounge.

'Why?' I can see my phone but can't grab it until there's no one looking.

'Because until we've worked out what to do, we need to all stick together.'

'He's right,' Sophie says and I stare at her. I thought she was different – I thought she was alright, but the bottom line is that she's an Elmer.

'Who's been looking at this?' Roger turns from where he's kneeling. Time stands still as all eyes turn to the TV. 'You.' He points at me. 'Is this what you were doing when we were eating? Is this why you were so desperate to get in here?'

Ann-Marie rises back to her feet and pushes past me in the doorway. All three of them are staring at the stilled image displayed on it, right at the moment where Dominic is tipping a slice of torte onto another plate.

'Well, of all the sneaky—' Dominic suddenly grasps my shoulder, digging his fingers into the muscle. Fear seeps into the core of my being. What will he do to me now?

'Owww – get off me!' I shriek.

'What the hell are you up to?'

'You switched the plates,' Sophie gasps, turning to him. 'But why?'

'I could ask the same question,' says Ann-Marie.

'I'm the one who should be asking the bloody questions.' I attempt to turn in Dominic's grasp but he holds me more firmly. My hand is in one of his hands, his other gripping one of my shoulders.

'It's a shame really.' His fingers dig deeper. 'Despite what you did to my friend, I quite liked you in the beginning. Until I found out the *full* story yesterday, that is.'

'What I did to what *friend*? I don't understand.'

'Kyle,' he says.

'You were friends with *Kyle*?' I stare at him in disbelief.

'As in Kyle from your university days?' Sophie looks puzzled.

They must have known each other before Kyle and I met. Has he really kept this from me for the whole of our relationship? Has everything I've ever believed about him, about *us*, been a sham?

'*She* was the one who stabbed him to death.' He jabs his finger so hard into my shoulder that I wince. 'I heard her shouting out in her sleep about it yesterday. And she's let her brother take the blame and serve time for her.'

'She *what?*' Ann-Marie is staring at me with her mouth hanging open. 'Are you sure about this?'

'And she's *admitted* this to you?' Roger shakes his head. 'What are you even *doing under the same roof* with someone like that?'

'You're joking,' Sophie says and the tone of her voice suggests I've lost my ally.

'I only found out the full story yesterday,' Dominic replies. 'Which is why I tried to deal with her my own way.'

Roger comes towards me. 'Even without all that, she's become a liability.'

'Please, no.' I try to step back, but with Dominic behind me, there's nowhere to go. 'I won't say anything – I won't do anything, I promise. Just let me get out of here.'

If I can just get away, I can call some help for Carla – it may still not be too late. My eyes fall once again on my phone. I have to get that, then I have to get out of here.

'Pass me that phone, Dad.' Dominic must follow my gaze for he removes one of his hands from me and holds it towards his father, jerking his head towards the sofa arm. 'It's *hers*. It wants doing away with.'

Roger gets to it and hurls it to the floor in front of Dominic.

'No! *Please!*'

There's nothing I can do to prevent him from stamping on it. Once, twice, three times.

Oh my God, he's a maniac. *What the hell am I going to do now?* Carla's probably dead, this lot have turned on me and I've no phone to call for help. While Dominic's busy stamping on my phone, I lunge towards the kitchen. This is it. This might be my last chance to get away from them.

I swing at the kitchen door handle but Dominic catches my arm in mid-flight and twists it behind my back. I screech out in pain.

'You're going nowhere.' Dominic crushes me against the door.

'Let me go. Get off me.' I slither and squirm but I'm no match for the weight he's exerting on me.

'What the hell are we going to do with her?' The pressure of his body against mine intensifies.

'Sophie, help me, please.' She's just standing there, watching. But I know she's not going to help me. She's *their* daughter, *Dominic's* sister, and it's unlikely that she's going to go against them.

'She could take the blame for what's happened to the other one for starters,' Roger's voice sounds behind me.

'That's not such a bad idea.'

'What are you talking about?' I gasp, going suddenly limp in Dominic's grasp.

'It was obvious how jealous you were of her,' Dominic says, his voice so close it tickles in my ear. 'It was inevitable that you'd snap eventually.'

'You've got *no* chance of pinning that on me,' I cry. 'The forensics will show otherwise anyway.'

'We'll have the lot of it cleaned up by the time *they* get here,' Roger says.

'This has gone too far, Dad – Mum, come on.' At least Sophie's suddenly trying. 'There has to be a better way out of this.'

I'm still trying to wriggle free of Dominic. 'Please just listen to her – and let me get to Carla. Then I'll leave. If you let me go, I won't say a word about any of this.'

'Of course you won't.' Dominic laughs. 'As if.'

'Do you really think we can pin what I've done onto *her*, Roger?' Ann-Marie says from somewhere behind me.

'As long as we get our stories straight and then all stick together. At the end of the day, who will the police believe – people from good stock like we are or someone with *her* kind of background.'

Dominic grips me harder. 'It's up to *us* to make sure she goes down for murder,' he says. 'Like she should have done in the first place.'

'*Carla* could still be alive in there.' Roger's voice hardens again.

'I doubt it, but go and see.' Ann-Marie's voice wobbles. 'I can't bear to go back in there.'

Despite being pressed up against the door, I haven't heard a single sound come from in the kitchen. All I know is that after the volume of blood she lost even in front of me, Carla can't *possibly* still be alive.

'Keep hold of *her*.' Roger nods at Dominic. 'And let me get through.'

I struggle to stay upright as Dominic tugs me backwards. Roger steps towards the kitchen door, pushes it open and peers in.

I hold my breath.

'You're not going to believe this,' he begins as he turns back to face us all. 'She's gone.'

TWENTY-EIGHT

'She can't have gone.' Ann-Marie races into the kitchen after him. 'She was practically dead before. She wasn't even conscious.'

'There's no way she could have got back up from that.' Sophie goes in after them.

Dominic frogmarches me back towards the door, presumably to see for himself. I can't stand being this close to him and am still reeling from the shock that he used to be *friends* with Kyle. He was so convincing when we first met. I still don't understand any of it. I need to know – I need him to tell me, but right now perhaps there's other priorities.

I wait for the shock of Carla's disappearance to make him relax his hold on me so I can make another run for it, but he doesn't. Instead he grips me tighter than ever.

'You saw what happened in here.' Ann-Marie's face is more pinched and white than usual as she stands beside the island, surveying the pool of blood she left Carla lying in. There's more blood splattered all up the cupboards beside the sink from where Ann-Marie lashed out with the blade.

Sophie shoots towards the back door. 'She must have gone out the back way?'

Roger darts after her. 'Surely there'll be blood all over the place if she has.'

I look along from the pool of blood in which she lay, and towards the back door, expecting to see a trail. But there's nothing.

'She's not likely to get very far, is she?' Dominic's voice is loud in my ear.

'Get after her then, someone,' Ann-Marie cries. 'Though I imagine that you're just going to find her face down somewhere.'

'And what about this one?' Dominic shoves me forward but retains the strength of his grip on me. 'The second I let her go, she's going to try to make a run for it.'

'I'll go after Carla.'

'You're going out there like *that*?' Ann-Marie looks Sophie up and down.

'I'll quickly get my coat and boots on.'

'Well, hurry up about it then.' She gestures towards the door as a clump of snow slides from a ledge above it, filling in whatever imprints in the snow were made from the earlier scuffle out there. 'The very fact that Carla's made it out of here shows how determined she is.'

Sophie pushes past us and dashes into the hallway.

'Ring when you find her,' Dominic shouts.

The door bangs behind her.

'On second thoughts.' Roger skids in the blood as he comes back towards us. 'Lock *her* in one of the outbuildings until we get everything straight and decide how we're going to handle this – the one furthest from the house – it's the most secure.'

'No – please!'

'Right, you're coming with me then.' Dominic rams his knee

into the bend of my leg, buckling me as he pushes me towards the open door.

'No – no – I'll freeze to death out there.' I tug against his grip on me. The chill cutting through the kitchen is as sharp as the blade that's done so much damage. 'Please, can't you just lock me in the bedroom? Please, Dominic, don't lock me up outside.'

'It's only until we've cleaned up and got the police here,' Ann-Marie says, her voice softer than before – as though that makes it all OK. 'Go on, Dominic, get her out of here.'

'And then you'll be off to a nice warm police station instead.' He unhooks a key from the rack as we reach the door. 'Which is where you should have been all along.'

The freezing air takes my breath away. 'Please, I'm begging you, Dom, don't do this to me. You know how cold I get.' Snow fills my slippers after only a few steps.

I glance around for traces of Carla's blood or footprints, but there's absolutely *nothing* out here.

After what Ann-Marie did to her, how can she even still be alive? And she can't just have disappeared without any trace. There should be streaks of blood dragging away from the pool they initially left her lying in. I remember only too well about blood seepage after what I did to Kyle.

Dominic doesn't reply – his concentration seems to be set on staying upright in the snow and getting me to the building that's coming into vision through the mist.

'Please, Dominic, I had no *idea* you once knew Kyle. But you didn't know the real him. Or what he put me through and how abusive he was.'

'Just shut it, will you?'

I'd never have gone anywhere near Dominic if I had any inkling. I was only aware that he knew the newspaper's version of my backstory when we first met, but then, *most* people did.

I twist in my husband's grip, trying to make eye contact with him – there must be *something* I can do to change his mind about what he's doing to me here. 'What I don't understand is how you could have come anywhere *near* me if Kyle was your friend and you felt so strongly about his death.'

'I thought your brother had done it. That was horrendous enough.'

'By *marrying* me?' I can hardly believe this.

'I liked you, Natalie. What you'd done was bad enough, but I decided you'd already been punished enough. Turns out that you haven't.'

'Honestly, Dom, he hit me, he verbally—'

'There's no way Kyle would have abused you like you accused him of. No way. I used to share a room with him.'

'I'm telling the truth.'

'It's easy to lie when someone's no longer around to defend himself. But it's fine – you're going to get what you deserve now.'

'You've no idea what a brute he was to me when no one was around.' My tears are the only thing keeping my face warm. After all Hayden gave up for me – I should have stayed on my own. What an absolute fool I was to risk *anyone* finding out the truth. I know now that I jumped out of the frying pan and into the fire. From what Carla's managed to tell me and from what I saw on that camera, Dominic's as much of an abuser as Kyle was.

'I always knew there was more to the story than you were letting on in court.'

'Hang on, you were in court?' Not that I'd ever be able to recall faces from the public gallery. The whole thing was a complete blur. The seats had been jam-packed with Kyle's supporters – their hatred rippling around the room and washing over us the whole time. I'm surprised they didn't burst into applause when we were eventually sentenced.

'Of course I was in court.'

'I stabbed him in self-defence, Dominic,' I sob. 'It was him or me.'

'Twelve times,' he snarls.

Hayden will tear Dominic limb from limb when he eventually gets out of prison, whether or not I make it back out of this building he's about to lock me into. Hayden promised our mother before she died that he'd *always* look after me, no matter what. He put me before himself over and over when we were teenagers, and living in foster home after foster home. His friends would laugh at him for letting his uncool younger sister trail around after him but he didn't care. He worked weekends to buy extras for us, protected me against the bullies at school and was there for me night and day – when things were tough. As they often were.

Then he did the *ultimate* putting me before himself.

Dominic pushes me forward. 'Time's up – we're here.' Even though we're now away from his parents, I still haven't managed to talk him around. 'At least by locking you in *there*, I can give you the justice the court never did.'

'Will you bring me my coat and some blankets out?' I twist my head, trying once again to meet Dominic's eye. There *must* be a hint of conscience in there *somewhere*. 'Please, Dom.'

'Don't call me that again. And don't even *look* at me,' he snaps. 'Not after what you've admitted to.' He shoves me up against the door, pressing his body into my back. My face grazes the splintering wood as he fumbles with the key and the hefty-looking padlock. That won't be kicked off in a hurry. I'll probably have more success kicking the inside walls to see if one of them will give way once he's gone.

He slides the padlock from the hook. 'Get in there.' He tries to push me forward but I dig my heels in.

'Don't do this to me, Dom. You must have loved me – you wouldn't have married me otherwise.'

'I never *loved* you. I married you mainly to get back at

Carla,' he replies. 'You were there. You were convenient. I thought it would make her jealous enough to bring her back.'

'You just said you *liked* me,' I cry. 'So which one is it?'

'Both,' he replies. 'What an idiot I was.'

'You had no chance with Carla,' I shout back at him. 'She's told me about her lucky escape from you – I just wish she'd let me know sooner. But you completely took me in, didn't you – with your lies and your empty promises.'

'You're not in a position to be dishing out the abuse, Natalie. Go on – get in there.' He pushes me forward with the intensity of the first push of a child on a swing.

I cry out as I land on the floor. 'Please, please don't leave me in here.'

'I'm doing it for Kyle.' He slams the door, then fumbles with the lock before it clicks, signalling that I'm well and truly incarcerated in here. Part of me welcomes him leaving me alone so I can straighten my thinking and work a way out for myself. The other part of me's terrified. Freezing to death is a real possibility.

I can only hope that wherever Carla is, she's still alive and is en route back to me with some help.

Shivering, I glance around at the daylight seeping through the corners of the outbuilding. It's totally empty in here and I recall overhearing Ann-Marie talking to one of her friends at the barbecue about how she was going to convert it into a garden room they could work in to get them out of the house.

I lurch from corner to corner, scouring the floor for something, *anything*, that I might be able to use to free me, or some old sack or cloth I can wrap around myself to get warm. But there's absolutely nothing.

My teeth are chattering with fear and cold and I don't know what to do. If they leave me out here, it will be dark in a few hours and the temperature will, no doubt, drop back to well below zero.

'Sophie.' I bang against the walls. She's out there somewhere, looking for Carla. Surely she'll let me out? She might be an Elmer but she's the most decent one out of all of them.

I scream and shout until I'm hoarse. But, really, I know that no one else has a chance of hearing me. It's a five-minute car ride to the nearest house. And this outbuilding is probably far enough from The Elms that even when Sophie comes back, she won't be able to hear me. They might just tell her that I've left of my own accord and then she'll be none the wiser.

I circle the space again, this time prodding and pressing at all the walls with my now-numb fingers. There are no obvious weaknesses I can push my way through, but the two shorter walls have a slight give when I push at them.

I lash out with my foot at one of them, grunting with the exertion. Then again, and again. Each time, the wall moves slightly, but it's a long way from collapse. But at least what I'm doing's keeping me warm. This is what I'm going to have to do, just keep moving, doing star jumps, whatever – until one of them lets me out.

Ann-Marie will sooner or later – she even said that my being here is only temporary while they clean the evidence up. *Then* she's going to call the police and say it was *me* who stabbed Carla.

I don't care if they try to blame what she did on me – the forensics will soon prove otherwise as there's no way they'll be able to clean *every* trace of evidence. I rub my face, peeling away the droplets of Carla's dried blood. Ann-Marie's right – at first glance, it probably *will* look like it was me that did it – I was right in the firing line of that first spurt of her blood. They'll tell the police how I was the jealous current wife, lashing out at my adversary in a rage, but somehow I'll get the police to believe me.

As for what happened with Kyle, if Dominic starts bleating about all that to the police, as my brother has already proven, he'll back me up to the ends of the earth. And after all that's happened in this house over the last couple of days, it shouldn't be *too* difficult to discredit Dominic. Particularly if I'm able to get out of here and join forces with Carla.

Her face swims back into my mind. 'Please be OK,' I whisper into the silence. I hope to God she's managed to get somewhere by now and is raising the alarm.

Wherever she's ended up after that kitchen floor, if she's still alive, she'll have no idea of just how much trouble I'm in.

TWENTY-NINE

I'm so cold I can't remember what it ever felt like to be warm. I close my eyes and try to bring to mind some home comforts – a steaming cup of tea, a cosy hug, a roaring fire, a fluffy jumper – but every time my eyes are closed all I see is spurting blood. And I don't know whether it's coming from Kyle or Carla.

Is she dead? Is she coming back to help me? Do I deserve to just be left out here to freeze until I die?

I rise from the floor, blowing on my hands as I hop from one foot to another. I can't give up – I've got to fight. Life might have been shit so far but things can get better – I've still got so much living to do that it can't end here – not like this.

Summoning every reserve of my energy, I begin star jumping again. If I close my eyes and use my imagination, I can almost pretend I'm doing the warm-up at legs, bums and tums. *Come on, ladies, get yourselves moving.*

I only manage around ten when I have to stop as I'm exhausted. And I don't feel any warmer. I rub at the sides of my arms as I stare at the door. Ann-Marie was supposed to come back for me – she said she would. But then what would she do with me?

I rush at the door again, banging and kicking with all my might. 'Sophie! Sophie! Please! Please help me! Please let me out of here.'

I don't know how their consciences allow them to stay locked out like this. Maybe they're hoping I've frozen to death by now and are inventing some story to cover themselves. The truth is that, unless I get back indoors within the next couple of hours, I probably *will* freeze to death.

After the meagre helping of brunch which was all I ate earlier, I'm fast running out of energy to keep doing these star jumps. But without them, I can't keep my blood circulating. However, even more than food, I need a drink. I desperately, desperately need a drink. There's all that snow outside that I could thaw and drink, but I can't get to it.

I stare at the cracks of fading light seeping through the corners of what's become my holding cell. I really am going to die in here and there's nothing I can do.

I lift my head from the ground. I must have dozed off. I'm numb from head to foot but I no longer feel cold. I'm not even shivering, so perhaps I'm already dead. I stab my nails into the fleshy part of my palm but can't feel a thing.

Where the hell is Carla? Is she lying somewhere, collapsed in the snow, a frozen corpse, waiting to be discovered?

I've been in here for so long that I've no idea what time it is or if it's snowed some more. If it has, it could be days before Carla's body is found, and as for *my* body, maybe it *never* will be found. Perhaps I'll rot away, here on my own, without anyone knowing or bothering to check up on me. There's only my brother who'll notice my absence and that won't be for two or three weeks when I don't visit him. Even then, it's not as though he'll have any power from where he is. I don't even know if he'll be able to report me missing. Maybe some of my nail clients will wonder where I am when they try to book their next Shellac appointment, but they'll no doubt just shrug their shoulders when I don't get back to them and go off to find someone else.

Nobody will be looking for me. Carla, if she's still alive, is my only hope.

I've only got myself to blame for this. And it's my own stupid fault for ever letting someone get too close.

I told myself Dominic's initial intensity was all part of his personality and because he wanted me so much – really, there was a glint in his eyes and an edge to his voice when he spoke to me which I could never put my finger on. It was like he wanted me but didn't want me, at the same time.

So the last thing I *ever* expected to hear from his mouth were the words, *will you marry me?*

My head had jerked up in shock as I peeled potatoes at the sink. 'What on earth's brought this on?'

He smiled then as he took my chin between his fingers and tilted it towards his face. 'Are you going to answer my question, or not?'

I hesitated – of course I did. We'd only been together for a matter of months, though he was at the house I was renting from his parents morning, noon and night before we moved into his place. His presence was so intense that, at times, I felt suffocated – especially after everything I'd been through with Kyle. And it wasn't as if Dominic was down on one knee in front of me – I was getting the impression that his proposal wasn't even planned.

But since Hayden had gone to prison, I hated being alone. I really, really hated it – feared it even – so perhaps I jumped too fast at the first man to show a flicker of interest in me.

'Come on, Natalie, we'll move in together *properly* then and we can make a real go of things.'

'But what about your parents? They can't stand me.' It was

the understatement of the century. Even before they ever clapped eyes on me, my card had been well and truly marked. I can't say I blame them, I'm not exactly dream daughter-in-law material with my record.

'You're marrying *me*, not my parents.'

'Have you even bought me a ring?' I looked down at his hands.

'Well, *no*, not exactly, but we can sort that out after, can't we? In fact, say yes and we'll head out straight away to choose one.'

And we did. He bought me a beautiful sapphire. It's so dark in here now, it's no longer glistening as I turn it this way and that. It will probably never see daylight again. Like me.

An owl hoots in the distance. Ann-Marie's words, the ones I was hanging onto, were clearly completely empty. None of them are coming back for me. They're probably all sleeping, warm in their beds, hoping I've died by now. I can't believe Sophie is going along with it all, but perhaps they've told her something else. Maybe she doesn't even know I'm locked in here.

I've gone beyond shivering now – it's as if my body's giving up on me. After all, there's little point in me trying to keep myself warm any longer – I'm probably going to die, no matter what I do. I haven't got the energy to get up off the floor again, so doing any more star jumps is out of the question. I'm all out of fight and I just want to sleep. If I'm asleep I'm less aware of my predicament and I don't want to be awake when the end comes. I just want to slip peacefully from this world to the next. But will I be permitted to do that? *After what I've done?*

As I try to drift back off again, heat seeps around my pelvis. Momentarily, I'm grateful for it, though my disorientated brain won't allow me to work out what's caused it. But as the stench of urine creeps around my nostrils, I realise that I must have wet myself. The smell makes me raise my head to retch, though nothing comes up. There's nothing *to* come up.

No one's coming to help and this is going to be my final resting place. Here on a shitty, hard floor, lying in a pool of my own piss, as the darkness limps towards a brand new day that I won't even get the chance to see.

Then Hayden's face slides into my mind as if urging me to fight.

Come on, sis. Do it for me. Get up off that floor and move.

My brother sacrificed everything for me – and for what? So that I could end up with another man who just wants to hurt me?

One thing's for certain, if I ever make it out of here, I'm going to admit to what I did to Kyle and why – I'm going to make sure my brother's released, which is what I should have done ages ago. I can't believe it's taken what's happened here for me to come to this realisation.

I'll serve time – of course I will. But at least my conscience will be clear at last.

It's no good, I can't get up. And the wetness I'm lying in is cooling. Soon it will freeze and will probably bring death even faster. My breathing is already slow and painful.

Surely I'll be put out of my misery soon.

CARLA

THIRTY

'Mum – Dad – this is Carla. Carla, meet my parents.'

'Hi,' I said. 'Thanks for inviting me over.'

'It's just so lovely to meet you at last.' Ann-Marie threw her arms around me, then as she pulled away, she reached behind her and produced a wrapped gift. 'It's just a little something to welcome you to the family,' she said.

Roger hung back, though the expectant look on his face said he was waiting for some attention from me too.

'Hi, Roger,' I said. 'I've heard lots about you.'

'All good, I hope,' he laughed. 'Come, let me give you a guided tour of The Elms, then we can finish up at our little bar in the drawing room.'

Dominic pulled a face behind his back and I fought the urge to laugh. Who on earth calls it a *drawing room* these days?

'If you play your cards right, Carla,' Roger said as we followed him into the kitchen, 'if you and Dominic marry, some day this will all be yours.' He swept his arms around.

'Oh, I've got my own business,' I laughed. 'My brother and I run a legal firm. I'm not with Dominic for what I might marry into.'

'So we've heard,' Ann-Marie gushed. 'Dominic's told us how successful your company is. Well done you!'

'So long as you won't be going in for one of those ridiculous prenup arrangements,' Roger added. 'As you can see' – he cast his gaze from one side of the room to the other – 'there's no need.'

'Well, we haven't actually got as far as—'

'You mean you haven't proposed to her yet?' Roger shook his head. 'Dominic Elmer – get her snapped up immediately.'

It was the third time I'd met the parents of a boyfriend and it couldn't have been any weirder. Ann-Marie and Roger treated me as though I was royalty – nothing was too much trouble, yet I felt almost smothered by them. They were far too keen for Dominic and me to rush things to the next stage and when two weeks later, he presented me with a beautiful ring, although the sensible side of me was saying *no-no-no*, I kept thinking about the many people I'd be disappointing if I rejected his proposal, and besides, we could always have a *long* engagement.

'Her eyes are moving, look. I'm sure of it. And did you see her fingers twitching?'

I don't recognise the voices, but machines are bleeping at either side of where I'm lying. I must be in hospital – and can't believe that somehow, I've survived. I've no idea *how* – after all, I didn't even make it to the house I could see in the distance. When my dizziness meant that I couldn't go another step, I flopped onto all fours in the snow, and then as soon as I landed there, and the cold gnawed into the core of my bones, I knew I wouldn't be getting up again.

The blood had seeped through the tablecloth I'd bound my arm in before escaping through the back door of The Elms and I really thought I'd die there. It became a toss-up as to whether the loss of so much blood or the icy conditions would kill me first.

'You're alright now,' a kindly voice says from beside me. 'You have another little sleep if you need to. One of us will still be close by when you wake up.'

Tears spring to my eyes as I sense the heat of someone's hand over mine. Wherever I am, I'm cosseted and safe. Warm in this room, surrounded by people who are looking after me, I can drift away again, though unfortunately, I have little control over where I drift away to...

'I'll have to speak to him,' I said to my PA as she announced Dominic's call for the fifth time in an hour. 'It's the only way we're going to get rid of him.'

'Are you really sure that's a good idea?'

'Put him through to my office, will you?'

'Do you want me to let Liam know he's bothering you?' She rose from her desk.

'Not just yet.' The last thing I needed was my brother getting involved. He'd handle things in his own way if he knew Dominic was doing this. And after everything that had gone before, it would probably involve either a golf club or a cricket bat.

'What do you want?' I sank onto my office chair and glanced out of the window at people hurrying about with their bags of Christmas shopping. I yearned for their normality – to be looking forward to the festivities with family, with the biggest challenges being over where everyone might sleep or how many vegetables to peel.

'Why the *hell* have you sold your shares, Carla?'

I couldn't pretend I wasn't expecting this question. 'Dominic, we're divorced and you're remarried now.'

'That doesn't explain why you've pulled out.'

'Why shouldn't I want a clean break? Furthermore' – I'd put my legal head on by this point – 'I no longer want any involvement in what's going on with your parents.'

'What about your promise to carry on representing them in court? I've heard you've backed out of that too.'

'I don't want to be—'

'But they're counting on you – as you very well know. You need to reconsider all this, Carla – for their sake, if not for mine. You know they still think of you as family.'

'I'm sorry, Dominic. I've made my mind up – on both counts.'

'You know as well as I do' – his voice had taken on the edge I used to fear – 'that they have *zero* chance of defending themselves at the trial – not with what they're up against. And how are they supposed to clear that tax bill without your investment?'

'It's no longer my problem, Dominic – I'm really sorry.' I wasn't, but trying to appease him was still happening naturally.

'Not as sorry as you'll be if you don't step back up, Carla.'

'Hang on a minute – are you threatening me? Don't you think I put up with enough of that when we were married?'

'Alright – if not the shares, then what about a loan? Dad's already rung you and run this by you, hasn't he?'

Were this bloody family ever going to leave me alone? 'I said no to him and I'm saying no to you.'

'For God's sake, what they're asking for is easily affordable for you. Five million pounds and a couple of days of your precious time in court?'

'I said no.'

'After everything they've done for you...'

'Such as?'

'Mum's treated you like her own daughter, you know she has.'

'That's because of what I've *got* rather than who I *am* – as you very well know.'

'It's not only their livelihood and freedom which you're putting at stake, it's mine and Sophie's inheritance we're talking about here. Come on, Carla, we were married once – surely that counts for *something*. And why would you want to punish my sister as well?'

So now we'd got to the only reason Dominic would be sticking his neck out. *His inheritance.* He'd so often bleated on about it. Although with the issues that were hanging over them, the Elmers would have to take all equity out of their house and what was left of their business just to clear the money side of things. But they might still be owing, even after that.

'You'll have to find yourself a different set of purse strings, Dominic. I'm having nothing to do with it.'

'Right, OK then – I'd hoped not to have to walk this line but you're leaving me with no choice.'

'What line? What are you talking about?'

'Surely I don't need to remind you about Liam's – what shall we call them? – legal aid indiscretions.'

'Pardon?'

'You heard?'

It was the first time he'd mentioned what Liam had done since the action against the Elmers first began. I'll always regret allowing them to hold me over a barrel like they have, but I regret even more the day I ever agreed for Dominic to take over our company's accounting. It was back in the early days when I was under the misguided illusion that I could trust him. But the confidentiality clause he once signed turned out to mean very little. Still, I wasn't going to let him think that he'd rattled me.

'Do your worst, Dominic. You can't prove a thing anyway.' It was true. Yes, he might have known about our situation back then, but everything had been meticulously swept under the carpet. Our company's wrongdoing has become nothing but dust – out of sight and out of mind.

Though parading his accusations and comments around to other businesses and clients would still be bad enough in terms of the harm it could cause to our reputation.

'Oh, I think you'll find that I can.'

'How?' I was asking this when, really, at that moment, I knew exactly *how*. The absolute snake.

'I've got everything documented in black and white. Call it my insurance.'

'I don't believe you.'

'You know me.' His voice oozed with smugness. 'I've always been one for dotting the i's and crossing the t's. After all, you never know when things might come in useful.'

I knew then what the saying *my blood ran cold* meant. He'd made copies of the paperwork I thought had long been shredded. My ex-husband was blackmailing me.

'So *this* is the reason for my phone call, Carla. And if you hadn't pulled out of everything with my parents, I wouldn't be forced to be doing this.'

'You've really made a copy of the paperwork?'

'You didn't think I wouldn't have taken advantage of my former access to your files, surely?'

I knew then that I'd have to stall him, *and* his parents – not only over the money, but also about continuing to represent them over the negligence charge. I'd been with them at the initial hearings, but knew I couldn't carry on. No way could I face defending them when they went on trial.

Maybe I could put on an act and keep up some sort of pretence until somehow, I'd get my hands on the papers Dominic had obtained. Without them as proof, he'd have no power to bring our company to its knees.

Which is why I found myself in the last place I ever wanted to be on Christmas Eve.

THIRTY-ONE

Yes, Liam *had* defrauded the Legal Aid Board. However, his claims had been made several years earlier and I'd thought the whole nightmare was behind us. He somehow thought he was doing the right thing as we were building the company up. To him, the legal aid side of things represented easy money.

I did consider giving in to the Elmers' demands for money and my continued representation, but I couldn't bear continuing any formal involvement with my ex *or* his family. Not when there was still something I could do to take away his leverage over me.

If Dominic had been a normal husband – if he hadn't been so abusive when we were together, perhaps there could have been scope for negotiation – even beyond our divorce. But after how he'd treated me when we were married, I wanted him as far out of my life as possible. But it would need one last foray into his family – and one last favour to call in.

Rather than his wife, Dominic had seen me as his rival. And he was as jealous as anyone can be. But he'd grown up that way. He and Sophie had always been jealous of any time, attention or gifts bestowed on each other by their parents. Dominic, especially, couldn't bear anybody being perceived as better than him or getting more.

'Not such a big shot now, are you?' he once yelled into my face. 'I saw the way you were looking at that idiot tonight.'

'He's just a business associate,' I said – well, croaked, as anyone might when someone's got hold of them by the windpipe up against a wall.

'Just because you earn the bulk of the money' – perhaps I was turning blue for he suddenly relaxed his grip on me – 'does *not* give you the right to treat me like an imbecile. I heard your "kept man" digs about me. I've got my own bloody business – did you tell him that?'

'So why don't you work at it then, instead of always leeching from me?'

He really grabbed me then, snapping my necklace and ripping my blouse as my head smacked against the wall. 'You're too fucking far up yourself for your own good,' he yelled. 'And I'm bloody sick of you looking down your nose at me.'

'I can't breathe, Dominic.' I grappled to get him off me, clawing at his restraint around my neck. I kicked out and writhed around – desperate to be free, desperate to—

'It's alright, you're safe now.' The weight of someone's hand rests on my arm. 'You're in hospital, dear. I think you must have been having a bad dream there.'

As I force my eyes open, the blurry face of a kindly-looking nurse slowly comes into view.

'How long have I been here?' I squint against the light.

'Don't move, sweetheart. I'll go and fetch someone.'

As she leaves, muffled voices echo outside the room, and another nurse enters.

'I'm Sister Leonard,' she says. 'It's good to see you awake – how are you feeling?'

'I'm not sure,' I say as I manage to open my eyes some more. It's true. I feel kind of woozy and tired, but it's not as if I've tried to move or get up yet. How can I possibly know how I feel. Just grateful, I guess. I thought that was it for me.

'What were you doing out in the snow like that?' Her voice is gentle as she turns to look at a machine beside me. 'You're incredibly lucky to still be with us.'

I close my eyes as it all swims back. The papers, the blade, the blood, the cold, the exhaustion. 'Who found me?' I turn my head to another nurse who's rushed into the room and is standing at the other side of the bed.

'We don't have any details yet,' she begins. 'We don't even know your name.'

I open my eyes again. 'It's Carla.'

'You didn't have any ID on you. In fact, you weren't even wearing a coat or shoes.' Her voice rises. 'What happened?'

'I left where I was in rather a hurry.'

The funny thing is, I can't really remember the details of being found. Who was there? A woman? Why won't my mind work?

'It's an absolute miracle you survived with the amount of blood you lost,' Sister Leonard says.

I try to raise my arm to inspect the damage but it's all bandaged up. 'How much *did* I lose?'

'Try not to move too much, Carla. The third bag's still transfusing.' She glances behind me. 'Around three pints. Can I ask what your full name is please?'

'Thwaites. Carla Thwaites.' I'm grateful every time I say this. One of the first things I did after I divorced Dominic was to change my name back. I'm very relieved not to be an Elmer anymore.

'I'm Doctor Taylor.' A man who can't be any older than I am strides into the room, with the first nurse following him back in. 'Carla, did I hear you say your name is?'

I nod.

'How are you feeling?'

'I'm not sure really. Shocked to still be here, if I'm honest. And incredibly lucky. Who brought me here – who found me?'

'You were airlifted yesterday afternoon,' he replies, his kindly eyes crinkling at the corners. 'You were extremely fortunate that even in the awful weather we've had, some people were still managing to get their dogs out for a walk. This particular dog was off its lead and managed to alert their owner to you being collapsed in the snow.'

'I owe that dog more than a few treats then. Am I going to be alright?'

'As far as we can see so far.' He smiles. 'You're clearly made of tough stuff. We've stitched your arm' – he points at my bandage – 'so there'll be some scarring there, but that's to be expected. Really, the cold temperatures probably saved you. It stopped your blood being pumped around your body so quickly and slowed everything right down.'

'So I got hypothermia?'

'*Acute* hypothermia.' He nods. 'However, we took your temperature around an hour ago and everything seems to have just about come back to where it should be now.'

'That's good. But my arm... I'd have expected to be in more pain with it.' Ann-Marie's face as she slashed the blade floods my mind, then the blood. All that blood. I honestly thought it was curtains for me.

'You're actually up to the max with pain relief,' he replies.

'When did you stitch it up?'

'We put you under a general anaesthetic when you first arrived yesterday. That was one of our first priorities – to avoid infection and start the healing process.'

'When can I leave?' I try to sit up. I just want to be back at home.

'You need to rest for now, Carla – and let yourself recover –

you've evidently been through a heck of a time over the last day or two.'

'I know, but you said yourself that I'm going to be alright.'

'Only if you look after yourself – you've sustained a severe wound to the underside of your arm, but thankfully' – he points at it – 'it looked far worse than it actually was when you arrived. I have to say though' – he steps closer to my bed – 'if just another twenty-degree turn had been effected, your artery would have been severed – and you definitely wouldn't be with us now.'

'If I were a cat, it sounds as though I've used up two or three of my nine lives then.'

'And some,' he says. 'Which brings me to the most important question now we know you're going to be alright – how on earth did you end up in that state? What can you remember about it all?'

'It's all a bit hazy at the moment.' There's something niggling at the back of my mind. Something I need to remember.

'The police are waiting to speak to you.' He nods towards the door, but following his gaze, I can't see anyone out there. I expect they won't be allowed into the High Dependency Unit.

'To be honest, I can't really remember exactly what happened. But I'll see the police, and tell them as much as I can.'

I'm not going to tell the full story – yet. I need to do this my way.

'You're seeing no one just now, Carla.' Gently, the doctor presses against my shoulder until I'm forced to rest back into my pillows again. 'For the next hour or two, you're staying with us in the High Dependency Unit.'

'Then can I go?'

'Once this final bag has finished transfusing' – he glances at it – 'we'll be able to transfer you to an ordinary ward for observation.'

'And how long do I need to stay there?'

'At least overnight. Listen to me, Carla – you've been through a heck of an ordeal and you need to give your body time to rest and recover from it.' He scribbles something onto a board at the end of my bed, before saying, 'I'll be back in an hour or so to check on you.'

I need the police to take me back to the house. Firstly, I need my things but mainly I want to face the Elmers head on, obviously with the protection of the police. If the police attend without me there, they'll try to squirm out of what Ann-Marie did to me.

Then it hits me like a train. I'm suddenly remembering the piece of information that was missing.

Oh my God. It's all I can do not to sit bolt upright and swing my legs around to the floor to get out of this bed. How has my mind managed to sideline the fact that Natalie's still in there? She needs my help. But I can't let anyone know about the danger or else they won't let me go anywhere near the place.

I turn to the ward sister. 'What happened to me is beginning to come back. I need to speak to the police *now*.'

THIRTY-TWO

Sergeant Alec Rowland looks at me, his eyes flooded with doubt. 'So you're telling me you can't remember how you sustained your arm injury. *Or* how you ended up unconscious in the snow.'

'Maybe I hit my head,' I say. I wish I could tell him the full story now. But I've got to get back there myself. I've already waited for two hours since the infusion completed for the police to get here.

'From what we've been told, there's no sign of any head injury.'

'Maybe when I go back to where I was staying, being there will jog my memory.'

'You were staying with your former in-laws, you said?'

I nod.

'That seems like a strange arrangement if you don't mind me saying. I can't imagine anything worse than spending Christmas with my ex-wife, her new husband and my former in-laws.' He smiles.

'I got stranded by the snow on Christmas Eve,' I reply.

'Being there was better than spending it on my own at my office.'

A complete lie, obviously. I'd planned to get into that office at the Elmers' and shred those legal aid documents at the earliest opportunity and then get myself back out of that house as quickly as possible. But I can't tell the officer any of this. If he finds out about any sort of confrontation between us all, there's no way I'll be allowed to step foot back in that house. And I've got to go back. I've got to.

'And was everything alright between you all?' His brow furrows. 'How do you and your ex get along?'

'So-so,' I reply. 'We've agreed to let bygones be bygones.'

'And how do you get along with his new wife?'

'I don't know her all that well. But I guess she's OK.'

'Presumably one of them might be able to let us know how you came about your injury and ended up in the snow.'

'Hopefully.' I stare straight back at him. 'Will you go there straight away?'

It might already be too late.

'Yes. That's the plan.'

'I'll come with you then if that's OK.' I push back the covers, but then stop as I remember that I'm wearing a hospital gown and the last person I want to be exposing my backside to is this rather good-looking police sergeant.

'I'm afraid that won't be possible.' He shakes his head. 'I believe you've had a pretty substantial blood transfusion. I'm no expert, but there'll be a recovery time associated with that, surely?'

'It's been a couple of hours since it was completed. And I feel fine now – I do. I've been lying in bed since yesterday afternoon, haven't I?'

I reach for my buzzer, ready to call for some help to find some clothes. I can hardly request what I was wearing yesterday.

Besides – what I was wearing will probably end up being needed as evidence. I wish I could tell the officer what really happened, but I need to go back there myself and make sure they can't wriggle out of anything. By now, they'll have their stories straight and where this might leave Natalie is anyone's guess. Especially after what Dominic tried to do to her on Christmas Day. The only way I can pin everything down is to go back there in person.

'Even if the hospital were ready to discharge you—'

'All my belongings are still at The Elms,' I say. 'My phone, my clothes, even my keys – I can't go home without my keys.'

All I know is that unless Natalie's somehow managed to get away from The Elms, she's in as much danger as I was in. But I can't tell them this until we get there. Nothing is going to stop me going back there with them.

Her face swims into my mind or, more to the point, the misery I saw on it in the last twenty-four hours we were around each other. I've often agonised about whether to warn her what she was getting into – especially at the point just before she and Dominic were married. But she'd have seen my interference as sour grapes and I'd have probably only succeeded in causing myself even more trouble. So I kept myself back. But now I've never regretted anything more.

'If you'd like to wait here while we speak to the Elmers, we can pick up your things – if you tell us where we can find them.' He plucks the notepad back from his pocket.

'I really want to come with you if that's OK.'

'I don't think—'

'I'll be able to find some other way of getting there if you're not able to take me. But it would be so much easier if you would.'

I look him straight in the eye so he knows I mean business. I'm sure the client who dropped me off on Christmas Eve would be only too happy to help me again – particularly if I promise to knock something off his next bill.

'May I remind you that you're an in-patient and you're under medical observation here?'

'I'm also a grown woman who can discharge myself if I want to.' I sit up straighter. 'Besides, The Elms is in the back of beyond and really hard to find. It isn't signposted and doesn't even show up on a satnav.'

'I'm sure we'll be able to manage.' The expression on his face is veering between irritation and amusement as he replaces his hat and steps nearer to the door.

'Please let me come with you.' I can't let him leave here without me. I'll go demented worrying about what's going on. 'I just want to get out of here, get my things and go home.' I give him what I hope is my most beseeching look. 'You seem like a man who'd be able to pull a few strings for me.' He's already mentioned an *ex*, so hopefully he won't be able to resist my 'damsel in distress' patter.

I really want to be there for Natalie too. I promised her yesterday that we'd stick together and we haven't. I didn't want to rock the boat too much until I'd shredded those papers but, really, I should have got the two of us out of there the minute I knew what Dominic had done to her dessert. I want to tell her how sorry I am – that's if she'll listen to me. That's if she's even *able* to listen to me.

'Right – OK, just wait here then. I'll go and have a word with the powers that be.' He rolls his eyes. 'But I'm not making any promises.'

Against the advice of the doctor, I've discharged myself. The nurse from the High Dependency Unit found me a pair of joggers and a jumper from lost property to wear since my clothes were soaked and bloodied and will, no doubt, also form part of the evidence against Ann-Marie Elmer once the police know what she did to me.

Really, I lied when I told the two officers I'm now travelling with I was feeling fine. Now that I'm out of bed, I feel as woozy as if I'd downed a couple of bottles of wine and each bump that this four-by-four goes over is hurting my arm. Perhaps the painkillers are beginning to wear off. They've given me more, as well as a hefty amount of antibiotics, but I don't really want to take them – I'm going to need my wits about me when we get there.

The roads are much clearer than I thought they'd be. Only three days ago on Christmas Eve, the UK was at a virtual standstill – but now the snow's stopped falling and the gritters have been able to get out, everything's become passable once more. Perhaps Natalie will have been able to leave The Elms by now – I really, really hope so.

We pass the church Dominic and I got married in, the row of shops I used to pop to, the school we'd earmarked for when we had children because *he* used to go there and the park we once walked around in together. Times when his true colours were only a flicker instead of a full-blown movie.

I'm still at a loss to accept how he could have stood by and allowed his mother to do what she did to me. Money, or a threatened lack of it, does strange things to some people.

It could be any normal car ride as we head through the village towards The Elms. However, with each turn, I know we're getting closer and my stomach knots with increasing anxiety. Who knows what we're going to find when we get there? At least I've got protection with me now and none of the Elmers can hurt me anymore. If only the same could be said for Natalie.

'Are you OK?' Sergeant Rowland twists around in the passenger seat.

'I'm fine,' I reply.

It doesn't look quite as easy to drive once we get to the entrance of the long driveway. The snow from Christmas Eve and Christmas Day has thawed slightly but their private road hasn't been gritted and the other police officer looks to be gripping the steering wheel with all his might. I wouldn't fancy having to drive through it myself.

'Up there?' Sergeant Rowland asks as I point. 'You weren't wrong when you said it was hard to find. I'd have driven straight past that entrance.'

'What did I tell you?' Despite how nervous I am, I smile to myself.

My panic levels begin to build as we head towards the building. Within minutes, I'm quite possibly going to be coming face to face with them all again. Perhaps two police officers won't be enough and what if the Elmers manage to win them over with their lies? Perhaps I should have told Sergeant Rowland the truth so more officers could have been drafted in for this. Who knows what we might be walking into?

Even in a four-by-four, we're sliding all over the road, and as I clutch onto the door handle with my good arm, while trying to protect my stitches, I wonder if we'll even make it up the drive to the house. The closer we get, the more piled-up snow we have to navigate, much of which has been drifting from the hedges flanking either side of the drive.

I'll be the last person the Elmers will be expecting. They'll be hoping that I'm lying dead somewhere, covered in snow – my absence unnoticed by anyone else. So this softly-softly approach of arriving with the police completely unawares is undoubtedly the best one. If I'd told Sergeant Rowland the full story, the rumble of an approaching helicopter might have offered the Elmers the possibility of escape.

'The main entrance is around the next bend.' I point. My heart is beating ten to the dozen and my head swoons at the realisation that three pints of the new blood being pumped around my body have been donated by someone else. It's a peculiar feeling.

The Range Rover is brought to a halt. Now that we're outside the house, what happened yesterday is flying through my mind in all its glory and the fear that floods me is like a tsunami. It's not as if any of the Elmers are going to be able to get past the police and to me, but the thing I'm most scared about is Natalie's wellbeing.

Sergeant Rowland twists in his seat. 'Now that we're here,' he asks, 'is anything more coming back to you about what happened?'

I shake my head. 'Perhaps it will when we get inside.'

As we walk towards the door, I cast my gaze from window to window. If Natalie heard the doorbell, she will no doubt be watching from one of them.

The room she was staying in is around the back. However, I'm still hopeful that she's managed to get away.

The door opens and Ann-Marie, looking every inch like she couldn't possibly be capable of what she's about to be arrested for, stands in the doorway. She's even wearing a pinny over her tailored trousers and blouse.

'Carla,' she exclaims as we lock eyes with each other.

THIRTY-THREE

'I'm Sergeant Alec Rowland, and this is my colleague PC Tom Dunhelm. Is it alright if we come in?'

'Yes, of course.' She calls back over her shoulder in a pleasant voice. 'Roger, the police are here, with Carla. Where have you been, dear? We've been so worried about you.'

I want to laugh but obviously I hold it in.

I follow the officers into the hallway and we all stand facing each other.

Ann-Marie looks as nervous as I've ever seen her. 'Oh, do come through,' she eventually says, gesturing towards the lounge. 'And thank you so much for bringing our daughter-in-law back safe and sound.'

'Natalie,' I shout up the stairs. 'Natalie?'

'Who's *Natalie*?' Sergeant Rowland turns back to me as we approach Roger, framed in the lounge doorway.

I glance towards the kitchen, to which the door is firmly closed. There's a faint whiff of bleach and cleaning fluid – as I suspected. They'll have done everything in their power to cover their tracks.

'Carla.' Roger can't hide his shock as we come face to face.

'Yes – it's me – still alive and kicking.'

'Ms Thwaite.' Sergeant Rowland's eyes narrow. 'Have you remembered something?'

'Ann-Marie and Roger should be able to fill you in on what happened,' I say pleasantly. 'Why don't we all have a seat? Where's Dominic?'

'I, erm, I'm not sure.' Ann-Marie lowers herself to the edge of the sofa. A fire's roaring in the grate and the Christmas tree's still twinkling merrily in the corner. They left me for dead and then carried on regardless. But they won't get away with it.

'What about Natalie?'

Roger and Ann-Marie exchange glances. Roger's face is ashen, which the two officers clearly haven't failed to notice.

'What's going on here?' asks Sergeant Rowland.

'You tell us,' replies Roger. It's like cat and mouse with no one sure who's going to pounce first. Once someone does, that's it – all hell's probably going to break loose.

'The officers want to know what happened to my arm yesterday,' I begin. 'How I came to be so badly injured and unconscious in the snow.'

Roger swallows. 'Right. OK.' He looks from PC Dunhelm to Sergeant Rowland. 'The truth is, and we really didn't know what else to do, but our daughter-in-law attacked Carla right there, in our kitchen.' He gestures towards it.

'Who's your daughter-in-law? Would this be the *Natalie* Carla was just looking for?' PC Dunhelm plucks his notebook from his pocket. 'Can you tell us exactly what happened?'

Ann-Marie glances at me and I'm certain she won't fail to notice the amusement etched across my face as I watch them lie through their teeth. I'll let them have their moment for a few minutes. When I was still lying in that hospital bed, I couldn't have predicted that I might have *enjoyed* any of this.

'They had a set-to in the kitchen,' Roger begins. 'You know, she was jealous, that's how it all started – and—'

'Natalie was?' Sergeant Rowland tips his head to one side as he awaits his reply.

'Actually, being here has helped me to remember what happened,' I blurt. Suddenly, I can't listen to any more of this crap. Just sitting here isn't ensuring Natalie's safe. Finding her is far more important than watching the Elmers squirm. 'Where is Natalie?' I ask.

'She just ran off,' Roger replies. 'After what she did – we couldn't stop her.'

'After what *she* did to me, you mean?' I point at Ann-Marie.

'Hang on.' Sergeant Rowland's eyes widen. '*She* attacked you.' He and his colleague exchange glances.

'With a food processor blade,' I reply, calmer than I could have ever envisaged. After all, there's nothing they can do to me now, not in front of two police officers. 'All because I wouldn't give them the money they were demanding of me, *she* attacked me and then they all left me for dead.'

'That's just not true,' Roger says though there's a wobble of unease in his voice. 'You must be confused, Carla. You're not remembering things right.'

'Better luck next time.' I stand from my seat. 'Oh, but there won't be a next time, will there? Because, by the time you two are let out of prison, you'll be too old and decrepit to do any damage to *anyone*.'

'It wasn't us, Officer – really it wasn't.' Ann-Marie folds her arms as she addresses Sergeant Rowland. 'It was *Natalie* who attacked her.' She gestures towards the kitchen.

'They're lying.' I turn to Sergeant Rowland. 'It was *her*.' I point straight at Ann-Marie. 'And I don't believe they won't have tried to hurt Natalie as well.'

'If you could just bear with me one moment.' Sergeant

Rowland lifts his radio from his lapel to his mouth. 'This is 4020 Sergeant Rowland,' he begins. 'Request further units to assist at The Elms, North Yorkshire.'

A voice comes back at him, confirming his request.

'Also request the availability of two interview rooms for a Mr and Mrs Elmer.'

'You want to interview us?' Ann-Marie gasps.

'Of course we do,' PC Dunhelm replies.

'But we haven't done anything. As we've already said, it's *Natalie* you should be looking for.'

Despite the circumstances they're in, Roger still looks pretty relaxed. 'It's only to make a statement, dear. Then when we've done that, we'll be able to come home.' He pats his wife's hand from where he's sitting next to her.

'If you think for one moment you'll get away with what you tried to do to me, you're mental – the pair of you,' I say. 'It's all on their video cameras anyway.' I turn to Sergeant Rowland. 'As I'll show you. That's the other reason I wanted to come back here. There's something else on there I need to show you.'

He looks towards where I'm gesturing at the TV. 'What?'

'Natalie's got a nut allergy. Dominic swapped the desserts around so that Natalie would eat one that would cause a reaction.'

'And how do you know this?'

'It's all on the cameras. And I actually saw this too.' I sit forward in my seat. 'He then went into Natalie's handbag and moved her EpiPens.'

'Why would he have done that?'

'That's not true,' cries Ann-Marie.

'It really is,' I reply. 'He wanted to make sure she wouldn't recover from the anaphylactic shock he knew she'd have. He attempted to murder Natalie as much as those two' – I point from Ann-Marie to Roger – 'wanted to murder me.'

'You won't find anything on the cameras.' Ann-Marie smiles

and in that moment her face says it all. She must have wiped them. But Natalie recorded some of the footage onto her phone. That'll at least prove what Dominic did to her. As for what Ann-Marie did to me, Natalie will be able to act as a witness for that.

'Do we really need to come to the station with you?' asks Ann-Marie. 'Can't we just talk here?'

'There's someone else you should be interviewing as well,' I say. 'Dominic, obviously but also Sophie. She's Dominic's sister,' I quickly add.

'She wouldn't be able to tell you anything,' Ann-Marie says. 'She left for home yesterday.'

'We still need to speak to her if she's been here over Christmas. If I could take some contact details for her please?' PC Dunhelm poises his pen over his pad.

I can't believe she's just cleared off back home. She might not have known anything about what Dominic did to Natalie, but she saw the whole of what they all did to *me*.

'So assuming we're willing to speak to you at the station?' Roger begins. 'I assume we can drive ourselves there so we can return home easily once we've cleared things up?'

'I'm afraid we'll be the ones to drive you there,' Sergeant Rowland replies.

'You need to be finding my ex-husband and taking him in too.' I shift my gaze to one of the officers. 'He was part of what happened. He had hold of me while she...' My voice trails off.

'Where's your son now?'

'He went out for a run. He often does at this time of day.'

'In the snow?' Sergeant Rowland raises an eyebrow. It's a load of rubbish and he probably knows it too.

'He runs in all weathers.'

'When our colleagues arrive, we'll need to take a good look around the house,' says Sergeant Rowland.

'You're not poking about in my house while we're not going to be here,' Ann-Marie says.

'We can very easily obtain a warrant,' he replies, 'but it will be far less intrusive for you to grant access to us without the necessity for us to force our entry back in here.'

As the second two officers arrive, the Elmers look at each other and I can see the defeat in their faces. It appears as though they're going to stick to the *Natalie did it* story, but I'm certain there'll be some evidence somewhere in this house to prove what happened here yesterday.

As all four doors of the car slam after the Elmers, I head towards the TV. 'I need to check if they really have wiped these cameras,' I say. 'She might have just been saying it.'

'Carla,' PC Dunhelm says from the doorway. 'You'll have to wait back in the car – now you've made the allegation that your former mother-in-law inflicted your injury, this house has become a crime scene.'

'But I need my stuff – my phone and my keys,' I say.

'I'll accompany you to get them.' He steps back into the room, brushing his fingers against what must be his taser gun as though he's checking it's still there. 'We'll get your belongings and then we'll head straight back to the car. What does your ex-husband drive, by the way?'

I glance through the window. The only car on the drive is Roger's SUV and there aren't any tyre treads in the snow to suggest anything's been recently moved. However, I've no idea when the last of the snow fell. I've totally lost a day with being in hospital. 'I don't know what Dominic drives nowadays,' I reply. 'They have a garage though – it could be in there.'

We head along the corridor to the bedroom – the same corridor I've walked up and down so many times whenever we've stayed here. I never dreamt in a million years that things would ever come to this. If only they could have just left me alone and allowed me to get on with my life after Dominic and I divorced.

'Are your things all there?' PC Dunhelm asks, from where he's standing at the doorway.

'Yes.'

Everything in here is just as I left it. I suppose it would be – no one was ever expecting me to come back to collect it all.

I'd have loved to have seen their faces after they went back into the kitchen and found me gone. Playing dead turned out to be easier than I would have thought – and without doing that, I'd have never got out of there. The Elmers would have just left me to bleed to death on the floor.

I stride across the room and pick my phone up. I only spoke to my brother yesterday morning so he won't have a clue that anything's amiss yet. I'll have to let him know what's happened soon. As I gather my belongings, our telephone conversation from a few days ago about our plans for Christmas swims back into my mind.

'I can't believe you're not spending it with us, Carla. Mum's not too happy either.'

'I know. I've already spoken to her.'

'Won't you at least just come for dinner? You can't spend it completely on your own.'

'I've decided I want to chill out in front of the TV and stuff my face.' Of course, I was lying – Liam would have been apoplectic if they'd known where I was really going. And so would my parents. There's no way any of them would have allowed it.

'What's with the sudden decision though. I thought you were planning to come.'

'I was, but a person can change their mind, can't they?'

'What about Boxing Day, then?'

'Have you seen the weather forecast, bro?' I asked. 'Look, I promise I'll spend the New Year with you all – how's that?'

Maybe by the New Year, I could have been honest and told him where I'd been and why.

As it happens, I won't be able to put off telling him what's been happening for much longer.

THIRTY-FOUR

I stuff the clothes strewn over the bed into my weekend bag, blinking away memories of previous times spent with Dominic, here in this room. It feels like a lifetime ago now.

I feel in the side pocket for my keys and my purse – at least I achieved what I set out to do – thanks to the tip-off about the exact location of those incriminating papers. I just need to know that Natalie's safe now. And once Dominic's locked up like his parents, I'll be much happier.

He's gone for a run. Yeah, right. He'll have seen the car when we initially arrived and he'll have run off, leaving his parents to face the music. That's the only run he'll have gone for. Either that or he's hiding somewhere. Until I know exactly where he is, and much more importantly, where Natalie is, I won't be able to rest.

I glance from the window, trying to recall whether there was a second car out on that drive when I arrived on Christmas Eve, but the truth is that I was too cold and focused on not falling over in the snow to take much notice.

'Can you check in there please?' As we leave the room, I

gesture to the door opposite us. 'Natalie was staying in there. They might have locked her inside.'

'I'm sure she'd have called out if they had.' But PC Dunhelm knocks on the door anyway. 'Natalie, are you in there?'

His words are met with a stony silence. I must admit, I'm beginning to feel nervous. With no sign of Dominic *or* Natalie, I can't help but imagine that something *else* might have happened. After what she found out about him on that camera footage, she wouldn't have gone anywhere with him willingly, surely?

PC Dunhelm tries the door and we both peer in. The room's still full of their belongings but there's absolutely no sign of either of them. The whole thing is getting stranger by the second.

'Right, now you've got your stuff, let's get you back to the car,' he says. 'Don't worry' – he looks back at me – 'my colleagues won't stop looking until they find her. And him.'

Sergeant Rowland and three of his officers are by the Christmas tree in the hallway as we descend the stairs. The twinkling lights are oddly juxtaposed with the darkly dressed, grim-faced officers.

'I thought the two of you were waiting in the car.'

'I needed my phone,' I say. 'I want to contact my family. I also wanted to find out what's going to happen now you've arrested Ann-Marie and Roger.'

'They're not actually under arrest,' Sergeant Rowland replies. 'Not yet. We still need to piece things together and part of that will be to get a full statement from you when we take you home. Then we can take things from there.'

'There's no sign of the son or any car other than the SUV outside,' another officer says as he ducks beneath the doorframe. 'Nor of his wife. It seems that they might have left together.'

'But there're no tyre tracks.'

With fingers that look like they're going to burst through the blue gloves squeezed around them, Sergeant Rowland closes the door to the drawing room where classical music is still playing. They're even more callous than I had them down for. They'll have been busy covering all the evidence and their tracks since I fled from here, all the while listening to Classic FM.

'I've also had a look at the camera footage, but at first glance, it does appear to have been wiped.'

'I thought as much – I could tell by the smug look on Ann-Marie's face.' The last part of my sentence is drowned out as the grandfather clock behind me begins chiming twelve.

We all look at one another as we wait for it to finish.

'Mrs Elmer is denying all your accusations,' another officer says. 'Both of them are adamant that it was Natalie who injured your arm and that you're either confused – or maliciously trying to add more charges to what they're already facing.' An apologetic expression crosses his face. '*Their* words, not mine.'

'It wasn't Natalie.' I let a long sigh out as I look out into the driveway. 'And I'm not confused in the slightest.'

'But you can't deny that your memory was hazy to start with, Carla. You couldn't recall what had happened when we first spoke to you this morning.'

I wish I could admit to Sergeant Rowland that I lied just to get myself back here but I won't. There's quite enough to face as it is. 'Honestly, I've never been clearer about anything.'

At least, for the time being, I know Ann-Marie and Roger are safely away from me – and Natalie, wherever she is. But if I can't *prove* what the two of them did to me, I know the legal system well enough to know they could get bailed instead of remanded, that's if they even get arrested and charged in the first place, especially if they appoint someone half-decent to represent them.

'I'll show you exactly where it all happened, shall I? There'll surely be some kind of evidence left in there.' The image of blood spurting from my arm emerges again, making me feel nauseous. 'Ann-Marie must have been covered in my blood and Roger was beside his wife the whole time so he'll have been covered too.'

'You can't go in there, Carla – we've cordoned it off now,' one of the other officers says as I start towards the door. 'Though it appears to have been thoroughly cleaned *and* bleached in there, so I don't know how much information, if any, the kitchen's going to yield for us.'

'What about their clothes?'

Sergeant Rowland shakes his head. 'There's a washing machine full of what they could have been wearing yesterday – we've bagged everything up as evidence – but if they've been on a cold wash, there might not even be any staining. Really, what we need is Natalie's testimony. As you said, she saw the whole thing. It will definitely be preferable as far as the Crown Prosecution Service is concerned. We also need to speak to the son and the sister.'

'And then will they be arrested and charged?' The alternative doesn't bear thinking about. I've no doubt the Elmers will hound me until the ends of the earth if they get let out of there. And there's still Dominic to worry about. I can't live any more of my life with him bothering me every five minutes.

'I really can't say at this stage, but even if they are, without cast-iron evidence, it might then come down to a jury having to convict them.'

'Their daughter will probably stand by them too – which will make convicting them even more challenging.'

'If there's evidence to be found in here, we'll find it.'

'Where have you looked for Natalie and Dominic?'

'We've been around the entire building – there's no sign of either of them so far.'

'Did you ask the Elmers again when you took them out to the car? Not that they're likely to give you the truth.'

'All they've told us is what you've already heard,' he begins. 'That Natalie ran away yesterday after *"what she did to you"*.' He draws air quotes around his last few words. 'And they're still maintaining that Dominic's gone out for a run. If there's any truth in that, then I suspect he'll be back soon.'

A vision of my ex-husband's face, contorted with rage, swims into my mind. If Natalie is with him, chances are that he'll have forced her to go with him.

'She does nails,' I blurt. 'You might be able to find her number online.'

'Leave it with us,' he replies. 'Look, we're going to have to secure the building for the forensics team to come in now.' He looks around the area in which we're standing. 'We'll take you home and get that statement sorted out.'

'And what about Dominic and Natalie? What if they're definitely not here.'

'We've already got officers on their way to their home address.'

'And Sophie?'

'Her too. Sit tight – you shouldn't have to wait long for some answers.'

'Are you unable to recall anything about his car?' PC Dunhelm peers at me as I slide my coat from the peg. It's unbelievable to recall how things were when I first arrived and Ann-Marie hung it up for me. When we were all play-acting at being jovial and I kept trying to push to the back of my mind the real reason I was here.

'No – I'm sorry. I didn't take any notice as I came in.'

'Could he have still been driving the same vehicle as when the two of you split up?'

'No – I'd paid for it so I kept it.' I pull at the other coats on the pegs. 'This is probably Natalie's coat. I can't imagine Ann-Marie would wear Superdry.' I widen the door. 'I need to get my boots.'

I tug at the door for the shoe cupboard, taking my boots out and glancing around. There, right at the back, are a very similar pair to mine.

'They must be Natalie's. Again, they're nothing like anything Ann-Marie would wear.'

Sergeant Rowland and PC Dunhelm exchange glances. I can tell they're thinking the same as me. Natalie wouldn't have just left this house, leaving all her belongings behind, especially her coat and her boots.

Which means that she's still here, somewhere...

THIRTY-FIVE

Defeated, I reluctantly allow myself to be led from the house, a dreadful foreboding gnawing at me.

'Will they check everywhere?' Two more police cars are here now, one on either side of the one I travelled here in. 'Even in all the cupboards? I wouldn't put anything past them.'

'Wherever they've gone, our colleagues will find them,' PC Dunhelm replies as he turns around. 'It's just a matter of time.'

'And will Dominic be arrested?' I duck into the car as the door's held open for me.

'He'll certainly be taken in for questioning, but a lot depends on whether his wife *wants* to press charges for the incident with her EpiPens,' replies Sergeant Rowland as he climbs in and rests his hat on the dashboard.

'From what you've already told us about him,' says PC Dunhelm, 'he could coerce her to stay quiet.'

Sergeant Rowland frowns at him as though that was the wrong thing to say.

'There's such a thing as a victimless prosecution.' I clip my seatbelt in, hoping I don't come across as patronising.

'I'm well aware of that – but I'm not sure the CPS could charge Dominic without either the camera footage you've mentioned or from Natalie making a complaint.' Sergeant Rowland fastens his too. 'They've got to have concrete evidence.'

'Well, as I mentioned before, Natalie filmed some of the footage on her phone.'

'Well, if we can get our hands on that, making things stick will be much easier.'

'I'll stand in the witness box and tell *any* court what Dominic did to her,' I say. 'I was there, wasn't I?'

I can't imagine her *not* letting them have the footage as evidence, but the nature of my work has proved again and again how easily abused women can change their minds and stand beside their abusive husbands – instead of taking the necessary action against them.

'You're Dominic's ex-wife when all's said and done,' says Sergeant Rowland. 'I'm sorry to say this, but when it comes down to it, your version of events won't hold nearly as much weight as the visual evidence of a video would.'

'*You* believe me, don't you?'

'Of course.' PC Dunhelm starts the engine.

'But it comes down to the likelihood of obtaining a conviction in court,' Sergeant Rowland continues, 'we know how difficult things can get without concrete evidence. It's nigh-on impossible to get things to stick.'

I feel like making a *duh* noise at him. 'I know – it's what I do for a living.'

'But right now,' he continues, without making further enquiry into what I do for a living, 'the most important thing is that we find Dominic and Natalie and make sure she's safe.'

I lean back in the seat. I can't believe we're leaving here without her. Then, as PC Dunhelm puts the car into gear, a movement in the corner of my eye grabs my attention.

'Over there,' I cry as I unclip my seatbelt. 'I just saw something move.'

'It'll just be one of our colleagues,' says Sergeant Rowland, turning around and then following where I'm pointing. 'They've been briefed to thoroughly comb the grounds.'

'It could even be wildlife,' adds PC Dunhelm. 'There's deer, foxes and all kinds around here.'

'Can we just check – I need to know.' I open the car door.

'Look, Carla – let's just get you home so you can rest, and we can keep you informed from then. I know you want to help her but, really, our colleagues have got this covered.'

I've already got one foot out of the door. I can't leave here – I just *can't*.

A branch cracks in the distance. It's a tiny sound but enough to make my blood run cold. 'Don't start the engine yet – did you hear that?'

I'm certain it's Dominic – in fact, I can almost sense him here. And if they don't catch him soon, I've no doubt whatsoever that he'll come after me as soon as I'm at home on my own – to perhaps finish what his mother started. I shouldn't have come back here – I should have allowed them to drop me off at home like they were trying to insist on. Better still, I should have stayed at the hospital – at least I was safe and well looked after there.

But if *I* don't look out for Natalie, *who will*? I sway through indecision for a moment. I should go home and rest but, really, I need to take one last look around for myself. Starting with where I heard that noise.

Sergeant Rowland's radio beeps and he raises it to chin level. 'Come in, Rob.'

'Permission to force the door to a locked outbuilding on the perimeter,' the voice says. 'It's the only one of them that's locked.'

I freeze as Sergeant Rowland and PC Dunhelm exchange glances. What does this mean?

'Go for it,' he replies. 'We've got the battering ram in the boot if you need it.'

My heart rate quickens and a cold dread creeps up my spine.

'We'll give it a go without it. It looks like it shouldn't take too much forcing.'

'Can we just hang on here until they've got in there?' I ask. 'I need to know what's going on and if she's safe.'

Sergeant Rowland shuffles in his seat, but he nods. He's become edgy too. He'll probably want to be there with his colleagues as they kick the door in. He winds the window down.

I hold my breath as their attempts at the door echo through the air. Once, twice, three times. Then once more.

'Perhaps I should get there with the—' PC Dunhelm tugs the keys back out of the ignition as there's another bang.

'They're in,' says Sergeant Rowland. There's a shout of *police*. They must be entering the building.

'Should we go, Sarge?'

'Just give it a minute until we know whether they've found anything.'

A few more agonising moments pass. I wrap my arms around myself, still half in and half out of the car. Then the radio beeps again.

'We've located what could be a woman's body,' the voice says.

'Oh my God.' My hand flies to my mouth. *They've killed her*. They've gone and killed her!

'Just one second – she's – we're not sure. Have you found a pulse there, Rob?'

'Oh my God. Oh my God.'

'I'm on my way.' As Sergeant Rowland opens the door, he

turns back to PC Dunhelm. 'We need the air ambulance and some more units to locate Dominic Elmer. And Carla,' he continues, quickly averting his eyes to me, 'you're to wait in here.'

I try to find comfort in the fact that they're summoning the help of the air ambulance. After all, there'd be no point getting it mobilised if Natalie was already dead, so there *must* be a chance for her, no matter how remote.

As PC Dunhelm starts to follow the instructions he's been given, I open the door and get after Sergeant Rowland. I have to see for myself what's going on. *What the hell have they done to her?* He's broken into a run in the direction of where the bangs were coming from, kicking up snow as he goes.

This is all my fault – I should have never been here in the first place over Christmas. I allowed the Elmers to control me yet again and I despise myself for it. Losing our reputation and our company is far preferable to someone losing her life. My being here has blown everything up.

'I'm so glad you're not one of my staff,' Sergeant Rowland snaps as I catch him up around the back of the house. 'You're not the most compliant of individuals, are you?'

'Do they think she's dead? Have they radioed through with anything else?' I'm having to sprint to keep up with him. But at least my previous wooziness has been replaced with a rush of adrenaline. I can almost hear my father's voice as I go, *She's made of tough stuff, our Carla.* It's inconceivable to think that just last night, I was clinging to life as I lay out there in the snow. I will definitely have to thank the dog walker who saved me.

'Let's just get there, shall we?'

At least he's acquiesced to me coming with him and has

accepted that I can't just sit in that car, waiting like a spare part. Not when it feels like it's all my fault that Natalie's where she is in the first place.

If only I could have made it to that house instead of collapsing like I did – if only I could have sent some help back to her.

THIRTY-SIX

The outbuilding comes into view with two police officers pacing around outside – it's the one Ann-Marie was talking about converting into an office for their business. Before things turned so badly sour for them earlier this year.

An officer rushes from the outbuilding. 'There's a very faint pulse, sir. She's still alive but it doesn't look promising. I really don't think she's going to make it. I've left PC Bamford monitoring her.'

'The air ambulance should be mobilised by now,' Sergeant Rowland replies. 'Let's have a look at her and see if there's anything we can do.' He darts to the doorway.

'I don't think there is anything, sir. Apart from trying to warm her up.'

'Wait there,' he instructs me as I get to the door behind him.

As I poke my head inside, the stench of urine assaults my nostrils. At first, all I can see is a hump in the centre of the floor. Streams of light filter from all four corners of the outbuilding, landing on Natalie at different angles. My eyes adjust to the dimness and I can see that someone's draped a jacket over her.

Beneath that, the clothes she wore yesterday are visible – clothes she'd have picked out for Boxing Day before she had any inkling that her husband was capable of hurting her so badly.

'She must have been in here all night.' My stomach churns. I can hardly believe what I'm seeing and just want to rush over to her. 'How could they do this?'

'If we hadn't found her when we did, Sarge...' PC Bamford's voice trails off.

'She's hanging in there.' Sergeant Rowland checks her pulse. 'It's very slow though – do we have an ETA for the air ambulance?'

'Hang on, I'll find out.' PC Bamford reaches for his radio.

'Can you radio through and have the Elmers placed under arrest please.' Sergeant Rowland drapes his jacket over Natalie's legs and rises from where he's been crouched beside her. 'They tried telling us she'd run off somewhere.'

'What offence are we giving?'

'False imprisonment for starters.'

'Two minutes, sir,' PC Banford says.

'They might have got away with blaming her for my murder if I'd died.' A prickling sensation rises up the back of my neck. It's inconceivable to think that she could have served a life sentence if I hadn't survived and been able to tell the truth of what happened.

'There's a reasonable chance she might not survive this yet,' Sergeant Rowland says to me. 'You probably need to prepare yourself.'

'Can I sit with her until the ambulance arrives?' I ask. 'It looks as though she's been on her own in there for long enough.'

'I'm sorry – but no. We want as few people in here as possible.' Sergeant Rowland rests his hand on my shoulder as he passes me to come back out. 'We need to preserve the scene for evidence. Can you ensure the area is all cordoned off please.'

He turns to one of the officers who's been kicking up snow outside as he wanders up and down. Then to another, he says, 'Can you get on to DVLA and see which vehicles Dominic Elmer is the registered keeper of.' And to the other remaining officer, he says, 'Get on to the station and ask them to find the most recent photo of Dominic Elmer. There must be something online, perhaps on his business page. We need it out there in circulation and in the next news bulletins.'

The rumble of a helicopter echoes in the distance. I glance all around for any more signs of the movement I saw when I was sitting in the car. It could have just been one of the officers who were still searching, even if my intuition was trying to tell me otherwise. But try as I might to quell things, I'm still feeling Dominic's presence here.

When we were married, I could usually sense when Dominic was in the house, even when he was sleeping. It was a negative sensation, a feeling that told me to be on my guard. And right now, it's stronger than ever. Of course, there's no way of knowing exactly which one of them locked her in this outbuilding – not unless she wakes up and can tell the police herself. And like Sergeant Rowland has said, I need to prepare myself. She really doesn't look too good at all.

'I really think Dominic could be hiding somewhere here,' I say.

'If he's still here,' he replies, 'we'll find him.'

The whirr of the helicopter is deafening as it circles overhead, whipping snow up in its breeze before it lands in a field just beyond the boundary of the Elmers' grounds. Well, it's their property for now, anyway. Who knows what'll happen after the tax bill and legal action has made a mark in their assets?

Much seems to hinge on Natalie surviving. Her recording

of the footage of Dominic with her EpiPens and his switching of the plates is needed. Her testimony on the Elmers' attack on me is also vital. Then, finally, she needs to be able to tell the police exactly who locked her in the outbuilding. Without her version of events, it could all sound like I'm merely a vengeful ex-wife. I know all too well that any defence they might employ would try to make mincemeat of me.

The paramedics are hurrying from the field. One brushes the snow from the fence and helps another climb over it. They're half-walking, half-running with the equipment that will hopefully save Natalie strapped to their backs. It's probably impossible for them to move any faster than they are, especially since the snow is untouched over there. I feel utterly helpless just standing around and all I can do is wait, hope and pray.

I stand out of the way as Sergeant Rowland leads them through the door and towards Natalie. One of them lays a flashlight on the ground while the other crouches beside her.

'Stay out there,' Sergeant Rowland commands of me. 'See that she does,' he says to PC Dunhelm, who's now joined us. The other officers have been sent to cordon the area off and to keep looking for Dominic until the dogs get here. The consensus, however, seems to be that he's probably made a run for it and is in hiding somewhere else.

'What's her name?'

'Natalie Elmer, age thirty-one,' replies Sergeant Rowland. 'And she could have been locked in here since yesterday afternoon.'

'Hello, Natalie.' The male paramedic feels at her wrist while the other is pulling equipment from the box she had strapped to her back. 'My name's Paul, I'm a paramedic and we're going to look after you now. We're going to give you some oxygen to help you breathe better.' He holds his hand out to his colleague.

'Is she going to be alright?' I call from the doorway, but no one replies. Probably because they can't possibly know the answer.

'We should wait in the car,' says PC Dunhelm, resting his hand on my arm. 'You've been through enough already without standing out here in the cold like this.' His words are tinged with kindness, which is what I need right now. He's right, I know he is – I *have* been through a lot in the last twenty-four hours, but it pales into insignificance somewhat in comparison to what Natalie must have suffered. At least I've been tucked up in a warm hospital bed overnight with people taking care of me.

'I don't want to leave her,' I say, without adding that we should have stuck together in the first place. As soon as I saw the video footage of Dominic, I should have got us out of there. Our safety was a million times more important than shredding those papers, but I just couldn't see that at the time.

I move to the side to allow two more paramedics in who must have parked near us on the drive.

'Let's get her off this cold ground and get the stretcher under her, shall we?'

She almost looks comfortable as a woollen blanket, then a foil blanket is laid over her.

'We need to get an IV in before we raise her. Then we'll administer the Mequ on the way to the hospital. How are her obs looking?'

'Her heart rate's at twenty, and her core temperature...' The other paramedic bends over her. 'Is at twenty-nine.'

'Her heart rate's at twenty?' I squeak, thinking of my own heart rate when I go to the gym. If that's all her heart is beating, she must be practically dead.

'We need to move her to the helicopter – sharpish.'

'What's Mequ?' I turn to PC Dunhelm.

'I'm no expert, but I think it's why they've put the cannula in her hand, they'll start injecting something to slowly warm her blood – I've seen it done before but that was with an elderly lady.'

'Did *she* survive?' I ask, not really wanting to know the answer but needing a sliver of hope to hold onto.

'No, unfortunately, she didn't make it,' he replies. 'But Natalie's younger and fitter and she's already hung on for this long.'

'It doesn't look promising for her though, does it?'

'She's still alive – so there's still hope.' He squeezes my shoulder.

'I can't believe they've done this to her.' I shake my shoulder from his grasp as it still hurts from where I was grabbed and pushed around yesterday. Instead, I begin pacing up and down where we've already flattened all the snow – I just can't keep still. 'And I can't believe what they tried to do to me. If they'd had their way, Natalie and I would be lying side by side in a mortuary by now.'

'Clear, please.' The four paramedics are heading back towards the door, each carrying a corner of the stretcher. Under normal circumstances, I'd ask if I could accompany her in the ambulance, but these aren't normal circumstances.

'They'll look after her,' Sergeant Rowland says as the helicopter takes off. 'They'll do everything they can to revive her.'

Revive is an appropriate choice of word. As they carried her past me just now, she looked dead. It wasn't just her stillness, it was also her colour. Grey, lifeless and, well, dead. Which is clearly what my ex-husband and his parents wanted. As for Sophie, her role in all this is still puzzling me. That's another piece of unfinished business.

'Let's get you home now,' he continues. 'We'll let you rest and then come back to get a detailed statement later today.'

Reluctantly, I allow myself to be led around the side of the house and back towards the car. Inside my boots, my feet are numb with the cold, even though I've now rescued them from the hospital-borrowed pumps. I have to admit that the idea of lighting my fire and curling up in front of it is a welcome one.

'And then I can get back to the station and see what the latest is with your in-laws.'

'*Former* in-laws. Will you keep me posted?'

'Of course.'

As we reach the car, a Crime Scene Investigation Unit van skids up behind one of the other police cars in the snow.

Sergeant Rowland opens up one of the rear doors for me. 'I'll just be a moment.' He heads back towards the two officers that are getting out of it. 'Start in the kitchen,' he says, gesturing back to the house. 'We've taped it all up and there are a couple of lads from uniform waiting in there for you. The dog unit should be here at any moment to comb the grounds for Elmer.'

As his colleague opens his mouth to respond, I rummage in my bag and then tap at my pockets. 'I've dropped my keys,' I gasp. 'I thought I heard something drop when I got out of the way of the paramedics. I'll be back in a couple of minutes.' I push past Sergeant Rowland and set off back to where I came from at a brisk walk before he can stop me.

'Hang on a second, Carla.'

'I'll be fine,' I call back over my shoulder. 'It's not as if any of them are still here, is it?'

As I get to the side of The Elms, I glance back to make sure Sergeant Rowland is still speaking with his colleagues and that none of them are coming after me.

I know where I'm heading. Straight to where I noticed the movement before. I can't feel my feet as I rush through the snow, nor can I feel my face and hands. I'm trembling with the cold, though it could also be fear at what I'm about to confront.

Sure enough, Dominic steps out from his hiding place. He's grinning – he's actually grinning at me. But then his expression changes and I know that only one of us will walk away from this confrontation.

THIRTY-SEVEN

'Help me,' I yell. 'Someone – please.'

'Carla!' Sergeant Rowland's shout echoes through the air. It's taken him longer than I thought to come after me, but I knew he would eventually.

'No – no, get off me,' I screech. 'Help me, someone!'

'Carla!' It's a more frantic call this time. 'Where are you?'

Another moment passes before Sergeant Rowland skids to a stop beside me, with PC Dunhelm hot on his heels. Then their faces crumple in horror at the scene that awaits them.

Dominic's lying on the ground with eyes glassy and gaping and his mouth wide open, still gasping as his wounded head bleeds into the snow.

'He was trying to choke me.' My hand flies to my neck. I can't believe what's just happened. I knew it was him though – I was right to trust my instinct, but maybe not so right in what's come next.

'Are you alright? Just try to breathe slow and calm, that's right, in and out, slow and calm.' I feel the weight of PC Dunhelm's hand on my back.

'I didn't mean to do this – but it was either him or me.'

'What the hell did you think you were doing in the first place.' Sergeant Rowland doesn't seem as sympathetic as his colleague. 'What did I tell you?'

I'm panting so hard that it's hurting my chest. 'I thought he'd be long gone with us finding Natalie like that – I really thought it was safe to come back.'

He grabs a fistful of his fringe and turns in the snow as he looks into the sky. His face says it all as he then drops down beside Dominic.

'I think we'd better take you to be checked over again,' says PC Dunhelm.

'This *is* him, I take it?' Sergeant Rowland looks at me, grim-faced. 'Dominic Elmer?'

I nod.

'Get an ambulance here, Tom,' he commands of his colleague. 'And looking at the state of him, you'd better tell them to hurry.' He leans further forward. 'Dominic, it's Sergeant Rowland here – can you hear me?'

He's making a strange gurgling sound.

PC Dunhelm leans into his radio. 'This is Police Constable Dunhelm 4092. We need an ambulance please at The Elms at Farndale in Yorkshire.'

He gives another reference and then says, 'We have a man with a serious head injury, potentially life-threatening.'

Dominic's stopped gurgling. I daren't even look at him now.

'It was self-defence,' I say as Sergeant Rowland feels for his pulse.

'We know that,' he replies. 'We heard your screams for help. But that doesn't mitigate against the fact that you shouldn't have been around here in the first place.'

'Did you hit him? Or did he fall and hit his head?'

'I had to stop him.' I point to the rock on the floor. 'I had to get him off me and I didn't know what else to do.' No doubt that'll be bagged up and taken away as evidence. But whatever happens, I'll come through this – I know I will. 'Is he dead?'

'It's not looking good for him.' He rises back to his feet and reaches for his radio, giving his control team the instruction to hurry the ambulance along.

'I need to sit down.' I fall back against the wall of the outbuilding and slide down into a crouch. 'I don't feel too good.'

PC Dunhelm rushes to my aid again, gripping my arm to lower my descent. 'Let me know when you're feeling steadier,' he says. 'Then we'll get you back to the car.'

As a siren wails in the distance, I steel myself to look down at the man I once pledged my life to, while trying to filter out the blood that's seeping into the snow at one side of his head. On the other side, his hair flutters in the winter breeze like it once did as the outdoor photos were taken at our wedding. He was charm personified before that. As soon as he had me where he wanted me, that's when it all changed.

'I'll guide them in,' says PC Dunhelm, breaking into a run in the direction they've just arrived from.

Sergeant Rowland follows my gaze after him and then drops back down beside Dominic, feeling around once again on his wrist.

I hold my breath.

'I wouldn't bother,' he calls after his colleague. 'He's already gone.'

'Oh my God – I can't believe it,' I gasp. 'I didn't mean to kill him. Really, I didn't.' I've killed someone. I'm a killer. Oh. My. God.

Sergeant Rowland rises back to his feet. 'I'm sorry, but we're going to have to take you to the station now, Carla.'

'But-but – you said you were taking me home to recover. You said I needed to rest.'

'We're going to have to get a recorded interview of exactly what's happened here first.'

'But it would have been me, if—'

'We know that,' he replies. 'This is just a formality.'

'Perhaps we should head to a different station.' PC Dunhelm joins us again, not taking his eyes off Dominic. 'The Elmers are at the North one.'

'You're not arresting me, are you?' Suddenly I'm gripped by panic. I can handle any general questions or just being asked to give my account of it all, but arresting me means they're *suspecting* me of something.

'Not at this stage,' he replies and I sag with relief. It's not a definite no but it's good enough for the time being.

As I'm led back to the car, the adrenaline I was so fuelled by drains from me. I've *killed* someone. Yes, it might have been my bully of an ex-husband, but I've still *killed* him.

'I need to go home.' I turn to Sergeant Rowland. 'I really don't feel so good.'

'We'll do what we've got to do as quickly as possible,' he replies. 'We need photos of what he's done to your neck while it's still fresh. As well as to see if there are any other injuries. It's all to help you.'

'But I'll definitely be allowed to go home after that?'

'I should think so.' He holds the car door open and beckons for me to get in. 'Let's just see what happens.'

This time I comply. There's nothing left to do or find here.

THIRTY-EIGHT

The last couple of days have been hell. I was treated well enough at the police station, but it's the guilt I'm struggling with. Every time I close my eyes, I see Dominic's face. I've been given a number for victim counselling, but perhaps they'd see Dominic as the victim more than me. *I* killed *him*, after all – self-defence or not. Although, I wasn't arrested or charged, thank God, and the two officers made statements of their own to say they'd heard me screaming for help as they came to my rescue.

But I wouldn't be anywhere else than where I am this morning. I need to know what's going on and I need to know firsthand. The magistrate has gone out to consider what he's going to do with the Elmers and I can't believe he even needs thinking time. I'm shocked at Sophie not being here. She *must* know that her parents are up for bail this morning, yet there hasn't been sight nor sound from her. The police still haven't spoken to her either – it's as though she's completely gone to ground.

'They're being brought back,' my brother says. 'The magistrate must have made up his mind.'

It's strange to see my former in-laws handcuffed to the dock officers as they're led back into the courtroom. After all, I've been more accustomed to watching them swan around their big house as they host their garden and dinner parties. They look smaller somehow – as if they've been shrivelled by their current circumstances.

A buzz of conversation rises in the public gallery as all eyes turn to the front of the courtroom.

'Look at her face. It's all impossible to believe, isn't it?'

'Not so smug now, are they?'

'You think you know someone.'

Their voices swim all around me and for a moment, I feel detached from the situation, as though I'm not even here.

'Are you OK, sis?' Liam nudges me. He's been an absolute rock since I phoned him from the station. Of course, he went nuts that I'd tried to sort the situation without involving him and even more nuts at how it all ended up.

'Yeah – I'm good, but I'll be even better if that magistrate doesn't grant them bail and remands them.'

'He will remand them – I'm certain of it. At the very least, they still pose a danger to you and to Natalie, don't they? There's every chance they could try to finish what they started.' After a night on my sofa, Liam looks as crumpled and tired as I feel. But I'm so glad he's here and that I don't have to face anything else on my own. 'They've been cuffed to the dock officers.' Liam gestures in their direction. 'In my experience, that means there's no way they'll get bail.'

'Let's hope so.'

'Hanging should be brought back after what they did to you. We could have been identifying your body in a morgue today.'

'You don't get rid of me that easily.' I nudge him as the court clerk clears his throat.

'All rise.'

Ann-Marie and I lock eyes across the courtroom. I can tell

she'd like to scream *murderer* or some other similar reference to what I've done to Dominic, but she will have to stay on her best behaviour until she knows whether they're going to get out of here today. She'll have been told it was *me* who killed her son and I can't imagine she'll accept it was self-defence.

'Stop staring at her,' Liam hisses as he nudges me back.

I shush my brother as the magistrate returns to the room. I study his face, searching for a clue of what he's decided to do with the Elmers until their trial, but he isn't giving much away.

'Please be seated.'

I drop to my seat in the public gallery, not taking my eyes away from the woman who was twenty degrees away from severing the artery in my wrist and killing me. Alongside her is the man who stood beside her while she did it. Before they both left me for dead.

I can imagine the magnitude of the hatred they're harbouring towards me after what I've taken from them. Yet, they've got no right – after what they did to me and Natalie, they deserve *everything* that's coming their way.

'Firstly I'd like to thank the legal representation for both the defence and the prosecution,' the magistrate begins. 'For putting forward the cases in respect of whether the defendants should be allowed to leave this court on bail until their next hearing.'

There's a maddening pause as he shuffles his papers. *Just tell us what we want to know*, I feel like shouting. I just want to get out of here. Being in such proximity to them is making my skin crawl.

'Roger and Ann-Marie Elmer,' he says as he faces them, 'you are already on bail for two very serious charges indeed – one for tax evasion and the other for causing death by your own negligence.' He looks from one of them to the other. 'Therefore, this next, even more serious set of charges, should be merged with those you're currently facing and be dealt with all at once.'

He pauses as he leans forward to consult with an official sitting on the bench in front of him, nodding as they confer before clearing his throat and sweeping his gaze back over the courtroom. The wait is agonising and I can barely sit still.

'Easy, sis.' Liam rests his hand on my arm.

'I'm also going to refer this third set of charges to the Crown Court,' the magistrate adds.

A hum rises again amongst the public gallery. As the clerk stands, looking as though he's about to say something to shut everyone up, an automatic hush falls again.

'As the charges against you are so serious,' the magistrate continues, '*and* the potential for you to attempt to interfere with witnesses in the case for the prosecution is so great, I am unable to allow you to leave custody.'

Ann-Marie's face drops like a stone and several voices rise again.

'Therefore...' His tone hardens even more than it was before. 'You will be remanded into custody until your hearing.'

'Don't you think we've been punished enough?' Roger cries out. '*She* killed our son.' He jabs a finger in my direction and I can see, even from here, that it's trembling.

'It was self-defence,' I shout back. 'He was a maniac.'

Liam squeezes my arm. 'You're going to get yourself into trouble if you're not careful.'

'Can I ask you all to control yourselves,' barks the magistrate. 'There will be plenty of opportunity for you to *all* have your say at the hearing. Roger and Ann-Marie Elmer, it has been decided that you will remain in the custody of this court until such time as your case can be prepared for a plea and directions hearing. This court is dismissed.'

'Well, I wouldn't have expected anything different, to be honest.' Liam lets out a long breath. 'How are *you* feeling?' He turns to me.

We watch for a few moments as the tussle to get Ann-Marie and Roger back down the same way they came in ensues.

'You're going to pay for what you've done to him,' she screams as she's dragged towards the exit. There's only one person her words can be aimed at. Me.

'Come on, let's get you out of here.' Liam tugs at my arm. 'We know what's going on now.'

'Too right,' I agree. 'And once their trial's over, hopefully, I won't ever have to set eyes on *any* of them again.'

There's still a question mark over Sophie though – since she's ignored every attempt the police have made so far to talk to her.

'How about a celebratory drink?' Liam suggests.

'I don't know about *celebratory*, but I could do with a glass of something after coming face to face with *them*,' I admit. 'It's really unnerved me.'

'We can celebrate that they're where they should be and that you're safe.' Liam takes my arm as we head back into the sunshine. The snow's all gone now – like so many things in life, it departed as quickly as it arrived.

'I still can't believe you went along with it all in the first place,' Liam says as he slides a glass of wine in front of me. 'You should *never* have gone anywhere near that house.'

'Would you have rather I'd just rolled over and given them the money they were demanding?' I yawn. All I want to do now is sleep. 'And continued to represent them and their dodgy dealings in court?' I nod in the direction of the courthouse we've just vacated over the road.

'Of course not,' he says, raising his voice above the lunchtime rush. 'But I wish you'd have told me – we're supposed to be in all this together.'

'And how would you have reacted if you'd known they were

blackmailing me?' I glance around to check no one's overheard me. Our conversation isn't exactly run-of-the-mill for a post-Christmas Wednesday. 'As well as what they were blackmailing me with? We could have easily lost everything – I really didn't know what to do for the best.'

'I'd have preferred to have lost our business than my sister.' He sips his pint.

'I've heard all this from Mum and Dad already.' I take a large sip of my wine.

'To be honest, they're just relieved that you're safe. Money and belongings can be replaced.' He wipes the condensation from his pint. 'You, however, can't. I know you thought you were acting for the best, but look at the scale of it all now.'

'They're behind bars and Dominic's dead,' I reply. 'So it could be worse. The main thing is that Natalie's going to be alright.'

He nods. 'And at least she can testify against them now,' he says. 'That's such a relief. As well as the fact that no further action will be taken against you.'

'They couldn't have charged me after what I've been through.' An image of Dominic's twisted face slides into my mind. 'The bastard had his hands around my throat.'

THIRTY-NINE

Most people hate hospitals with a vengeance. However, I'll never forget how safe I felt when I woke up in that High Dependency Unit bed the morning after Boxing Day, surrounded by the people who'd saved my life. After all, the people I'd once counted as family, my in-laws, had attacked and left me completely for dead.

I stride through the double doors and into the welcoming foyer where patients and visitors are milling around the shop or sitting with drinks under the sunlit roof. The new year is around the corner and while I don't usually put much store in the new beginnings feel that's always in the air, this year I will try. All I want to do is to put everything behind me and move on with my life.

I head into the shop as I can hardly turn up at Natalie's bedside empty-handed. From what I've learned about her so far, her parents are dead and her brother's serving a hefty stretch in prison – so I'm not sure how many visitors she'll have had, if any. I doubt anyone will have treated her to anything – so I'm making it *my* job.

I fill a basket with chocolate, fruit, toiletries and magazines and head to the checkout.

As suspected, there's no one at her bedside as I'm directed into her room at the edge of the ward. As I reach the door, I hover for a moment. *Will she even want to see me?* Dominic's ex-wife, the woman she looked at with such dislike and mistrust only a few days ago? It was obvious she thought I was only there to snatch her husband back from her.

I kept wanting to tell her why I was really there, and also to find out how Dominic was treating her. I could only hope he'd done some work on himself and was no longer making the same mistakes he'd made while married to me. But witnessing his actions towards Natalie on Boxing Day, I had my answer.

'Hey.' She must sense me loitering in the doorway for she turns to face me. Her head barely makes a dent in the pillow and she looks as frail as an elderly woman beneath the hospital bedclothes.

'Hi.' I walk towards her bed and thrust the bag of goodies at her. I point at the chair. 'You don't mind me sitting down, do you?'

'Go for it. And thank you.' She gestures to the bag. 'That's really kind.'

'I thought you'd be able to use a bit of food that the hospital hasn't served up.'

'I've not really been eating.' She points at a drip. 'I only came around a few hours ago.'

'I know,' I reply. 'They've been keeping me posted. I've been so worried about you.'

'Really?' Despite her thanks and the fact that she hasn't turned me away, her eyes still glitter with suspicion. I thought we'd formed more of an allegiance than perhaps we really have.

'How are you feeling?'

'Weak, tired. Lucky.' She attempts a smile, but that's all it is – an attempt. She's clearly been through it. I can't imagine what it must have been like in that dark, freezing shed for all that time. The closest I've ever been to it was the two hours Dominic locked me in the garage and that was bad enough. I'd had to hammer on the door until, eventually, the next-door neighbour heard me as he was parking his car up for the evening. Dominic had joked that locking me in there had been an accident, but I knew full well it wasn't. He'd wanted to prevent me from attending an important business function and if it hadn't been for the neighbour, I dread to think how long I could have been left there.

Thankfully, it wasn't long after that I managed to get him out of the house for good. I packed all his belongings and stuffed them into his car whilst he was out for a run. My brother was also on hand to help me change the locks. Dominic kept coming back, issuing his threats and ultimatums whilst banging on doors and windows until eventually, when the police wouldn't do anything, I asked Liam to stay with me. At least he's not here anymore to be bothering Natalie in the same way.

'You really *are* lucky.'

'The police told me you suspected I'd left The Elms and gone somewhere with Dominic.'

'He moved the car and parked it in the housing estate – perhaps he was hoping to make it look like you'd both left.'

'I think he'd have moved my things as well, if that's what he was trying to do.'

'Who knows?' I shrug. 'Ironically, they found his car close to where that dog walker found me.'

She reaches out and lays her hand over mine. 'We've both been lucky, haven't we?'

'Thank God for that dog and thank God the police did a thorough search of the grounds, that's all I can say.'

'When I was lying on that freezing floor' – her eyes glaze

over with sadness – 'after a while, I didn't even feel cold anymore – that's when I accepted I really was going to die. I didn't even have the energy to try getting up again.'

'You must have done something right.' I shuffle my chair closer to her bed. 'Sergeant Rowland said an overnight stint in those sorts of temperatures, and the fact that you weren't even wearing a coat and shoes would have killed most people.'

'Were you there when they found me?'

'Yes. The whole time. I waited until they put you in the air ambulance.'

Mine and Natalie's relationship will go one of two ways after this, I should imagine. It'll either bond us for life and we'll have a firm, if unlikely, friendship, or seeing each other will become too painful and be too much of a reminder about a time we'd rather leave behind. I hope it's the former and I hope it's what she wants too.

'I can't remember a thing about it.'

'You were as close to death as I've ever seen anyone.'

Tears fill her eyes. 'Perhaps I would have deserved it. To die, I mean.'

'Hey.' I rest my hand on her arm. 'Never in a million years.'

A tear spills from her eye and slides down the edge of her cheek before soaking into her pillow. 'You don't know what—'

'Natalie.' I gently shake her arm. 'It really is all over now.'

FORTY

'Thank you.' I smile at the lady who leaves two cups of tea and some biscuits on Natalie's table. 'There's not much that tea and a biscuit can't fix. Do you feel strong enough to sit up?'

I help Natalie with her pillows as she shuffles up to a seated position and then push the table across her bed. She's still so pale and fragile-looking.

'You OK?'

'Still light-headed, that's all. Hopefully, these might do the trick.' She reaches for a biscuit.

'I really can't believe he locked you in there – the evil bastard.'

'I always had a feeling in my gut that there was something a bit *off* with Dominic, but never in a million years...' Her voice trails off and she places the biscuit back on the plate.

'He can't hurt you anymore.' I slide her tea towards her. 'He can't hurt either of us.'

I take a sip of my own tea, the liquid warm and comforting as it slides into my stomach. I wrap my fingers around my mug. If anything, my brush with death has taught me to appreciate the little things in life – to be grateful for the ordinary.

If someone had asked me before how I'd feel about taking a life, I'd have said, *consumed with guilt and unable to live with myself.* But in Dominic's case, I'm at peace with what I've done. I can't say there's no guilt whatsoever, but it's not as severe as I first thought it would be. With the right counselling, I'll be able to work through it. Natalie's forgiveness and understanding would be a positive start – after all, no matter *who* or *what* Dominic was, he was still her husband and until encountering me on Christmas Eve, she didn't know the man he really was.

'Are *you* OK?' It's her turn to give me a scrutinising look.

I take a deep breath, steeling myself to steer the conversation in a new direction. One that could make or break the amicable situation we've currently found.

'How do you feel about me after what I did to Dominic?'

'I totally understand,' she replies, though her eyes appear to cloud over. 'You did what you had to do. The sergeant who came to see me said Dominic was trying to strangle you.' Her eyes fall lower as though scanning for any damage he's caused.

My hand flies to my scarf. 'I've been wearing this ever since – it covers a multitude of sins.' I smile, sadly.

'Honestly,' Natalie continues, 'I had a sense of foreboding about Christmas from the moment Dominic told me where we'd be going.' She places her cup on the table. 'I already knew Ann-Marie and Roger weren't too keen on me and then when I found out *you* were coming—'

'I hope you can see now that I'm not the ogre Dominic might have made me out to be.'

'I was more worried that there might still be something between you.' She sniffs. 'Ann-Marie was certainly trying to push things that way, wasn't she?'

'I know, but the very idea's ludicrous.' I smile. 'I wouldn't have touched him with a bargepole. I'd already more than learned my lesson.'

'What do you mean?'

'People like him don't usually change. Once an abuser, always an abuser.'

'I just thought that you could do no wrong in Ann-Marie and Roger's eyes. And were far more favourable daughter-in-law material than me.' She looks away. Their rejection of her seems to have cut deep.

'They only wanted what they were trying to get out of me,' I reply. 'This blackmail thing over those papers and the money they wanted had been going on for a while.'

She glances up at the clock. 'I've been told they were in court this morning, weren't they? Did they get bail?'

I shake my head. 'Nope, they didn't stand a chance.'

'Thank God for that.'

'They've been remanded until their trial and I reckon with the other stuff, they'll be inside for a pretty long time.'

Natalie lets a long breath out. 'Roger could have been taken to the same prison as Hayden for all I know.' Her voice dips.

'Is Hayden your brother?' I sip my tea and sink further back into my chair. I'm still feeling pretty washed out myself. After I've left here, I'm going to go home and probably sleep until tomorrow morning.

She drives her head back into her pillow and closes her eyes. 'Yeah. And he shouldn't even be in there.'

'What do you mean?'

'Oh, it doesn't matter. What's done is done – the story of my life, really.'

'You can tell me what happened, Natalie.' I shuffle my chair closer to her.

She meets my eye, a good sign that she's willing to talk. 'But how do I know I can trust you?'

'Since I'm now technically a killer myself, I might be well-placed to understand.' Blimey, what a thing to have in common.

'You're *not* a killer.' Her voice softens. 'He had you by the throat – just like *my* ex had me. There's just a couple of major differences between us.' She looks *really* uncomfortable now as her eyes flit away from me.

'Like what?'

'Is everything OK in here?' A nurse pokes her head in.

'Yes, thanks,' Natalie calls back.

'Don't be staying for too long,' she says as she returns to her trolley. 'Natalie really needs to rest.' Her words die away along the corridor.

'You're not the only one,' I tell her. 'I could sleep for a week. Anyway, about what you were saying – about your ex having you by the throat.'

'You'll be able to use the *reasonable force* argument.' She looks so depressed, I want to hug her. I've got my brother, parents and friends out there, but when Natalie's discharged from here, she's got no one from what I can gather.

'I'm not sure I know what you're getting at.'

'I'm talking about the *twelve* stab wounds I inflicted on my ex.' She looks at me directly now. 'My brother was sent to prison.' Her voice is small. 'But my brother wasn't even there.'

FORTY-ONE

'Hang on… but I thought—'

'It was *me* who stabbed Kyle a dozen times. I completely lost it. Months and months of being bullied and controlled made me snap – not that that's an excuse.'

'But it's a *reason*.'

Bloody hell. Looking at Natalie, she doesn't look capable of inflicting such violence on another person, but having lived with an abusive narcissist myself, I know only too well the depths they can force any sane person to plunge to and how much they back you into a corner. It's how a narcissist thrives in the first place.

'When we were both first arrested,' she continues, 'after they eventually found Kyle's body where we'd left it, Hayden and I had agreed with each other that we'd both give *no-comment* interviews.'

I wait for her to continue.

'We were advised to do that by the duty solicitor. So there I was, with my no comment, no comment, to every question, while Hayden was telling them it was *him*. That *he'd* stabbed Kyle and killed him.'

'But why would he do that – if it *wasn't* him?'

Her face falls. 'After our parents died, my brother and I were all each other had in terms of family. We've been through thick and thin together.'

'I can't imagine my brother doing that for me.' Then, I think of Liam and, actually, I think he possibly would. He hated Dominic with every fibre of his being, and when I consider what I've risked for Liam, perhaps Hayden's sort of loyalty *is* conceivable. I didn't just want to save our company and our reputation – I was also desperate to keep Liam out of prison for legal aid fraud. From what I know, he'd have served at least three years for it. He's full of bravado, my brother, but he'd struggle to survive behind bars. As soon as I realised it was a possibility, I knew I'd do whatever it took to prevent it.

'All I ever wanted was to *belong*,' Natalie says. 'Having spent my teens in foster care, I couldn't wait to be part of my *own* family, which is why I jumped at the first man who showed an interest in me. But then I went for someone like Kyle. He might have come across as a pillar of the community to everyone else – with his teacher job and his oh-so public good deeds that he always made sure everyone else knew about – but he was bloody dreadful to me.'

'The notion of *behind closed doors* is a very true one,' I say. 'Nobody ever knows what goes on.'

'Nobody ever did.' She wraps her fingers around her cup. 'Only Hayden, and even he didn't know the full story. He knew enough to be seriously worried about me though.' Her lip trembles and I reach for her hand again. She has to know she's not on her own here.

'From everything I know...' My voice becomes more authoritative as I slip comfortably into my legal mode. 'You'd have had a really good chance of being acquitted on the grounds of diminished responsibility.'

'But I couldn't see the woods for the trees at the time.' She stares into her cup. 'And neither could Hayden. We were both just panicking.'

I stare out of the window at the end of the room, the blue sky and wisps of clouds beyond it reminding me of the life and freedom we can enjoy once we get over this.

'Where's Dominic now?' Natalie's voice wobbles.

My eyes fall on her ring finger. She's taken her wedding and engagement rings off. 'He's still here, in the hospital mortuary. Apparently, they're planning to move him today.'

'Move him?'

'To a funeral director's.'

'Have you seen him?'

'No, I couldn't bear to – after all, I put him there.' The vision of his glassy stare enters my head. 'Will you?'

'Maybe. If only to ensure he's definitely dead.' She looks at me straight in the eye, her voice filled with so much certainty that I can tell she's tougher than she looks.

'Do you forgive me, Natalie?' I hold her gaze. 'For what I did to him?' If she can, then there's far more chance I can put it behind me.

'Of course I do.' It's her turn to rest her hand on my arm. 'I just can't fathom what they did to you. As far as they were concerned, you were dead in a pool of your own blood. They wouldn't let me in or out of the house to get help – I honestly thought you were dead in that kitchen.'

'I nearly was according to the doctor in HDU.' I point upwards, to where the High Dependency Unit is on the floor above us. 'What Ann-Marie inflicted was a whisker away from my main artery.' I raise my arm from where it's been resting in my lap.

Fresh tears fill Natalie's eyes. 'It was terrifying, Carla.' It's the first time she's used my name – hopefully a sign of our newly formed allegiance. 'I tried to get to you, but I had the three of them doing everything they could to stop me. Then they stamped on my mobile so I had no chance of calling for help.'

'I reckon that once we make it through all this – we've probably got a lot of living to take care of. After all, we're both still alive by the skin of our teeth, aren't we?'

'How can I even think about living? My poor brother's locked up for something I did.' She jabs her finger towards her chest. 'So one thing I decided when I was lying on the floor of that outbuilding was...' Her voice trails off and she looks uncertain, as though she's suddenly doubting whether to continue telling me whatever she was about to say.

'What?'

'I decided that night, that if I survived being locked in that building, if I made it out of there, I was going to own up.'

'And are you?'

She nods, slowly. 'It's time. How can I sit back and allow Hayden to serve nearly another three years for something I did?' Her voice cracks. 'The truth is, I can't. He's been in there for almost four years already. I can't believe I've done it to him.'

'So what are you going to do?'

'Sergeant Rowland said he'd be back to take a full statement about Boxing Day when I was feeling more up to it, and that's when I'm going to tell him everything.'

'Have you spoken to your brother about what you're planning to do?'

'He doesn't even know I'm here yet. But confessing is what I should have done in the first place. By the time I'd got out of the police station when Hayden and I were arrested, he'd already been shipped out of there and remanded by the court.'

'Did you not get any chance to speak to him before that happened?'

She shakes her head. 'No, they wouldn't let me. It crucifies me every time I visit him. I'll never fathom why he sacrificed what he did for me.'

'Did he ever meet Dominic?' Just saying his name feels awful and I spit the word out like it's a piece of stale chewing gum.

'No, thank goodness.'

'I don't think I'll ever trust another man again.' I shake my head.

'Me neither – just look at my track record. Talk about jumping out of the fat and into the fire. I was so desperate not to be alone after Hayden was sentenced – I mean, I was really struggling. So I was probably easy pickings for someone like Dominic.'

'He could be very plausible to those who don't know him well.' I'm talking about him in the past tense, at least – a sign, perhaps, that I'm coming to terms with it all.

'To be honest, I think I was so tormented by guilt that I just jumped at the first man who showed a flicker of interest in me. I think it was the distraction I was after.'

'I can't imagine you'll be making that mistake again.' I force a laugh.

'I won't be here, will I? I'll probably get a hefty sentence after what I've done. Not just for what I did to Kyle but also for allowing Hayden to take the blame for it.'

'No, you won't. And I'll be making damn sure of it. I'm going to be by your side every step of the way.'

I reach for her hand and her fingers curl around mine. Our eyes meet and a bolt of solidarity passes between us. We don't need to say anything else. We are bound together by our past, our present and now, it seems, whatever becomes of our future.

FORTY-TWO
THREE MONTHS LATER

'In conclusion, Your Honour...' Our barrister's voice takes on an edge of extra authority as she moves to the final stage of her summing up. I, however, feel ill. We're nearly there. We're nearly at the moment we've been both dreading, yet willing to arrive in equal measure. My eyes meet Natalie's and I try to convey as much as I can in the look I give her across the room, *we've got this*.

But have we?

'As we've heard from the defendant, her brother and now a neighbour who has bravely come forward, what we have here is a situation of a desperate woman' – she gestures towards Natalie – 'a woman so driven out of her mind with month after month of being isolated, after month after month of being ridiculed, abused and attacked, until she eventually snapped. We've heard that this was not without reason. No, her bigger and far stronger partner snapped well before she did and if she hadn't acted in self-defence, she wouldn't be standing here in this courtroom today.'

The judge isn't taking his eyes off Natalie as the barrister speaks. She must be able to feel his gaze boring into her. But what's going through his head? Is what the barrister's saying holding sway or has he already made his mind up?

'Sadly, as we've already heard in Natalie's own words, a red mist of rage descended on her, leading to behaviour that even now, she still finds difficult to understand of herself. But who knows how *any* of us might respond when we've been ground so low within a relationship that we feel as though there's little else to lose? Or when someone has their hands around our throat?

'As we know' – her voice lowers again – 'Natalie Elmer has already pleaded guilty to the manslaughter of her former partner Kyle Parkes. However, Your Honour, I would urge you in your sentencing to find her guilty of manslaughter with diminished responsibility. We've heard numerous examples of how she was treated, we've heard how her partner had succeeded in cutting her off from the world in order that everything could take place behind closed doors.'

Tears fill my eyes as how Natalie used to live is described. There are so many parallels with how Dominic used to treat me. We're both free of these dreadful men but we'll bear the scars forever.

'Of course, as outsiders, we can never know for certain what did take place, not only on that fateful day but also in the lead-up to it.'

The barrister pauses as she now faces Hayden where he's sitting in the public gallery. Hopefully, having her brother here is helping Natalie to feel more positive – I just pray she can walk out of this court with him shortly.

'But what we do have is Natalie's brother's testimony, which I strongly urge you to take into account. A brother so bereft at being unable to protect his sister from an abusive man that he offered the ultimate sacrifice to her – his freedom.

'Your Honour, I'd like to further add that nothing can be achieved by sending this woman to prison. The guilt she has already endured has punished her enough. I would suggest that a custodial sentence would only serve to exacerbate her already fragile mental health even further.'

The tears in my eyes are threatening to spill over – she's not wrong there.

'Whilst her actions were admittedly in self-defence, Natalie herself has said she *wants* to atone for her behaviour, in particular, her actions after Kyle's death in not reporting the truth of what had happened and also the time in prison that her brother has endured as a result of what later transpired.

'Before you, Your Honour, is a woman who is deeply sorry for her actions, has never committed any kind of wrongdoing before and is unlikely to ever again. For these reasons, I would recommend a community order and hope you will allow her to provide recompense for her crime in this way.'

We nod at each other as she retakes her seat. I've gone all out for Natalie over the last couple of months to get her the most lenient sentence possible and would hope that appointing someone from King's Counsel for Natalie's defence will have made all the difference.

I stare at the judge, trying to gauge what's going through his mind. Is he going to send her to prison? I rest my hands at my sides and cross my fingers. *Please, please, please don't send her to prison.* She's well aware that what she did, particularly what she did after she'd killed Kyle, is more than enough to be put away for a hefty stretch but, hopefully, her extenuating circumstances, as they keep calling them, will be what saves her.

'I'll retire to consider my verdict.' He nods towards the defence bench. 'All rise.'

I stand, feeling light-headed as I look towards Natalie. She, too, looks like she could faint. At least she's not handcuffed to the dock officer – as Liam's said so many times when we've been in court together, it's always a good sign of things.

The officer says something to her as the judge leaves the room through a door behind him. She sags to her seat and seems to be searching the public gallery for her brother. I glance over at Hayden, now allowed to sit in the courtroom after giving his evidence first thing this morning.

I can't be sure from the distance we're at, but I think he winks at her. He's right at the back, and understandably sitting well apart from those expecting justice for Kyle – his parents, his brother and some acquaintances from the school he worked at. Their hatred emanates towards us – no doubt they'll be thinking we've been told a pack of lies about Kyle.

With the judge out of the room, Hayden rises from his seat and heads towards where I'm sitting at the defence bench, pushing up the sleeves of the suit jacket which is slightly too large for him after all the weight he says he's lost in prison. He's probably eager to get away from the bile surrounding him in the public gallery. I stand and walk towards him.

'How do you think it's going to go?' he says, his voice shaky.

'It's like anything,' I reply. 'It could really go either way. We're just going to have to wait and see.'

'It'll boil down to whether the judge believes what we've all said about her being abused. Or whether he'll believe that lot.' He jerks his head in the direction of the public gallery.

We both look that way. According to what's been said, Kyle was a very different person when in his work and community. However, I'll bet that if his family were to have been forced to take an oath and tell the truth to the court, there would be a different version of Kyle to the one that's been portrayed. Someone who can treat someone he's supposed to love like he did must have also shown his true colours to his family to some extent when he was growing up.

'According to the barrister,' I say, 'the judge has a reputation for being firm and fair. He's got daughters of his own, so perhaps the presence of domestic abuse should go some way to sway him. At least that's what we're hoping.'

'She's told me that she won't appeal if this doesn't go her

way.' He looks over at her. 'She's said that she couldn't go through all this again.'

'We'll cross that bridge if we come to it.' I rest my hand on his arm. 'But listen, Hayden, like I've already said, the fact that she was granted bail after her confession was a really good sign. If she'd posed any sort of risk, she'd have never been granted bail to begin with.'

We both stare at the door where the judge went.

'Right, all we can do is sit tight and hopefully we'll all be out of here shortly, Natalie too. Through that door and not that one.' I point at the door behind her which we'll all give *anything* for her not to be taken to. But she knew what she was risking when she told the truth. And she maintains that it's all been worth the risk to finally do the right thing.

'All rise.' The court falls silent as the judge reappears. He's been less than ten minutes. Oh. My. God.

This is it.

FORTY-THREE

'Cheers.' The three of us clink glasses over the table. 'Here's to freedom.'

'And new beginnings,' Hayden adds. 'God, when the judge started giving his spiel back there, I thought...' His voice trails off and his eyes, exactly the same blue as Natalie's, are as wide as jar lids.

'Me too.' Natalie sips from her glass. 'My blood ran cold, what was it he said, *no matter what the circumstances, violence should not beget violence.*'

'It was the words, *I have no choice other than to impose...*'

'I nearly stopped breathing at that moment,' I say. 'But, anyway, three hundred hours is a hefty community service order, in fact, it's as much as they're able to give you, but it's a million times better than the alternative.'

'Just think, I could have been sharing a cell with my former mother-in-law,' she says. 'At least I don't have to clap eyes on her for another five years.'

'Only three for *him* though,' Hayden says. 'You should get out of this area really, sis. If you want a proper new start. I've been toying with the idea myself.'

'I can't think that far ahead yet. Until today, everything's just been about trying to survive this and stay out of prison.'

'It could have been me up there today,' I say, before taking a long drink of my wine.

'No – as we've said all along, you used reasonable force to defend yourself.'

'And at least you didn't try concealing what you'd done to Dominic afterwards.' Hayden closes his eyes. 'It was absolute madness, what we did. All I can say is that I've never felt panic and fear like it when I walked into the kitchen that day.'

'You've been punished enough.' I reach across the table and squeeze his arm. 'As they said when they dealt with you, four years in prison is more than time enough for your part in it all.'

Within minutes, our glasses are empty. After the last couple of days, it's no wonder.

'Another?' Hayden gathers our empties and gets to his feet.

'That would be great.' We watch as he threads his way through the other afternoon drinkers towards the bar.

'It's so good to have him back,' Natalie says. 'I'll never forgive myself for standing back and allowing him to do what he did for me.'

'You've got to forgive yourself,' I reply. 'Or you'll never be able to move on.'

'I know.' She stares down at her hands. 'But it feels impossible at times.'

'If you don't, your life will be as over as theirs is. Is the counselling helping you?'

'Kind of.' She has a faraway look in her eyes. But it's a troubled look. 'Obviously, it was self-defence and I'll always believe the first two knife blows were justified but—'

'Stop right there.'

'No, let me finish. The rest of what I did to Kyle wasn't justified, the other *ten* knife blows, I mean. And neither is allowing Hayden to continue taking the blame for me.' The pain on her face is palpable.

And I have the power to take some of it away.

'Diminished responsibility.' I look at her pointedly. 'Unlike *me*.'

Her head jerks up. 'What do you mean, *unlike you*?'

'I wasn't ever going to tell anyone about this, but I think it'll make you feel better.'

'What?' There's a quiver in her voice and for a moment, I waver. Am I doing the right thing by telling her? After all, Dominic was her husband and until Christmas Eve, she really thought something of him. 'Tell me – please.'

'Alright.' I pause again. I'll have to tell her now. I've started so there's no going back. 'Nobody knows what I'm about to tell you. Not even my brother.'

She stays silent as she waits for me to continue.

'I planned what I did to Dominic.' I carry on looking her straight in the eye.

'How do you mean?' Her eyes don't leave mine.

To everyone else here, in the pub, we could just be a couple of close friends having an intense conversation, not the ex-wife and the widow of the *second* man we've killed between us.

I take a deep breath and hope she'll understand what I'm about to tell her.

FORTY-FOUR

The wait for the paramedics to stabilise Natalie in that outbuilding was endless and I've never felt as helpless in my life. All I could do was pace up and down in an attempt to hold my anxiety at bay as well as to keep warm in the snow.

As I continued to pace and I reached the far corner of the outbuilding, there was no mistaking who I saw lurking behind another of the outbuildings. And it *wasn't* a police officer. At first, fear stole over me at the sight of my ex-husband but a steely resolve quickly replaced it.

I opened my mouth to tell someone but then closed it again. Natalie was probably going to die.

And without her evidence, Dominic might walk from all this scot-free.

It was up to me to make sure this didn't happen.

So the whole time I was heading back to the police car, I knew I had to create a reason to return and deal with him *my* way. The presence of the Crime Scene Investigation Unit and the distraction it provided to Sergeant Rowland turned out to be a welcome one.

While Sergeant Rowland spoke with his colleagues, I sent

Dominic a message on Snapchat, knowing these messages auto-delete after being read. Even if the message didn't reach him, I was *still* going back there.

Wait where you are and I'll be back in a few minutes. I've got a proposition for you.

He came back to me straight away. Clearly, there wasn't much else for him to do with himself while hiding away on the fringes of his parents' grounds.

Sounds interesting. Well you know where to find me.

With the officers' voices ringing in my ears, ordering me to stop and go back, I ran, or should I say, slid, as fast as the snow would allow me to, back towards the side of the house under the pretence of having dropped my keys at the outbuilding.

As soon as I was out of their sight, I kicked around in the snow until I found a suitably sized rock, then tested it out in the palm of my hand for size. It was small enough to conceal in the pouch of the hoodie I'd been given from lost property at the hospital, but big enough to cause the damage I would need it to. Then I continued towards the spot where I had previously spotted Dominic.

It took a couple of anxious moments for him to step out of his hiding place but eventually, curiosity of what I wanted to suggest must have got the better of him.

'So, you've come back then?' Dominic grinned. 'I might have known you wouldn't be able to stay away from me.'

'Is that what you really think?'

'Ah come on.' His manic smile widened. 'We belong together, you and me.'

'I don't know what I ever saw in you.' I couldn't believe how he was acting, so casual, so brazen, as though nothing had even happened.

'All this, I reckon.' Dominic swept his arm over the grounds and towards the house. 'All that's ever interested you is *money*.'

'Hark at you,' I replied. 'As you and your family have demonstrated, you'll literally *kill* to get your hands on it.'

'Now that's not strictly true, is it?' He pulled his coat more tightly around himself. 'No one's actually died, have they?' There was an edge to his voice as he looked at me and I could tell that he'd held back on using the word *yet*.

'Why did you do it to her, Dominic? Why did you lock Natalie in there all night?'

'How do you know it was *me*?'

'It's exactly the sort of thing you'd do.' I was quaking but I was also standing firm – I knew what I'd come to do and I wasn't going to let him overpower me. Not for one second. 'You're sick in the head.' I thrust my hands into the pouch of my borrowed hoodie, feeling each contour and point of the rock beneath my fingertips. It was nearly time to find out whether the rock could inflict the damage I hoped for. I'd have to stun him quickly so he'd be less able to fight back.

'There are no cameras this far away from the house, are there? So who's to know?'

The bastard. I curled my fingers around the rock, its sharp point digging into my palm. If all I'd wanted was Dominic's arrest, I would've just let Sergeant Rowland know he was still hanging around – that I'd definitely seen him. The team would have surrounded him within seconds. But I wanted something more permanent than that. It was down to me alone to ensure that Dominic Elmer got exactly what he deserved. But I had to make it look like self-defence.

'I know what you did to her with her nut allergy as well – and I've told the police.'

'You have?' His voice rose as though he was shocked – as

though I'd somehow betrayed him. Then his expression relaxed. 'But can you prove that?'

'What the hell is wrong with you? I can't believe that I once thought I knew you.'

He stepped closer to me, with an expression that caused the hairs to rise on the back of my neck. 'I had my reasons for what I've done.' He leaned in so close to me that the vapour we were breathing into the cold air merged.

'All I've got to do is scream and the police will come running. They'll be coming after me in a few minutes anyway.'

'So why don't you? Go on, what's your plan here, Carla?' He rested one hand against the wall at the side of my head. 'You said you had a *proposition*. When I first saw you, I thought you were going to help me.'

'As if.' I held our eye contact.

'And there was me thinking you still cared.' He rested his other hand at the other side of my head.

'I've come back to make sure you can't hurt anyone again. You *or* your warped family.'

'And how are you intending to do that?' His smirk was back.

'Do you think I'm just going to let you walk away from all this, Dominic – whether Natalie dies or not?' There was a shake in my voice by then, after all, I knew what I was about to do. And once it was done, there'd be no going back.

'I don't see how you're going to stop me.'

If I didn't do something there and then, there was every chance he could walk away from what he'd done. If Natalie died, and without any concrete proof of anything, the police might not even have been able to charge Dominic.

So, holding our eye contact and smiling right back at him, I forced my knee up as hard and as fast as I could between his legs, watching with pleasure as he cried out and staggered back from me.

Then plunging my hand back into my pocket, I grasped the

rock and with all my might brought it crashing into the side of his head, the sound of stone against skull making me gag. But it was no time to be squeamish.

He didn't go down the first time. Instead, he came back at me, trying to grab my throat but his attempt was so feeble, it was almost laughable. I curled my fingers more tightly around the rock that had become my saviour, gripping it harder against my palm before crashing it against his skull for the second time.

He let go of me then and wobbled back, his hand flying to his bloodied head and his face twisting even further. But he was still on his feet.

'Carla.' Sergeant Rowland's voice echoed towards me. It was close enough to suggest that he was on his way around the side of the house. He must have heard Dominic cry out.

Whatever I did next would make the difference between whether Dominic Elmer would go on to turn on the charm with other women, lulling them into a false sense of security as he had with both me and Natalie. Or, in that moment, I had the power to prevent him from ever infecting someone else's life.

If I let him off the hook, he'd possibly recover from his wound to the head, then he'd come after me again, and Natalie too, if she pulled through. So I had to finish what I'd set out to do.

'This one's for Natalie.' I kept my voice as low as possible as I smashed the rock against the side of his head for a third time. Blood spurted into the air as he collapsed onto the ground with a yowl.

'Carla.' A more frantic call that time.

'No – no, get off me,' I screeched. 'Help me, someone!' I tore and grabbed at my throat to create some marks.

Dominic was jerking around on the floor. A fourth blow was tempting, just to make sure, but that would be pushing my luck, especially with Sergeant Rowland on the way.

I stared at him for a moment. My former husband. Would I be able to live with what I'd done to him? Damn right.

'Help me,' I yelled out. 'Please.' I lurched out from the side of the outbuilding, still clutching the rock.

'So they didn't know?' Natalie stares at me.

'Didn't know *what*, exactly?'

'That you had that rock in your pocket in the first place?'

I shake my head. 'I told them it was on the ledge beside me. That I'd grabbed it when he had his hands around my throat.'

'But he didn't have his hands around your throat?'

'No. I think what I've done places you and me on a level playing field, don't you?'

'Pretty much.' Her eyes are still wide. With shock, probably.

'You understand why I did it, don't you?' I'm gabbling now. 'To stop him ever being able to come after either of us again.'

She nods slowly. 'Of course I do.' She glances towards the bar. 'Hayden's coming back. I don't want to lay all this on him after everything I've already put him through.'

'Given what Dominic did to you,' I say, 'I think he'd understand.'

'I know, but let's leave the past where it is now. It's time for us all to look to the future.' She reaches for my hand.

EPILOGUE

I can't fathom how I've ended up here today. As I crunch along the pebbles towards the newer graves, at the edge of the cemetery grounds, I keep trying to work it out. Am I visiting to ensure Dominic's definitely gone, or is some guilt over ending the life of another human starting to gnaw at my edges?

As I head towards the plot I looked up on the cemetery's website, I stop dead. I'd recognise that figure anywhere, even though it's been five months since I last clapped eyes on her.

She didn't attend court when her parents were sentenced, nor have our paths crossed anywhere else since. I tried contacting her at first but eventually gave up when she wasn't responding.

I shuffle forward a bit more before stopping a metre or so behind her. Who knows what sort of reaction I'm going to get now.

'Sophie.'

She spins around. 'What are *you* doing here?' Her tone is neither friendly nor accusatory, so knowing how this unplanned encounter might turn out is impossible.

I've never seen her hair so unkempt or her face so bare of

make-up, which makes me feel even more responsible. Aware that I'm staring, I glance at the flowers she's laid in front of the wooden cross. Carnations. Cheap. They've never been a carnations sort of a family so I'm quite surprised at this. But then Sophie's always set herself apart from the rest of them.

'I never thought I'd come here, to be honest.'

'So why *have* you?' She squints at me in the sunshine.

'I guess it's to do with, um – closure.' There I have it – I've answered my own question. Unburdening myself to Natalie two months ago wasn't quite enough for me to put everything behind me and to move on. I needed to come *here* as well. After this is done, I hope I can walk away and never look back.

'Closure,' she echoes, looking puzzled. At least puzzled is better than angry. 'But if it hadn't been for what *you* did to him, you wouldn't need *closure*, would you?'

'Look,' I cut in. 'I know you must be blaming me but you know—'

'I know better than anyone what he was like.' She turns to look back at the grave and I find myself wondering who might have wanted to attend his funeral. Sophie, obviously, and maybe his parents, though they'd have been handcuffed to prison officers. Perhaps a few business associates or so-called friends, though he spent most of his life so filled with his own self-importance that I doubt he'd have had anyone genuinely grieving over him. I wouldn't have attended in a million years – how could I have done when I was the person who ended his life?

I follow Sophie's gaze back to the wooden cross, glad of a moment's silence to gather myself back together. Her being here is something I really wasn't reckoning on.

Dominic Elmer, aged 34. Beloved son of Ann-Marie and Roger and sister of Sophie. Those we love don't go away. They walk beside us every day.

I shudder. The thought of him walking beside anyone isn't a pleasant one.

'I'm really sorry, Sophie.'

'What are you sorry for?' Her look is bordering on accusatory.

'Just this – you know— I've tried contacting you, Sophie. But you've ignored all my calls and texts.'

'I was always going to answer you *eventually*,' she says. 'I've just been trying to work things out.'

'What things?'

She looks back at me, and for a moment, I see Dominic's eyes. The same eyes I looked into as we were facing each other beside that outbuilding. Right before I slammed that rock into his head. But what I don't see in Sophie is the same sneer as her brother or any intention to hurt me. Instead, it's a face that also needs closure.

She gestures at the grave. 'He made my life hell growing up, you know.'

'I can imagine. I only spent a couple of years with him and that was more than enough.'

'I never really talk about the past,' she continues.

'Maybe you should. Perhaps it could help.' I stare at her. I don't know if she's getting any support from friends or the partner she mentioned at Christmas, but as far as family goes, she's completely on her own now. All because of me.

'I come here every month with flowers, you know. There's only me who ever visits.'

It's on the tip of my tongue to say, *it's no wonder*, but instead, I say, 'I'm sorry, Sophie. Really, I am.'

Still, she stands in front of me, not moving, not reacting. But this is a woman who's lost her entire family and her entire existence as she knew it. It's going to take more than the five months that have elapsed to get over it all.

'Do you visit your parents?' I don't know why I'm asking

this. *Do I even want to know?* I guess I'm trying to keep the conversation going. It's too rude to just walk away. I'll hang around for a couple more minutes and then I'm out of here.

She shakes her head. 'I've been trying to distance myself from them for as long as I can remember.'

'At least you aren't cut from the same piece of cloth as they are.'

'Aren't I?'

'Not as far as I can see.'

'Well, whatever you can or can't see, it hasn't stopped them all from trying to control me for all these years, has it – constantly telling me that I should be prouder of where I've *come from.*' She draws air quotes around her last two words.

'You should be prouder of the fact that you're different if you ask me.'

'I can't stop feeling guilty though.' She breaks our gaze and returns her attention to Dominic's grave. 'I might not have liked my brother much but I didn't want him dead. Nor did I want anyone to get hurt.'

'What on earth have *you* got to feel guilty about – it wasn't you who hurt anyone.' I stare at the plaque attached to the wooden cross again until the words blur in front of my eyes. I often wonder where Dominic's gone after here – whether such a nasty soul can be ever allowed to rest in peace – it's certainly peaceful here, amidst the birdsong and the rustle of leaves.

I also wonder where I'll go when I die after what I've done. I might have had my reasons for doing what I did but I still played God with someone else's life and if it wasn't for me, Dominic would still be alive and most definitely kicking.

'Without me getting involved in the first place, none of it would have ever started.' She looks down at her feet, her shoulders sagging some more. In black jeans and a black T-shirt, she looks every inch the mourner in this place.

'You told me where those papers were.' I step closer to her.

'When it would be much easier for you not to have done. For that, and for you giving me the chance to be able to shred them before they could do any more damage, I'll *always* be grateful.'

'It wasn't just the papers.' She raises her eyes to meet mine. They look piggy and tired – she probably hasn't slept properly for all these months. 'Who do you think alerted the authorities about my parents' tax evasion in the first place?' she asks.

'What do you mean?'

'And who do you think told the police about them falsifying their gas safety checks?'

'*You?*' I stare at her. 'Really? But why?'

'I was sick of playing second fiddle to Dominic. Every time they went away, they left the running of everything to him. It was the last time they left it all with him that I made the calls. My own business had failed and my dad had made some quip about how I couldn't be trusted with theirs.'

'So it was a heat of the moment thing?'

'It ran quite a lot deeper than that.'

'Wow.' I'd never have thought Sophie would have had the guts to go against her family so spectacularly.

'But it all went wrong. If I hadn't reported them, they wouldn't have come after you for the money they needed, would they? You'd have never been there over Christmas.'

'Natalie's days would still have been numbered even without me being around.'

'I had no idea that Dominic was once friends with Natalie's ex,' she said. 'He went away to university so I didn't know any of his friends.'

'So you knew about what she'd done when you first met her?'

'Only what I'd read in the original article after her brother was sentenced.'

'I can't believe what she went through,' I say. 'But at least she can get on with her life now.'

'Unlike my brother,' she replies, her face darkening. She looks more like Dominic again.

'I'm sorry.' It's my turn to look down at my feet. As if the word *sorry* is going to cut it.

'Anyway, as I've been telling myself over and over again, everything happens for a reason.' Her voice lifts. 'Perhaps we were all exactly where we were supposed to be at exactly the right time. Like now.'

'How do you mean?'

'We have something to discuss.'

'Me and you? Do we? What?'

'Money.'

'Oh no, I don't think—' I squint at her, the sunshine in *my* eyes now.

'My family's money has practically all gone.' She steps closer to me. 'I assumed I'd get at least ten times the amount that I'm ending up with. Some might say it's my own fault, but I thought The Elms would sell for a hell of a lot more than it has.'

'What's this got to do with me?' There's a sudden shift in the air between us. I might have known our initial conversation was going too smoothly.

'That money you were supposed to give my parents.'

'I wasn't supposed to give them anything.'

'Well, you can send it my way now.' The tone of her voice suggests she's telling me rather than asking me.

'Hang on a minute – what are you talking about?' I've never seen this side of Sophie before, but then, as a pair of sisters-in-law go, we barely really got to know each other, not properly. She remained in the background, watching and obviously waiting for her chance to step forward.

'I made copies of those legal aid papers you shredded.' Her voice is passive and even as if it's a normal run-of-the-mill thing that she's done. 'I wasn't sure at the time whether I'd do anything with them but after what you—'

'So it's your turn to blackmail me now? Is that what you're saying?' I step back from her. I should have just walked off as soon as I saw her, but by the sounds of it, she was planning to come after me anyway.

'You killed my brother. You pay me, I destroy that legal aid evidence and then we're quits.'

I don't believe this. Or maybe I do – Sophie's an Elmer, after all.

'I think you're underestimating me here, Sophie. You're forgetting what I do for a living.'

'There's also the matter of the CCTV recording.'

'What CCTV recording?'

The one which shows you picking up that rock at the side of the house,' she goes on. 'It's as clear as a bell.'

My breath's coming more rapidly now. I thought I'd got away with what I did. Oh my God – there must have been a camera out there.

'Things were a little more premeditated than you've been letting on, weren't they, Carla?'

'The police never said a thing about CCTV to me?'

'They never saw it.'

'So how did you?'

'I had remote access on my phone. I was watching everything.'

'But how— what—'

'I wiped the main server.'

'But I take it that you've made your own recording?'

I don't really need to ask her this. What a ridiculous question – of course she has.

I stare back into the eyes of the last remaining Elmer.

The one who's possibly more dangerous to me because she pretends not to be.

A LETTER FROM MARIA FRANKLAND

Dear reader,

I want to say a huge thank you for choosing to read *The Night Before Christmas*. If you enjoyed it, and want to keep up-to-date with all my latest releases, just sign up at the following link. Your email address will never be shared and you can unsubscribe at any time.

www.bookouture.com/maria-frankland

It was an accident my husband, Michael, had that sparked the idea for this story. Last year, he bought an all-singing-all-dancing food processor that looked like it did nearly everything apart from actually cook dinner. Whilst experimenting with it, he dropped the blade, causing a very nasty gash in his leg that required swift and extensive hospital treatment.

Of course our families were like, *yeah, yeah,* when we shared the details of what had happened and were making jokes about 'the psychological thriller author' and the fact that somewhere, a food processor blade would make it into one of my stories. So of course – it did! Who knew that a kitchen gadget could cause so much damage – or inspiration?

Cue an ex-wife, and a new wife, both with histories, a venomous mother-in-law, a father-in-law with everything to lose and a controlling misogynist man who's playing everyone off against each other. Set against the backdrop of Christmas during a snowstorm no one can escape from and bring in the food processor. Ta-da!

I'd love to know your thoughts on the story and would hugely appreciate a review on Amazon or Goodreads, or both if you're feeling generous. Or even better, come and find me on social media or my website.

www.mariafrankland.co.uk

facebook.com/writermariafrank

instagram.com/writermaria_f

tiktok.com/@mariafranklandauthor

BOOK CLUB DISCUSSION QUESTIONS

1. Discuss how the dynamic changes between Natalie and Carla as the story progresses. What are the ties that bind them?
2. Have you ever encountered a true and enduring friendship arising from an ex-wife and a new wife situation?
3. Discuss the motivations of each character in relation to their flaws.
4. How is it possible that some men can mask themselves throughout the early stages of a relationship? How do they do it?
5. Discuss the factors that might have kept both Natalie and Carla in their relationships for longer than they should have stayed.
6. What personality traits and experiences might a perpetrator drag in from his childhood?
7. Imagine Kyle and Dominic's friendship when they were at university. How might they have bonded? How might they have spent time together?
8. One of the subplots was the trouble the Elmers were in with a large tax bill plus a pending case for landlord negligence. How do these wrongdoings fit in with the personalities of the characters you got to know?
9. What did Sophie's childhood look like? What might

she have been trying to gain, if anything, through her involvement with each of her brother's wives?

10. Explore the brother and sister dynamics which exist in this story.

11. Was the judicial system right in not handing down custodial sentences to Natalie and Carla but in giving them to Ann-Marie and Roger?

12. What might happen when Ann-Marie and Roger are eventually released?

13. The common themes in this book are being trapped and guilt. How are these emotions intertwined?

14. What are your feelings about what Natalie and Hayden did to Kyle? Have they been punished enough? Or not?

15. What were your feelings about Sophie at the end of the story?

ACKNOWLEDGEMENTS

Thank you, as always, to my amazing husband, Michael. He's my first reader, and his opinion is vital with my editing process for each of my novels. His belief in me means more than I can say.

My next huge thank you goes to Susannah Hamilton, my editor at Bookouture, who is a joy to work with. I love bouncing ideas around with her and what she doesn't know about the psychological thriller genre isn't worth knowing! I'd like to also acknowledge the hard work of Jade Craddock, my copy editor, and Becca Allen, my proofreader, as well as David Grogan at Head Design for his amazing cover design.

A special acknowledgement goes to my existing community of wonderful readers, especially those in my FrankFans reader group, who give me so much support and encouragement.

I will always be grateful to Leeds Trinity University and my MA in Creative Writing Tutors there, Martyn, Amina and Oz. My master's degree in 2015 was the springboard into being able to write as a profession.

And thanks especially to you, the reader. Whether you are new to my work or have read every book, thank you for taking the time to read this story. I really hope you enjoyed it.

PUBLISHING TEAM

Turning a manuscript into a book requires the efforts of many people. The publishing team at Bookouture would like to acknowledge everyone who contributed to this publication.

Audio
Alba Proko
Sinead O'Connor
Melissa Tran

Commercial
Lauren Morrissette
Hannah Richmond
Imogen Allport

Cover design
Head Design Ltd

Data and analysis
Mark Alder
Mohamed Bussuri

Editorial
Lucy Frederick
Nadia Michael

Printed in Dunstable, United Kingdom